THE TAKERS

A SAM POPE NOVEL

ROBERT ENRIGHT

In loving memory of Arthur Baker.
My Poppa.

CHAPTER ONE

The rain hammered down relentlessly from the grey clouds that hung over London. The city was illuminated by a plethora of lights, bathing the wet city in a shiny glow. London was still a hub of activity, the midnight crowd just getting started for another Friday night of hard drinking and senseless drugs. Although not as vibrant as Camden or as colourful as Soho, Holborn was equally busy, the large, dual carriage main road separating the bars and pubs on either side of the street.

Despite the inclement weather, every bar was packed, and groups of drunks were huddled in tiny smoking areas, all of them shaking as they had their nicotine fix.

Sam Pope watched intently.

Perched on the first floor of a fire escape which hung to the building like a tumour, Sam shivered slightly as a drop of rain snuck under his collar, before sliding an icy descent down his spine. He grimaced, before shaking it off and refocused, annoyed that the tarpaulin he had draped over the balcony hadn't done its job. Not only was it acting as a barrier between him and the ferocious November night sky, it was also obscuring him from the eyes of the public.

The eyes of the police.

The eyes of his target.

It had been six months since Sam had started down his current path, all of it triggered by the bomb that had obliterated mile seventeen of the London Marathon and shook the city to its core. Despite the instant headlines of another terrorist attack, Sam, on account of one hunch regarding an officer, ended up uncovering a conspiracy, headed up by a Chief Inspector of the Metropolitan Police, his subordinates, and one of the most dangerous criminals in the country. As he fought desperately to uncover the truth and keep his therapist, Amy Devereux and her husband alive, Sam had lost his best friend.

Theo Walker.

The very thought of it caused his muscles to tighten and he removed his finger from the trigger. His hands gently held the L85IW SA80 assault rifle, the stock pressed into his shoulder as naturally as holding a baby. His gloved fingers hovered near the trigger, safe in the knowledge that his years as one of the UK's most deadly snipers made this shot seem like a walk in the park. He had over sixty confirmed kills from his time serving abroad, the tours through the bloodstained streets of Baghdad had seen him hone his skills to almost unprecedented levels.

That was when he joined Project Hailstorm.

The "need to know" missions soon came thick and fast, and while two years of his record would soon disappear, the two bullet wounds that scarred his body like a tattoo were permanent.

That was when he had returned home.

Not long after that, he lost everything, which soon became the catalyst that had put him on this path. Losing his faith in the justice system had caused him to seek his own, using his job as an archive officer to find 'innocent' men who had beaten the system. His violent attacks soon brought him to the attention of DI Adrian Pearce, who eventually became his only ally.

It had been a crazy week in spring, which not only saw him become one of the most wanted men in the country, but had also seen him break his promise to his son.

He had killed again.

A bitter wind whipped through the side alley where he was perched, shaking the metal staircase and chilling Sam to his bones. It was certainly a contrast to the blazing heat of Africa where he had been deployed numerous times.

Now the missions were on home soil.

Sam knew the ramifications as he uncovered the truth six months ago when he had stormed the headquarters of Frank 'The Gent' Jackson. The 'High Rise' was infamous as a place where the law wasn't allowed, yet the police still went. Officer after officer were soon in The Gent's pocket, his offerings of drugs and cheap sex too much for many.

Sam had brought it all down.

Floor by floor.

Room by room.

Man by man.

When he'd confronted Jackson himself, Sam had put a bullet in his shins. It was only when the threat of Amy's future was spat out that Sam unloaded the rest of the gun into the crime lord's chest. That should have been the end of it.

But here Sam was, following the trail for the last six months that had led him to this stairwell on this freezing, rain-soaked night.

The rumours of a second High Rise.

The mission had become clear and Sam knew, with his new-found status as a wanted man, he needed to keep moving. But he couldn't let the same thing happen again. He couldn't allow another haven for the criminal underworld of London to establish itself, its allure too strong for the corruptible officers and politicians.

Sam had to bring it to an end.

He had spent the last few months knocking down doors, hijacking a number of illegal gambling facilities, and holding the proprietors at gun point. The money and drugs were coming through somewhere, and Sam knew that Jackson would have contingency plans. The man may have run what was essentially a criminal hotel, but he was connected.

He had links to the people bringing in the drugs, the money, and the women.

Sam had followed the bread crumbs, starting with a few street dealers who had set him onto their handler. A few broken bones later, Sam was working his way through the underground gambling world. A few men had ended up in the hospital.

A couple of properties had burnt down.

Then he was given a name.

Elmore Riggs.

Further digging had uncovered Riggs's volatile history, with several felonies relating to violence and gun crimes. The man was the living embodiment of the London gang culture that was tearing the city apart. Having watched his father get arrested during the Brixton riots, Riggs had found his way on the street. His lack of compassion had seen him rise fast, and he soon went from a dealer to a hired gun.

Riggs spent two years in prison for his role in the London Riots back in 2011, the culmination of rising tensions and a police shooting. Riggs found his way out and soon made his way to the High Rise. Apparently, the 'Mitchell Brothers' had labelled him a loose cannon and had advised Jackson to move him to another location.

The Mitchell Brothers were Jackson's two most trusted

henchman, Brian Stack and Mark Connor, both of whom shared similarities with the *EastEnders'* characters.

Sam had come face to face with them six months prior.

Both were now dead.

As Sam had delved deeper into the murky waters of the London Underbelly, he had learnt that Riggs wasn't too good with the numbers. That he needed a right-hand man to oversee the details, to ensure that what he had taken over was being distributed correctly.

That man was Sean Wiseman.

And at that moment, as the ice-cold rain clattered that metal platform and echoed like a shaken rattle, the headlights of his car turned onto the main road, illuminating the downpour and the clear road ahead.

Sam readjusted, pulling the stock back, lodging it into his meaty shoulder and locking it in place.

With a swift, natural swing, he drew the gun up to his eye level, closing one brown eye and casting the gaze of the other down the scope of the rifle, the cross hair locked on the moving vehicle.

His finger looped back into the trigger loop.

He took a breath.

He squeezed.

The bullet blasted from the chamber, travelling through the silencer attached to the barrel, cloaking the roar of the rifle. With pinpoint accuracy, it travelled through the night sky, slicing through rain drops before burying itself in the rubber of the tyre and instantly bursting the tyre of the black Range Rover. A sharp squeal pierced through the air as the driver tried to turn into the swerve, instead causing the 4x4 to spin out completely before colliding firmly with the concrete barricade.

It was all over in seven seconds.

Sam was already stepping off the bottom step and into

the alleyway, the wet trash greeting his nostrils with a pungent 'fuck you'.

Out on the main road, a trail of ripped rubber followed a skid mark all the way to the wreckage. The side panel and bonnet of the car had been heavily dented, a small trail of smoke escaping up into the downpour. The streets were flooded with gawping pedestrians, all of them trying their best to record the incident to post online in the hope of garnering a few extra 'likes'. Sam was sure a few of them may have had the common sense to call the emergency services beforehand.

After a few moments, the driver side door shunted open, and a burly man stumbled out, his eyebrows stained with blood from the gash across his forehead. He wore a black jumper and jeans, with a thick gold chain and watch. In his left hand, the driver held a Glock 19, the wet metal shimmering the street light.

The sight of the gun sent the watching crowd scarpering, the audible panic of shrieks echoed down the main road.

A bus sped past, barely missing the stumbling driver, who from his wayward steps, was nursing a severe head wound.

Sam stepped out into the street, marching across the other side of the road and straight towards the totalled car.

The driver, frantically trying to regain his composure, locked his eyes on Sam. They widened as Sam pulled up the assault rifle once more.

The driver tried to raise the gun, but Sam expertly dropped to one knee, stock against shoulder, eye down the sight, and shot a small burst.

Two bullets ripped through the left leg of the driver who collapsed instantly to the pavement in agony. His screams were masked by the panicked mayhem of the

London public and in the distance, the familiar faint wailing of police sirens.

Sam moved quickly.

He hopped over the concrete barricade and stormed towards the fallen gunman, who was desperately trying to scramble towards his weapon. Blood pumped out from the bullet wounds in his leg, the rain pushing it further out and staining the road red.

Without breaking his stride, Sam violently twisted the gun downwards, crashing the stock of the rifle into the man's temple. He was unconscious before he fell back onto the pavement, the rain attacking his lifeless body.

Sam raced to the smashed car, letting the rifle drop and hang from its sling, approaching just as the backdoor slowly pushed open.

Sean Wiseman slowly turned his body out of the door, his wiry, thin frame shaken by the collision and he clutched his neck. The obvious whiplash had stopped him making a break for it and now, as he tried to step out of the car, he came face to face with Sam.

The colour drained from his pale face, his blond hair shaved short. He had two lines shaved in his eyebrows, but Sam could see through the faux gangster act.

Sean Wiseman was a numbers guy.

And, judging by the terror in his eyes, was absolutely petrified.

The sirens echoed loudly, only a few streets away and Sam reached out and grabbed Wiseman by the face, forcing him back into the car before stepping in, thankful for some respite from the downpour. He tightened his grip on Wiseman's jaw, his fingers digging into the cheeks as he held his head in place.

Calmly, he pulled his own pistol from his side holster, pressing the barrel against Wiseman's head and thumbing the safety.

The unmistakable smell of urine flooded the car as Wiseman abandoned any tough guy act.

He feared for his life and Sam knew it.

With the metal pressing against Wiseman's skull, Sam stared deep into his bloodshot eyes.

'Address. Now.'

Wiseman let out a pathetic whimper and Sam pushed the gun harder, pressing him back into the seat. Sam raised his voice.

'The address of the new High Rise. Give it to me or I'll blow your goddamn brains out.'

Wiseman shook with fear before he stammered a few words out.

'The old Kodak factory in Shepherd's Bush. Please, please don't kill me.'

Wiseman began to weep, and Sam shook his head in disgust. The man worked for a violent criminal, brokering deals and shipping drugs and women through the city. Yet here he was, stripped of power, begging for his life in piss stained trousers.

Sam pulled the gun away from the young man's forehead, the pressure leaving an indent in the skin. Wiseman breathed a palpable sigh of relief.

The sirens pierced through the night sky and Sam could see the flashing lights through the blurry, cracked windscreen. He snatched Wiseman's wrist and pressed his hand down against the white leather seat. He then, much to the young gangster's horror, pressed the barrel of the gun against it.

'This is your last night as a criminal. Do you understand me? If I find you again, this bullet will be between the eyes.'

Before Wiseman could protest, Sam pulled the trigger, a cocktail of burning gun powder, splatters of blood and bone, and anguished screams filled the back of the car as he stepped out, Wiseman rolling on the chair in agony, clutching his shattered hand.

Two police cars sped as fast as they could up the main road, their lights and sirens announcing their arrival as elaborately as the cabaret shows in the nearby theatres.

Sam didn't have any time to think about it. There was only the next phase of the mission.

He had the address. As Wiseman wept with uncontrollable pain, Sam reached into the man's coat and withdrew his mobile phone, pocketing it instantly. Wiseman begged for help, but Sam ignored him, allowing the rattle of the rain against the window to drown out the man's pitiful pleas. He would need to regroup, draw up his plan of attack, and hit it as soon as possible.

Riggs would be expecting him, especially when news of this filtered back to him.

Sam wasn't going to disappoint him.

Under the blanket of the torrential rain, Sam sprinted off towards a nearby side street, allowing the dark, interlinking backstreets of London to swallow him.

CHAPTER TWO

Mark Harris held the newspaper open, scanning his eyes across the article and slowly shaking his head. A disappointed sigh left his immaculately dressed body and he ran a manicured hand through his well-maintained brown hair. As the leading candidate to replace the current Mayor of London, Harris was aware of how important his image was. The youngest candidate to ever get this close to the chair, his entire campaign was based around the rise of crime within the city, boosted considerably by the bomb attack six months previous. Now, as he read about a reported shooting in Holborn the night before, he could already hear his next speech.

Gun crime needed to be stopped.

His office, a minimalistic yet expensive room, sat overlooking the wonderful grounds of Regent's Park, the vast, sprawling fields in the heart of London which housed London Zoo, and, when the weather was more accommodating, the London Food Festival. Not far from his office was Harley Street, a plethora of private hospitals charging vast amounts for the sort of healthcare most people could only dream of. A short twenty-minute walk would take him to Holborn itself, the scene of the alleged shooting. The details were murky, the only eyewitnesses were either drunk or ducking for cover, but apparently a man blew out a Range Rover's tyres, before shooting one man in the legs and the passenger in the hand.

Harris knew exactly who it was.

The man making the headlines for the last six months.

On a rainy night in London, Sam Pope had once again handed out his own brand of justice.

Frustration surged through his body like an electric shock, causing his hands to ball into fists and the pages to crunch. Harris took a deep breath and set the paper down on his oak desk, atop of the closed laptop. He needed to calm himself. His entire campaign was hinging on the capture of a known vigilante, the extra effort to reduce a gun-toting maniac would surely solidify his seat. From there, it would only be a few years until he would undoubtedly be prime minister, the entire country at his fingertips.

He pushed himself from his leather chair and slowly walked to the window, hands clasped behind his back as he stared out over the city he was hoping to govern. The extra effort hadn't gone unnoticed, and he had already received word of a large crowd outside the building, ready to listen to his next speech. They would devour every word, cheering his strong stance on making the city safe once more. Journalists would eagerly lift their recording devices, struggling against each other to ask him a question like they were fighting for the last life jacket on the *Titanic*.

Mark Harris knew he was big news. He was handsome, smart, charming, and pushing all the right buttons. Three months shy of his fortieth birthday, his hair was starting to grey at the edges.

His wife thought it made him look more endearing.

His mistress didn't seem to care at all.

Carl Burrows, his executive assistant, was the only

other person who knew of his infidelity, arranging the secret meetings and the removal of evidence. Burrows was a stern, well-educated man who had a permanent sneer across his world-weary face. Tufts of grey hair framed his bespectacled head and did so that day as he opened the door and stepped into the office.

Harris didn't even turn from the window.

'Good morning, sir,' Burrows said approaching the desk, a stack of folders resting in his arms. He placed them on the desk before unbuttoning his blazer and taking his seat. Rain gently pattered against the window, each droplet exploding on impact.

'Do you ever think it will rain hard enough that it will wash the streets clean?' Harris eventually offered, his eyes still transfixed on the streets surrounding the vast park, the trees clinging desperately to their final leaves.

'I very much doubt it, sir,' Burrows said without emotion. 'It would take an unseemly amount of rain.'

'Quite.' Harris turned, smiling warmly at the stalwart of his political party. Burrows had been in the same position for years, serving as the assistant to the last mayor from Harris's party. The man may have been a complete stick in the mud, but he knew his job and knew it well. Harris nodded to the files as he took his seat. 'What are those?'

'They are all the reports about last night's, shall we say, incident?' Burrows removed his glasses before wiping them with a small cloth. 'Several different angles, but all similar details.'

'Pope?' Harris asked, picking up the first file and flicking it open.

'Definitely.'

'Hmm.' Harris shook his head, his eyes flaring with anger as he read the red-top headline. 'This isn't great, especially with the election only a month away.'

'You have nothing to worry about, sir,' Burrows spoke, his words robotic. 'We have already prepared you a statement to read to the gathering press outside. The usual.'

Harris tossed the folder back onto the desk in frustration. He massaged his temples before looking around the room. A sofa with a coffee table was pressed against the far wall, adjacent to a book case that stood proudly next to the door. Harris wasn't one for reading, but Burrows had demanded its inclusion in the office. Apparently, it boosted Harris's intellectual appeal.

'The usual isn't working,' Harris eventually offered.

'But today, you will not be alone.'

Before Harris could respond, Burrows leant forward and pressed his finger on the small, red button atop the phone. Instantly, the speaker produced a ring before Peggy, Harris's secretary, wished them good morning. Burrows leant forward, his mouth near the speaker of the phone.

'Send them in, please.'

The phone hung up as Burrows stood. Harris copied, confusion on his face as he slipped his arms into his blazer.

'Them?'

Before Burrows could answer, the large, wooden door swung open and in walked Assistant Commissioner Ruth Ashton of the Metropolitan Police. A veteran of over twenty years, Ashton was the prototype for any senior police official. An immaculate record on the beat, with three commendations for bravery. Six years working within CID, heading up a task force that brought down an inner-city drug ring as well as spending three years on Project Yewtree. Since then, Ashton had taken a back seat, working the political ladder and progressing all the way up to the third highest rank in the entire police service. Juggling that with a marriage of over twenty-five years and two kids in further education, and Harris understood exactly why she commanded respect as she entered the room. With her hat tucked neatly under her arm, she marched to the table, extending her hand and firmly shaking Harris's.

'Assistant Commissioner, what a lovely surprise.' Harris flashed his brilliant, white smile.

'Mr Harris,' Ashton spoke with well-honed gravitas.

'To what do I owe the pleasure?' Harris motioned to the seat which Burrows had respectfully vacated. 'First off, would you like a drink? Tea? Coffee?'

'A tea would be lovely.'

'Burrows.'

Without a word, Burrows nodded and vacated the room, as loyal and obedient as ever. Harris knew the man deserved more respect than that, but there were times when he caught himself testing to what lengths Burrows' obedience stretched. As Burrows left, Harris took his seat, pressing his fingers together in front of his chest.

'Mr Harris…'

'Please, call me Mark.'

'Mark.' Ashton corrected herself. 'As you know, there was another incident last night.'

'Yes. I'm aware.'

'Well, your confidant, Mr Burrows, invited me in this morning to discuss the plan of action. As you're well aware, the Metropolitan Police has had some severe problems this year, especially within its own ranks.'

'Yes. That whole mess with Inspector Howell.'

'That was handled internally and as you can imagine, we'd like to keep a lid on that as much as possible.'

'Quite.' Harris offered his smile once more.

'Since then, Sam Pope has been a strict priority. Again, you can see the sensationalism of the press with regard to an armed vigilante supposedly cleaning up the streets.'

'Well, as you're aware, Assistant Commissioner…'

'Please, Ruth.'

Harris smiled politely before continuing.

'Ruth. My entire campaign is all for the apprehending of this man and the reduction in gun crime within this great city. I'm due to speak to the press this morning in relation to yesterday's incident and impact on my campaign. I'm sure I can play my part in extinguishing any flames of excitement.'

'Thank you. Do you know that the press has given him a nickname now?' Ashton asked rhetorically, shaking her head. 'They are calling him *The Watchdog*.'

'Pathetic,' Harris chimed in, disappointed at the press for branding a man who was breaking the law. Burrows re-entered the room with two cups of tea. He placed them on the wooden coasters on the desk before taking his leave once more. Ashton took a satisfying sip, allowing the piping hot liquid to warm her on a bitterly cold and wet morning. 'As I said, I was invited here.'

'I can't say I'm too sure why. You know Carl, he's full of secrets.'

Both of them smiled politely at the lame joke and Harris sipped his tea, annoyed at his own intimidation at the powerful woman before him.

'Well, in light of yesterdays incident, we have released extra funding to not only increase our search for Sam Pope, but to launch a task force dedicated to his apprehension.'

'Well this is excellent news.' Harris beamed.

'Of course, this will be run through the Met, but as you know, many of our officers are fully behind your campaign and have suggested you would like to officially launch the task force today.'

Harris shook slightly with excitement. Although he was the clear favourite for the next election, being the face of a dedicated task force was only going to increase his standing in the eyes of the citizens. He took another swig of his drink before placing the mug down, his eyes wide with glee.

'Ruth, I would be honoured to announce it on your behalf, and I look forward to working with you.'

'Oh, I won't be leading the task force.' She smiled politely, a few wrinkles framing her blue eyes. Her auburn hair was tied neatly into a ponytail.

'Oh?' Harris raised an eyebrow and Burrows stepped back into the room, stepping to the side and ushering in Detective Inspector Amara Singh. Despite her lack of height, Singh walked with purpose, her police tunic immaculate and her fierce brown eyes locked on Harris. Her brown skin complimented her striking face and Harris was slightly taken aback by her immediate beauty. Singh marched towards the desk as both Harris and Ashton rose from their seats, stopping in front of her superior and offering a salute. Ashton nodded her acceptance and they both turned to Harris.

'Mr Harris, meet Detective Inspector Singh.'

Harris extended his hand as well as his dazzling smile. Singh took it, looking less than impressed.

'It's a pleasure.' Harris couldn't help but have a quick scan of her body, her petite frame clearly carried some muscle. He could tell she was a strict trainer, without a shred of fat on her. 'Are you up to the task, ma'am?'

'Sir, I've spent the last four years on the Armed Response team, leading several successful raids as well as working alongside Assistant Commissioner Ashton on Project Yewtree. I have extensive field and command experience and to be honest, sir, I just want this scum bag off our streets.'

Harris felt a jolt of arousal as he regarded the stern, highly strung Singh who stood powerfully before him.

'I couldn't agree more, Detective.' Harris waited for Singh to offer her first name but she didn't. The situation was clearly too important for niceties. Harris respected it and even saw it as a slight challenge. 'Tell me, and please exclude the usual reasons, why is this task force important to you?'

Singh stood to attention at the question, aware the eyes of the mayoral candidate and her superior falling upon her. She cleared her throat and began.

'With all due respect, sir, it's the duty of every officer to uphold the law, regardless of rank. This man is a criminal. On a personal note, a friend of mine who I trained with at Hendon eleven years ago, was shot twice last year. He was attending a noise complaint and was murdered for doing his job.'

The office fell silent for a moment. Harris, determined to steer the conversation back to a positive, shook his head.

'I'm sorry to hear that, Detective. You have my full support and if you need anything, please don't hesitate to ask.'

Harris once again offered her a smile which she acknowledged. Her brown eyes sparkled with an eagerness to begin. Harris found it as attractive as he did impressive. He wondered if Burrows would be able to instigate a private meeting between them. A little presumptuous, but he was sure he would be able to seduce her. With his mind wandering, Burrows stepped forward.

'Sir, if I may, the press is gathered downstairs and would like to speak with you. I suggest, with us all having made our introductions, there would be no time like the present in launching this task force.'

'Quite right.' Ashton nodded approvingly, fixing her cap onto her head and turning to Harris, who was gathering his belongings. 'Shall we?'

'Of course.' Harris began to round the desk, aware both police officials were watching him. 'What's the name of the task force?'

'Project Watchdog,' Singh said coldly.

'Clever.' Harris smiled, hoping to break the stern exterior. Unsuccessful, he turned to Burrows, who stood passively by the door. 'Let's go shall we?'

All four of them headed to the stairwell and towards the hungry swarm of questions and photo flashes of the waiting journalists.

CHAPTER THREE

As the rain clattered against the lone window of the kitchen, trying in vain to wash away years' worth of grime, Sam turned the volume of the TV up. His flat was as depressing as the early winter weather. Situated above Store 'n' Go, a storage facility run by a Greek man named George Tsillis, Sam had tried his best to make it homely.

Originally a dumping ground for the soiled or abandoned goods, Sam had offered the man five hundred a month in cash for the next year, slapping six grand on the table. As the greedy man's eyes lit up, Sam knew there would be no questions asked. The facility was in North Wembley, the multicultural streets alive with traders and small business owners, all of them trying to get by. The surrounding streets were filled with fast-food chains, a car hire service, and a few dodgy bars with delusions of grandeur. Late at night, as Sam passed through the droves of people still out wandering the streets, he marvelled at the illuminated arch of Wembley Stadium, the lights bending over the tops of the houses.

Despite the glamour of the national stadium and the

cash injection in the surrounding areas, the majority of the town was in poverty, with a number of estates overrun with gangs and knife crime. Reportedly, there was on average at least one stabbing a week in the borough, a statistic the media liked to roll out in their never-ending quest for hyperbole.

Sam wanted to do something about it, but his focus was on the mission.

It was only about the mission.

Now, sitting in the dingy kitchen of his crummy flat, he watched the early afternoon broadcast, the reporter stood in front of Holborn station, giving a reasonably accurate account of what Sam had accomplished the night before. What they failed to mention was the information he got.

The second High Rise's location.

Shoveling a spoonful of porridge into his mouth, he clicked the TV off as it cut to a well-dressed man in front of a weather map, trying his best to make a torrential downpour interesting. Finishing his porridge, Sam stood, walking across the bland kitchen to the porcelain sink, the bowl stained from years of filth.

When Sam had moved in, the walls were peeling, mould and damp pushing the outdated paper from the wall, and the electrics were out. As fastidious as the armed forces had demanded, Sam had stripped them all and then applied an anti-damp treatment to the required areas. He had ripped the carpets from their rusted grip strips, exposing the perished underlay and a few sunken floor boards. Several trips to the local rubbish tip soon cleared them away and Sam found himself replacing some of the boards.

While he was at it, he had left two boards loose, allowing easy access to the small compartment that he stored his sports bag in. It contained over twenty grand in cash, and was more than enough to see him through the next few years.

The kitchen, now painted a neutral white, was small and compact, but it had a working fridge and a cupboard to store his dry food. It was stocked with packets of porridge and army issue meal packs, all in nondescript wrappers, all of them tasting more or less the same.

It didn't matter.

It was enough to sustain him, to keep him focused on the mission ahead.

Marching back across the kitchen and living room, he passed his dusty two-seater sofa and his one luxury: the bookcase. As he took a moment to look at the surprising collection he had amassed, he felt a twinge of guilt for his reason for reading.

A hobby he had taken up as a promise to his late son.

His Jamie.

Sam closed his eyes and drew in a breath, all his senses rushing from his body as they shot back through time to that warm night in North London. As he stumbled home drunk from the pub to celebrate another successful day of training at the Met's training facility in Hendon, he soon collided with his worst nightmare. In a drunken haze, he and his friend Theo had failed to stop a drunk man from driving home.

The smell of the night flooded back to him, the heat resting in the air, alleviated by the gentle breeze.

He could hear the panic of the passers-by. His ex-wife, Lucy howling with heartbreak.

The drunken man was being helped from the wreckage, blood covering his face and vomit down the front of his shirt.

Sam remembered it all. Every sound. Every smell.

His body shook as he recalled losing all power in his

muscles as his eyes rested upon his son's body, broken and motionless under the front of the car.

His cold, lifeless eyes staring into oblivion.

Sam startled, returning to his flat and finding a tear forming in the corner of his eye. It had been nearly four years since he had lost his son. Just under three since Lucy had left him. Every day, he awoke in a single bed, dreaming of the times when he had both of them beside him.

That life had long since left.

Sam had begun to make peace with it, accepting his son's death and using it as the catalyst to drive him to seek justice. The man who had killed his son got off on a reduced sentence, serving just under a year for erasing his son from the earth. Sam stopped himself from remembering the night he paid him a visit.

The horror of discovering what he was truly capable of.

His son had been a keen reader and Sam, who had spent his life in the army, was never an academic, but promised to show an interest. As their son excelled, Lucy encouraged him to get involved and Sam had taken to reading.

He promised his son two things.

One; he would read more.

Two; he would never kill again.

Now, as he stared at his burgeoning book collection, he knew he had to make good on that promise.

Especially as he had broken the second one.

Six months earlier, the capital was shaking from a terrorist attack. The London Marathon, a British tradition and one of the most eagerly anticipated days of the year, was ripped apart by a detonated bomb. A few people were killed, including a young police officer.

Officer Jake Howell.

The nephew of the revered, Inspector Howell.

Sam had mourned the young man, having seen a number of people die in the line of duty during his tours. When a few things didn't add up, Sam eventually unveiled an inside job, commissioned by Howell himself. They had been on The Gent's payroll, and Howell had signed off on the murder of his nephew.

All for greed.

Having only broken his promise not to kill out of self-defence, Sam decided to take the High Rise by force, executing over ten of The Gent's soldiers, before unloading an entire round into the criminal's chest.

He left Howell for the police, who duly sent him to prison, where after two months of assaults, he was found hanged in his cell.

It was suspected suicide.

Sam didn't care.

As far as he was concerned, it was another criminal eradicated from the world and he marched on. He scolded himself for his broken promise, but had balanced it by investing more time into his books. As he stepped from the living room into the dim bedroom, he spied his latest read on his bedside table. *War and Peace* loomed large and Sam was struggling to make any headway into it.

Still, he would persevere.

For his Jamie.

Sam walked past his single, battered mattress that rested on top of rickety camp bed and opened his wardrobe.

An array of weapons greeted him.

After Theo had been killed and his house destroyed by a grenade, Sam had recovered his 'rainy day fund'. A stash of weapons he had hidden, a paranoia that his past discretions while part of Project Hailstorm would reappear somewhere down the line.

The things they'd done wouldn't stay hidden forever, and Sam was sure that one day, those sins from his past would rear their head.

But it was the injustice of the Metropolitan Police, the death of his friend, and the safety of an innocent woman that had put a gun back in his hand.

That had made him do the right thing.

Sam glanced at the weapons, all of them polished and cleaned weekly, a regimen he had performed blindfolded to the delight of his comrades. During a few of his tours in Afghanistan, he had been christened 'The Silent Death', for his streak of headshots without ever giving away his position.

The L85IW assault rifle was affixed to two hooks on the inside of the door, Sam making a mental note to clean it thoroughly when he returned. On the inside of the other door was a Remington Model 870 pump-action shotgun, used by the British Special Forces as a breaching weapon. The barrels were clean, and at the bottom of the cupboard were several segmented shelves, all of them filled with boxes of bullets or full magazines.

Two Glock 20s were hanging on the back wall of the cupboard, their larger magazines stacked neatly below. The powerful handguns were regularly cleaned by Sam, and he usually carried one in the inside of his jacket while on a recon mission.

He reached a muscular arm into the cupboard and withdrew one of them, quickly sliding back the chamber and inspecting the inside of the weapon.

It was good to go.

He pulled up a full, fifteen round clip and satisfyingly snapped it into the gun. Sam gave it one more admiring glance and tossed the weapon onto his bed, before reaching for the large, black case that rested atop his makeshift armoury.

With a large heave, he pulled it down, taking the weight of it onto his broad chest, before carefully lowering it to the recently swept floorboards. The case was locked with a combination lock, which Sam quickly set to his son's birthday.

The case pinged open.

A smile crept across his stubble covered jaw.

His sniper rifle.

The Accuracy International Arctic Warfare bolt action sniper rifle had been with him through thick and thin.

It had been with him on the cliff face on the outskirts of Kabul when he single-handedly took out a squadron to protect his own.

It had been the instrument of over sixty deaths.

He had taken great joy in cleaning it two weeks previously, sliding the plastic tubing down the forty-six-inch barrel and removing the flakes of gunpowder that would eventually cause a potential impact on his shot. He had taken himself to Cassiobury Park in Watford one night, speeding up the M1 to Hertfordshire and found a dark, quiet spot on a pitch-black field.

He fired two rounds into a tree from over a hundred yards. It was a simple shot to make, but he needed to iron out the first few potential skewed shots which always happened after a clean.

Sam needed the gun to be accurate.

Just not tonight.

But soon. He could feel it.

Sam slowly ran the palm of his hand across the stock of the rifle, feeling every groove of his war-torn weapon and trusting every single inch of it.

It had become an extension of his body.

Sam patted the rifle and then slammed the lid shut. Pushing himself up again, he turned, stretching his lower back before heaving the case up once more and sliding it back atop of the cupboard. Before shutting the door, he unhooked his assault rifle from its hook, the trusted gun ready for another night of action. With a smile, he felt the rifle's weight in his muscular arms as he turned and faced the opposite wall.

A map of London was pinned to the white wall, the recent paint work a poor attempt at injecting some brightness to the wall.

The map was littered with markings, with different pins denoting different points of interest.

Blue were known drug hot spots.

Green were the vicinities that willing snitches patrolled.

Yellow were strategically placed 'emergency stashes', which consisted of fake documents, weapons, and cash.

Red was his favourite, recording all the places he had hit since he'd begun his crusade.

Seventeen separate drug dens or gang hideouts had been successfully cleared down. All of them without killing.

But now, he marched to the map and slammed a pin into the Kodak factory in Shepherd's Bush. Long since abandoned, he now knew it was the makeshift High Rise being run in memory of the one he had torn down six months ago.

All that bloodshed would not be for nothing.

He glanced at his wrist, the watch telling him it was a little after two.

With the rain refusing to relent, he snatched his parka from the back of the door and slid it around his muscular frame. Sam pulled a black sports bag from under the bed and laid it on the sheets, carefully placing the rifle inside. Lastly, he picked up his Glock 20, slid it into the back of his jeans, and headed to the door.

Sam knew it would take him roughly forty-five minutes to drive to Shepherd's Bush and he wanted as much time as possible. Once he had scouted the area fully, he was planning on returning with his rifle.

Because tonight, he was going to introduce himself to Elmore Riggs.

He was going to shut down the final door of the High Rise once and for all.

CHAPTER FOUR

'Come in.'

DI Adrian Pearce didn't even look up from his blank computer screen, his scowl furrowing a brow that was turning grey. His hair, closely shorn to his scalp was already a faded grey colour, contrasting strongly with the darkness of his skin. Having passed his fiftieth birthday that summer, he knew he looked youthful for his age. But time was starting to catch up with him.

A creak here.

A crack there.

And his utter contempt for computers.

The door to his small office opened, clattering against a metal filing cabinet that had been shoehorned into a corner that was just too small. The gap was just big enough for people to slide through, which wasn't a problem for Amara Singh, as she eased through the gap and into the room.

The sleeves of her white shirt were rolled up, revealing her delicate forearms. The lapels of her shirt wore 'pips', the proud insignia of an Inspector and she cast her dark eyes around the room, a look of pity on her face. Pearce looked up, peering over the top of his mandated spectacles and caught her silent judgment.

'Hardly the Ritz, is it?'

She forced a smile, ignoring the obvious elephant in the room. It was an elephant that had followed Pearce around ever since he had arrested Inspector Howell at the top of the High Rise. In the six months since, he had been moved from the Department of Professional Standards to working internal cold cases.

They hadn't reallocated him.

They had neutered him.

His office, stuffed away behind the printing room on the fourth floor of the iconic Met building in Westminster, was a place to hide him from the world. After exposing the 'terrorist attack' as an inside job, Pearce knew what was coming next. The powers that be ensured that Howell was put away, but they swept a laundry list of indiscretions under the rug. Pearce's access had been restricted, and they soon removed him from a number of potential internal investigations.

Now he sat, in a dark corner of the police service, killing time until they gave him his golden handshake and a strict confidentiality agreement.

Pearce leaned back in his chair, his head just missing one of the overstuffed shelving units above him. He regarded Singh with an experienced eye, noting how she carried herself, the sternness of her expression and her clear obsession with proving she was more than a pretty face. Eventually, she offered him a smile that he was sure turned plenty of heads on a daily basis.

'DI Pearce.'

'Please, call me Adrian.'

'Very well, sir.' She shuffled as he raised his eyebrows. 'I mean, Adrian. I'm Detective Inspector Si…'

'Singh. I know.'

'How?' she asked, her posture as straight as an arrow.

'It's my job to know.' Pearce flashed her a warm smile. 'How long have you been with us now?'

'I transferred just over three months ago, sir,' Singh said.

'They still let you carry a gun?' Pearce asked, nodding towards the holster that was strapped securely to her curved hip. Singh flashed a glance down at the Glock 26 pistol that rested against her, the halogen light bathing it in a menacing sheen. 'You transferred from AR, am I right?'

Singh raised a perfectly tweezed eyebrow. She smiled.

'I served in the Armed Response unit for over two years sir, with distinction.' She smiled warmly. 'As did you, am I right?'

'A *long* time ago.' Pearce motioned to the small unit in the corner which housed a rusty old kettle and a small jar of instant coffee. Singh waved away politely. 'I'm essentially a bookkeeper nowadays.'

Pearce chuckled to himself, clicking his mouse in frustration as his computer still refused to burst into action. Singh cleared her throat.

'That's not entirely true, is it, sir?' Singh asked rhetorically. Pearce could see the effort she was putting into being authoritative.

'Excuse me?'

'With all due respect, sir. The reason you have been blackballed in this organisation is due to your involvement in the Sam Pope case from six months ago.' Singh carefully selected her words. 'So it hasn't been too long since you were seeing some action.'

Pearce smiled again, linking his fingers together before letting his hands drop into his lap. Singh stared at him, her tenacity threatening to sour the mood between them.

'You mean the Inspector Howell case, for which he was

arrested for the murder of his own nephew?' Pearce corrected, adding a sternness to his words for extra impact.

'Forgive me, sir. But I'm not here to sully the name of a peer who has passed away.'

Pearce raised his eyebrows, conveying his difference of opinion. After arresting a bloodied and bullet ridden Howell at the top of the High Rise, Pearce had followed Howell's descent with intrigue. He was sentenced to life in prison, which came to a non-surprising end after only a few months when they found Howell dead in his cell from suicide. Singh spoke again, breaking his train of thought.

'My focus is on Sam Pope, the man who killed over a dozen men, including Frank Jackson, and who is still at large. A man who, and I mean no disrespect, you're accused of aiding and abetting.'

'Allegedly,' Pearce stated calmly.

'Well, for someone who has worked for years to ensure that the police uphold the law, the evidence against you is rather damning.'

Pearce rose from his chair, his athletic frame evident through his grey suit and which was impressive for a man of his age. His reputation as a crack shot on Armed Response had followed him into his job of investigating his own colleagues, as well as his unbeaten record in the boxing ring. He was well aware of how imposing he could be and he noticed just a flicker of nerves on Singh's face.

It was what he was trained to notice.

It was all he needed.

'DI Singh, if you have come here to test my knowledge on that case then you are succeeding in only testing my patience.' He fastened the top button of his suit, the jacket clasping across his yellow tie. 'Now, I'm assuming you didn't come all this way to insult me, so why don't you tell me what it is you want?'

Singh straightened her stance, her hands clasped

behind her back. Pearce admired her attempts at standing strong.

'I have been assigned to the Sam Pope Task Force, sir, and I was hoping I could lean on you for information or maybe even entice you to join.'

'Join?' Pearce raised an eyebrow again, never tiring of leading people to their point.

'Yes, sir. With your knowledge of the previous case and your alleged dealings with Pope himself, your contribution in bringing this violent criminal to justice could be huge.' Pearce chuckled and Singh's face scrunched in frustration. 'I don't see what is so funny, sir?'

Pearce shuffled around his desk and sat on the edge of it, gently pushing a few files to the side. He regarded Singh carefully.

'So, let me get this straight. You have walked in here, have almost accused me of aiding and abetting a criminal and now you want my help?' Singh went to speak but Pearce held up an authoritative hand. 'Let me offer you some advice, Detective. Don't let your ambition cloud your application. I may be under my own cloud at this moment, but I've been doing this job a long time and I know how to play the game. I know where all this fire comes from, I do. You're a female and you're Indian. That's two ticks against you and you have knocked it out of the park. But just remember, I'm a black man who did all of that through the seventies and eighties.'

'No offence, sir. But I didn't ask you for a character assessment.'

'You keep saying no offence.' Pearce shook his head once more. 'Tell me, Singh. What do you want from me?'

'I want you to help me catch Sam Pope,' Singh said firmly. 'Assistant Commissioner Ashton has assigned me to track him down and that's exactly what I'm going to do. Even our mayoral candidates are backing our campaign.'

'Well, that must mean it's a *really* dumb idea.'

Singh ignored him and continued.

'Sam Pope is a dangerous man, highly trained in conflict and clearly has access to deadly weapons. No matter how well he served his country, he cannot take the law into his own hands. He has killed a number of people and will be held accountable for his crimes.'

'Crimes?' Pearce interrupted. 'There are those, not just in this station but in the press, who think he is just cleaning up the streets.'

'Are you one of those people, sir?' Singh shot an accusatory glare at him and Pearce found himself liking her even more.

'People will believe what they want to believe, Singh.' Pearce carefully sidestepped the question. 'But a few years ago, there was a gentleman called Lucas Cole who took down one of the most notorious crime gangs in London. Killed all four of the siblings and left the head of the snake for the police.'

'Then he was a criminal, just like them,' Singh said, crossing her arms in frustration.

'They raped and killed his pregnant wife and we did nothing,' Pearce responded solemnly. 'The Met stood back and tried to sweep it under the rug. Lucas Cole fought back. It may not have been legal, but I wouldn't tarnish him with the same brush when all he sought was justice.'

Singh shifted on the spot uncomfortably.

'What happened to him?'

'He died.' Pearce shook his head. 'He gave his life to avenge hers. While that was a different story, I wanted to paint a picture for you, Singh. I understand that you have orders and you have your eyes on the headlines you will make if you succeed. But if you really want my help on this, all I can offer you is my advice.'

'Which is?' Singh asked, a hint of anger in her words at being rejected.

'Sam Pope is a good man. You might not think it and this organisation has gone above and beyond to put him in everyone's cross hairs. But that man has been through more than you know and I believe, as a man who has hunted down corrupt 'good guys' for a living, that Sam Pope is on the wrong side of the law for the right reasons. My advice is the same advice that Howell gave me. Advice he should have heeded then. When it comes to Sam Pope … leave that man alone.'

Pearce smiled warmly and slowly eased himself off the desk, his back creaking once more as a mocking reminder of his age. Singh burnt a hole through him with her stare and he shimmied back around his desk to his battered leather chair and lowered himself down, the muscles aching in his legs. Singh stepped forward, pressed her hands to the desk and leaned forward, a whiff of her perfume snaring Pearce's attention for a split second.

'I'm going to take down Sam Pope. The man is a vigilante and belongs in a cell.' She leaned in further, doing her best to intimidate. 'And if I find a shred of evidence that you have helped him in any way, I'll make damn sure they throw you in one too.'

With that, Singh turned and wrenched open the door, the frame rattling against the file cabinet and echoing loudly around the measly office. She slid through the gap, slamming the door shut behind her as Pearce heard her boots stomp away and back to the real office. He sighed, annoyed that his likeness for her was outweighed by his disdain for her blind ambition. Pearce may have rattled a number of cages over the years, but he always did it with respect.

As he contemplated exactly how Singh's attitude would eventually be her undoing, he leaned back in his chair and thought of Sam Pope. Despite being shunted to the outskirts of the force, Pearce still had his ear to the ground and through hearsay and the reports in the press, he knew Pope was still fighting the good fight. Then, as a smile crept across his face, he wondered just how Singh would react if she ever did meet Pope.

Especially when she realised what he already knew. That she, nor anyone in the Metropolitan Police Service, had a hope in hell of catching him.

———

As she marched down the staircase, her boots echoing loudly in the bright corridor, Singh did her best to compose herself. She had heard stories about Pearce being a tough nut to crack, but she found her fists clenching in frustration. The man was one of the most highly regarded detectives in the Met, but he had pulled at too many threads and was now being punished. Whether or not that was fair, Singh had hoped that the chance to redeem himself by helping her would have appealed to what she had quickly discovered was a non-existent ego.

As she passed a few officers who respectfully nodded at her, Singh continued downwards, heading for the freedom of the bitterly cold day and to allow the crisp air to clear her head.

She was going to catch Sam Pope.

That was what she'd been tasked to do, and she was damn sure going to do it. Pearce had been right when he'd pointed out the shit she'd been through. She knew that a lot of her male colleagues saw her promotion as nothing more than a tick in the diversity column and she was determined to prove them wrong.

Yes, she was female.

Yes, she was Indian.

Yes, she was attractive.

But she was damn good at her job too and she'd underline that when she pulled Sam Pope in through the doors she was rapidly approaching, with his hands in cuffs. And after his non-compliance, she wondered if maybe she could do the same to Adrian Pearce, too. Singh pushed open the doors to the reception area and marched past the reception desk, shaking her head in pity as the young officer sat patiently in front of a distressed man, tears streaming down his face as he berated him.

'Please,' the man cried, his fist clenched. 'They have my girl and no one will help me.'

Singh could smell the booze emanating from the man from a few yards away and she strode with purpose towards him.

'Excuse me,' she said firmly. 'But unless you have a real problem, the only one here is you. Kindly leave so this man can do his job.'

The young officer smiled thankfully as the man turned to her. He was in his mid-forties, white with thinning, wiry blonde hair. His blue eyes were bloodshot, the bags beneath them evidence of a sleepless night. His face was covered in stubble and he looked the picture of someone going through a traumatic experience.

Judging by the stench of alcohol surrounding him, she imagined it was to do with needing another drink.

'Please,' the man repeated, his voice cracking with desperation. 'I don't know what else to do.'

Singh shook her head in disappointment, stomping towards the outside world and the chance to regather her thoughts. As she approached the automatic door, she called back to the drunken gentleman.

'Go home, sir,' she said without looking back. 'Get a good night's sleep and stop wasting police time.'

As the door slid shut behind her, Singh headed towards

the Thames, wrapping her arms around her petite frame to shield herself from the bitter cold. Approaching the metal railing, she watched with a sense of victory as the drunken man stumbled out of the station, stuffed his hands in his pockets, and hurried up the road. Singh watched him disappear around the corner, not realising that his desperate pleas were the truth and that he would become more important to her task than she could imagine.

CHAPTER FIVE

'Like I said, that motherfucker wants to step to me, I'll put him six feet deep.'

Elmore Riggs flashed his usual grin, the gold tooth gleaming among the pearly whites. His dark skin, courtesy of his Ghanaian family, was covered in faded tattoos, many of them from the gangs he had rolled with during his youth, or the seven years he'd spent behind bars for blinding a man during a gang attack. His hair, tied into thin corn rows, was pulled back into a ponytail, the intricate plaits slapping against his broad back.

His body was well toned, the ink work wrapping over a defined torso that was bare, beyond the gold chain that hung from his neck and the gun holster he still had strapped across his chest. Standing on the top floor of the 'new' High Rise, he glared at Sean Wiseman, who shook his head in fury. The makeshift building wasn't a patch on the old High Rise, which they'd been invited to enjoy by Frank Jackson on a number of occasions. Now, The Gent was dead and Riggs had found a new location.

Sure, it wasn't elegant, nor did it have a concierge. It was an abandoned office, with enough rooms for him to throw a number of mattresses and hookers into, and start making some serious cash. Once that rolled in, so did the drugs and so did the punters.

Now, he was sitting atop the seedy side of London and Riggs was sure as hell not going to let it go. Which is why, as his trusted friend begged for them to give it all up, he could feel his fists clenching with anger.

'Elmore, we been together since back in the day,' Wiseman pleaded. 'This guy ain't gonna stop. I say we go. Tonight.'

'Why? Because you told him where we at?' Riggs took a menacing step forward. On the sofa against the far wall, two of his trusted guards sat, scantily clad women writhing on their laps. Lines of cocaine sat on top of the table, alongside piles of money and loaded hand guns.

'Look what he did to me,' Wiseman protested, lifting his bandaged hand, the bullet hole severing several nerves and any hope of a functioning hand again. 'He did this to me, to get to you.'

'Part of the job, son.' Riggs shrugged. He looked around at the makeshift penthouse with pride, the drugs, the goons, the weapons. All he had ever wanted to be was a gangster.

'Not part of our friendship,' Wiseman spat, before prodding a finger into Riggs's bare chest. 'I'm out.'

Riggs's eyes widened in fury and quick as a flash, he swung a hard, back hand, his ring clad fingers clattering into the side of Wiseman's head. As blood sprayed from the gash that appeared above his eyebrow, Wiseman stumbled back, crashing over a side table, the clatter echoing over the hip hop music thumping out of the nearby speakers. Wiseman dabbed a hand at the blood seeping down his face, before looking up at Riggs with terror, whose eyes were wild with rage.

'Out? *Out*?!' Riggs roared, spit flying from his mouth.

'You know how far we have come, Sean. We were out on the fucking street, watching these white motherfuckers get rich off of us selling drugs for them. They sat in leather seats, getting fat and paid while we were out there, dodging bullets and running from the fucking pigs. Then, after I got out, I told you we were gonna get something more for ourselves. We were gonna get a seat at the adults' table. Look at us, Sean. We ain't fighting for scraps from the table anymore. We are the motherfucking table. And this shit, is not something you can just walk away from.'

One of the barely dressed women handed a towel to Wiseman, who pressed it against his bloodied face as he slowly got to his feet.

'And what if Sam Pope turns up here, huh?' Wiseman yelled, his eyes watering from the pain. 'What then? You gonna kill him?'

'Kill him? Shit, I'm gonna shake his damn hand, bruv.' Riggs beamed another grin. 'He cleared the path to the throne.'

'He didn't clear a path. He cut down everything in his way,' Wiseman said, shaking his head in anger. 'He'll do the same thing here.'

'Then maybe it is best you leave. Seeing as how you acting like a little bitch.'

A few sniggers came from the thugs sat on the sofa, both of them glaring at Wiseman as he shot them an angered glance. Suddenly, Sam Pope's threat from the night before wasn't so bad. Sure, he had been terrified and had a bullet blasted through his hand. But now, as he looked around at the lack of professionalism and care, he realised that if it wasn't Sam Pope, it was going to be someone else. It was time to get out. Taking a deep breath, Wiseman forced himself to look at Riggs.

'Fine, I'll go.'

He turned, heading towards the door, when the largest

member of the crew, imaginatively named 'Tiny', stepped in front of the door, his massive arms folded across his barrel chest like two pythons coiling each other.

Wiseman swallowed hard, before turning back to Riggs, who had a look of regret on his face. He was also holding a gold-plated Glock in his hand.

'Sean, you motherfucker. Why you put me in this position, man?'

'Look, El, you don't have to do this...' Wiseman began to beg, holding up his damaged hand. 'Please, let me just go and I'll never say anything to anyone. I swear,'

'I can't let that happen. You know too much about our set up, about our plans for expansion. In here, I can protect you. Out there, they gonna eat you alive. Sam Pope got you talking like that.' He snapped his fingers. 'And I'll handle that when he makes himself known. But I don't want any more wolves coming to the door, ya feel me?'

'Then let me stay,' Wiseman offered, his body shaking with fear. 'I'll stay and we can take this whole city like you wanted.'

Riggs gritted his teeth and shook his head, tossing a troubling thought around in his mind. The music had been turned off and now all eyes were on the two men and the mounting tension. Riggs had grown up with Wiseman, the two of them had been neighbours on the eighth floor of the same building in Neasden. The estate was riddled with gangs and before their tenth birthdays, they were already acting as lookouts for some of the bigger boys. They eventually dropped out of school together at the age of thirteen, running their own corner and making more money than their parents ever had. Wiseman had never met his dad, but he knew that Riggs's was a crack addict and violent and Riggs turned up to the corner on more than one occasion in a broken state. On Riggs's sixteenth birthday, his father died from an overdose.

Wiseman knew that Riggs had done it and his friend had never denied it. But they trusted each other, with Riggs even removing the eye of a man who had attacked Wiseman with a baseball bat. That had got him seven years in Pentonville and when he was released, Wiseman was off the streets and working his way through an Open University course in business management.

Now, years later, the two of them were standing a few metres apart, with Riggs tossing up the idea of their loyalty to one another, to his place on the throne ever since The Gent had been left bullet-riddled by Sam Pope.

Their friendship.

Or his power.

With a deep sigh, Riggs lifted the pistol, the gun suddenly feeling very heavy in his hand, and he aimed it squarely at Wiseman, whose tear-stained face lost all its colour.

The same way everyone's does when they realise they're about to die.

A gunshot rang out.

Suddenly, the window collapsed into a million shards and a bullet ripped through the room, ripping through Tiny's kneecap, shattering it instantly and splattering the entire door with blood. The large guard went down, screaming in agony as he held his wrecked leg, rolling side to side in an ever-increasing pool of blood. The cries for help were drowned out by the sheer panic of the rest of the room, with the women all screaming and racing for the other door, while the men all reached for their guns, all of them pointing them towards the shattered window and into the downpour of the night sky. The wind whipped through the opening, flicking rain droplets across one of the tables.

Riggs had dropped to the wooden floor, tipping over one of the tables and covering the floorboards in a plethora of drugs and money. Leaning against the wood, he held his pistol in his hand, yelling at his men to stay cool and to get down. As they obliged, he noticed Wiseman tending to Tiny, a sharp pang of guilt shot through him like the bullet had Tiny's knee.

He was going to kill his best friend.

For power.

Just as he began to process what that meant, the entire room looked at each other in shock at the next noise they heard. With all of them expecting heavy fire to rain down upon them, and a myriad of bullets to riddle their penthouse, they all looked at each other blankly.

A mobile phone was ringing.

Riggs's phone.

As the cold wind whipped through the empty window, Riggs reached around the table with his free hand and retrieved the phone from a small pile of cocaine that had been tossed across the floor.

The screen said 'Wiseman.'

Scowling, he answered.

'Mr Riggs. It's Sam Pope.' The voice spoke calmly. 'I believe you have been expecting me.'

———

As the rain clattered the city of London, Aaron Hill stumbled through a group of kids, ignoring their jeers and idle threats before they continued on towards Shepherd's Bush station. He knew this wasn't the safest neighbourhood in London, yet here he was. He trembled as his drunken state slowly morphed into a hangover, his brain pressing against his skull as if it wanted to escape.

It had been several hours since he had been to the Met, drunkenly yelling at them to help him find his daughter.

They had written him off as just another paranoid

drunk, trying his best to get thrown in the cells to shelter himself from the bitter night ahead.

What he was, was a man at the end of his rope. A loving single father, who had waited up all night for his fifteen-year-old daughter to return home.

A man who now had nothing to lose.

As the elements crashed against him, the bitterness of the evening shook him from his drunken haze and clarity sprung to the forefront of his mind. Ever since his wife had tragically passed away, he had been so protective of their daughter.

Jasmine.

She was a good kid, always well behaved and clearly set for big things after school. But as a single father, there were parts of her life he couldn't guide her through, and he had made up for that by being overbearing. Which had pushed her to rebel.

Which had forced him to let her go to that party the night before.

Tears joined the rain water that was cascading down his face as he stumbled past the entrance to the BBC grounds, the large, glass-covered buildings lit up brilliantly in the night sky.

In the distance, the roar of the QPR fans vibrated from Loftus Road stadium, the floodlights bathing part of the night sky in a magnificent glow, illuminating the torrential downpour from above as the Saturday evening kick-off was well underway.

Jasmine had never returned home from the party.

None of her friends knew where she'd gone, with one or two of them mentioning a boy who had led her outside. The thought of his daughter being sexually active filled him with dread, but worse was unthinkable.

He had tracked her phone to the abandoned Kodak

offices just on the outskirts of the borough, the building was rumoured to be a haven for crime.

For drugs.

For rape.

Shaking with a mixture of fear and rage, Aaron slipped his hand to the back of his jeans and retrieved the loaded Glock he had bought that afternoon. It hadn't been hard, a few terrifying conversations and the parting with a thousand pounds. He had spent the entire day staring at it, drinking himself to a drunken stupor, where his desperation not to use it had carried him all the way to that police station. The petite, pretty woman who had demanded he left had set in motion a series of events that would likely get him killed.

He knew that.

But without his daughter, he would have nothing left to live for.

Approaching the front door to the building, he noticed a number of lights on within, undoubtedly groups of criminals getting down to their business. His biggest fear was finding her in one of the rooms, hooked on drugs and being passed around from demented sicko to demented sicko.

Or her body, violated and disposed of.

That rage struck him, just as a clap of thunder roared through the night sky, like a physical manifestation of his mindset. Taking a deep breath, he fumbled slightly and eventually managed to slide his finger over the trigger.

The gun felt heavy in his hand.

Just as he stepped in through the door, the onrushing wind whipped around him, slamming it shut and blocking out the noise of a rifle shot that Sam Pope had just sent through the top-floor window.

CHAPTER SIX

'You one crazy motherfucker, you know that?' Riggs said, shaking his head. With his back pressed against the upturned table, he knew somewhere in the cold, wet night, Sam Pope had a gun fixed on his position. Riggs scanned the room, the mayhem the one bullet had caused. Rain fell through the shattered glass onto the shards below the window. Three of his soldiers had taken cover as well, all of them snarling and gripping their pistols.

Tiny had reduced his screams of agony into pathetic whimpers, the blood loss slowly ebbing away his consciousness. Wiseman, his hand heavily bandaged, looked panicked at the situation. The floor was scattered with loose bank notes, cards, and drugs.

Sam Pope could see it all.

From the building across the street, he lay flat on the hard, cold, wooden floor on the fifth floor. The building had long since been abandoned, a derelict office block that was once alive with activity. From the faded signage in the lobby, this particular floor had once homed an elite recruitment agency, specialising in IT software engineers. Now, as the thin windows gave little resistance to the wind that was lashing at his body, Sam was using it as a sniping spot. With the distance between the two buildings no more than a hundred yards, he had elected not to bring his actual sniper rifle. The weapon had forged his fearsome reputation and had been used to obliterate a number of skulls. As he stared down the scope, he adjusted his grip on his trusty assault rifle, the crosshairs focused on the table he knew Riggs was behind. He could have littered it with a flurry of bullets, ripping the man apart before systematically assassinating the rest of his men.

But he didn't want that.

He had enough death on his hands.

Riggs's voice wormed its way through the Bluetooth headphones Sam had attached to his ear.

'You still there, Pope?'

'I am indeed,' Sam replied politely, adjusting his gloved finger on the trigger. His Glock was pressed against the small of his spine. A flash and smoke grenade hung from a sling across his chest, which he had pushed to one side.

He was there. And fully equipped.

'So, what you gon do? You gon wait there like a pussy all night, or you gon come see me?' Riggs spat, his bravado as fake as the gold chains he had round his neck. 'Because we already sent word we under fire. That's right, white boy, we gon have two Beamers full of some hard motherfuckers here in five minutes. But they ain't comin' to my building, they'll be comin' to you.'

'Is that right?' Sam said dismissively.

'You damn right,' Riggs said triumphantly. 'You took a shot at the king and guess what, you missed.'

'I didn't take a shot at you,' Sam corrected. 'I took a shot at your biggest dog and by the looks of things, he might need to be put down.'

Silence sat between them, as well as a torrential downpour and an empty street. Sam knew Riggs wasn't bluffing.

Very soon that street would be filled with some more of his soldiers, all tooled up, all looking to find his vantage point.

Then, once word hit the police of a suspected gang hit with high powered guns, the whole of the Met would be swarming over the streets, not resting until they'd overturned the last paving slab if it meant they had a chance of finding him.

Sam had to end this soon.

As if he knew what Sam was thinking, Riggs finally spoke up.

'So what the hell you want, man? You already hurt two of my boys. You want me?'

'I want you to shut it down,' Sam said calmly.

'Shut it down? Are you dizzy, bruv?' Riggs chuckled. 'I got more money, gear, and pussy in this damn room than you will get in your lifetime. I ain't shutting it down.'

'The last man who ran the High Rise, he decided he didn't want to listen to me neither. It didn't work out so well for him.'

'Yeah, well he was too polite for his own good, ya feel me?' Riggs said. 'We don't play by the same rules.'

'I'm going to give you to the count of three, Riggs, to do the right thing and shut it down. Or else I will.'

The rain clattered all around Sam, the open, damaged building offering little protection from the winter evening. He readjusted his grip, pulling the stock of the rifle tight against his shoulder.

'You wanna shut me down? Give it your best.' Riggs yelled defiantly. 'Like I said, there is only one of you and from what I heard, you ain't killed anyone since you put a bullet in Jackson and saved me a job.'

Sam shuffled uncomfortably on the stone floor, the image of ramming a knife into Colin Mayer's stomach flashed to the front of his mind. The warmth of the blood rushing over his hands as he gutted the corrupt cop before leaving him for dead on that small boat in Dawlish.

The last time he broke the promise to his son.

As he stared through the scope of his rifle, the crosshairs still aimed at the overturned table that sheltered Riggs, he felt the temptation to break it once more. He took a breath and spoke.

'One.'

'I'm hanging up the phone now, Sam. You wanna come see me, you come across now. Before my boys turn up and tune you up.'

'Two.'

'Congrats. You can count,' Riggs retorted, craning his neck to the side, signalling to his eager henchmen to aim at the window. Sam could hear his words shaking, the fear in the gangster's voice betraying his apparent bravado. Sam took a deep breath before responding calmly.

'Three.'

At that moment, the door to the top floor of the new High Rise burst open and a middle-aged man was hurled over the threshold, stumbling forward and falling flat onto his chest. Two hulking men, both with cane rowed hair and several tattoos followed, laughing, with one of them holding a handgun. Sam quickly scanned the situation through his scope, squinting hard through the torrential rain to piece together the situation. The man was clearly terrified, scrambling to his knees and looking around frantically. Sam could hear the commotion over the phone, the noise calming down to a laughter before Riggs piped up.

'Well, what do we have here?' he said, standing up from behind the table and looking out of the window, daring Sam to fire. 'I thought you worked alone, Pope?'

'I have no idea who that man is,' Sam responded, smoothly shifting his line of sight from Riggs, back to the panicked man who feebly held his hands up in surrender.

Sam could see blood trickling from the man's eyebrow, evidence of a beating that Riggs's henchman undoubtedly enjoyed giving. As Riggs sauntered across the room towards the terrified man, Sam assessed the man's situation and quickly concluded it wasn't good.

The man was as good as dead.

Sam told himself to stick to his spot.

To keep his focus on the mission at hand.

Riggs interrupted his internal struggle.

'Let's find out the name of our contestant, shall we?' Riggs cackled, the laughter of his henchmen audible behind him. Sam watched through his scope as he leaned down towards the frightened visitor. 'Who the fuck are you?'

'I-I-I…' the man stammered, and Sam watched as Riggs lashed out, the clunk of the gun colliding with the man's head echoing down the phone.

'Leave him alone,' Sam demanded, his fingers tightening around the rifle.

Stick to the mission.

'Nah, this prick ain't a customer of mine and my boys found him creeping through the corridors with a fuckin' gun in his hand. So I ain't gonna leave him alone.'

'He isn't with me,' Sam said through gritted teeth.

'Well I don't give a fuck what you say, Pope. He turns up the same time you do so you know what I'm gon do? I'm gon put a bullet in every one of his joints and then, when my boys pick you up any minute now, I'll keep him alive long enough for him to watch me kill you. How does that sound?' Riggs turned to the window, awaiting a response.

Sam lowered his head, closed his eyes, and thought about his son.

His Jamie.

Memories began to flood into his mind like a broken

dam, from his son showing him his favourite books, to them play fighting on the sofa in front of a Disney film.

The memories always ended the same way, with the image of his son's dead, lifeless body staring up at him from the pavement. The swerved car, driven by a drunk that Sam could have stopped.

All the guilt.

All the pain.

It flooded back, along with the empty promise to Jamie that he wouldn't kill again.

A promise he had broken several times when he took down the High Rise.

A promise, he would break right now.

'Sorry, Jamie,' Sam uttered quietly.

'Jamie? What the fu—' Riggs's question was cut off, as a bullet sliced through the glass window, zipped through the room, and penetrated the side of his skull. With a loud crack, it ripped out the other side, spraying the wall with brain matter and a fantastic red mist. Riggs fell to the floor lifeless and for a moment, the only sound was the crashing of the rain as it hammered the capital. Then, a barrage of gunshots echoed, along with shattered windows and cries of anger as Riggs's men emptied their guns into the dark of the night, hoping to catch their unknown attacker with a stray bullet.

Sam stayed calm.

He was trained, and he pushed himself up onto one knee, resting a foot in front of himself and steadied himself. He pulled the gun tight to his chest, resting it in the groove between his pectoral and shoulder. It felt natural and despite the bitter chill of the rain, he felt back in Afghanistan all those years ago.

Scanning the top of the building, he noticed the terrified man crawling towards the door, when one of the thugs stepped towards him, clearly intending to lay down a marker of who was in charge.

The man raised his gun.

Sam pulled the trigger.

Silently, he saw a burst of red explode from the man's chest as he spun and fell to the floor, lifeless. With the phone somewhere in the chaos, Sam could hear the cries of terror from the rest of the gang, as they rushed towards the door, all of them looking to escape the onslaught. Sam pushed himself up, his drenched clothes clinging to him as he ran across the fifth floor of the derelict building and he stepped through an empty doorframe onto a rickety, metal fire escape. The wind shook it like a baby's rattle, but Sam carefully navigated down the steps, his boots gripping against the slippery metal, as he kept his gun trained on the building. The front door flew open and three shifty business men ran in any direction they could, clearly paying customers who had heard the commotion and realised they were a long way from home.

Sam continued down the metal staircase, his boots thudding on each step, when suddenly, the blast of gunfire shook the night sky followed swiftly by the ricochet of a bullet on the steps behind him. Sam instinctively ducked down, jumping the final three steps to the second-floor platform and swiveling on his heels, the scope of his gun peering between two of the railings that surrounded him.

Two of the gangsters had their gun drawn and aimed at his location, their faces plastered with murderous intent.

Sam aimed low and squeezed twice.

The first man cried out in agony as the bullet shattered his knee cap. The second followed suit, only that bullet had snapped his shin in half. They both fell into a crumpled heap onto the cold, wet pavement and Sam leapt to his feet, scaling the last two floors two steps at a time.

Sirens wailed in the distance, their volume increasing

with every second as they rapidly approached his location. Any reports of gunfire were met with a swift and armed response by the Met, who worked tirelessly to protect the good people of their district. But Sam knew they were after him and even the slightest hint that he may be involved, and he was sure they were sending everyone they had.

He had to move.

Fast.

Just as he approached the final staircase to the street, two 4x4s screeched around the corner, the booming music and the over the top stylisation to the vehicles told him it was Riggs's aforementioned backup. Sam whipped up the rifle once more and despite the obscuring downpour and speed of the vehicle, he sent one bullet straight into the front right tyre of the first vehicle.

The rubber exploded, blowing out instantly and the driver clearly panicked, the large car turning sharply to the right and screeching like a banshee as the metal wheel scraped the pavement. The second car collided into it at full speed, spinning it even further and sending it careering into a lamp post in a magnificent display of sparks and flying metal.

The second car, now crumpled from bumper to windscreen, slowed to a stop a few feet from the two fallen gangsters, whose cries of pain had silenced as they lost consciousness. Three of the doors opened and three men stumbled out, all of them dazed from the collision. The driver, a broad man of Indian heritage, had blood trickling from a head wound and he lazily raised a gun as Sam jumped from the final few steps onto the street in front of him. Sam dropped to his knee.

He lifted the rifle.

Three shots this time.

Three more legs were ripped apart by the severity of his ammunition.

Sam surveyed the situation. Five men were littered across the street in various stages of consciousness, all of them immobilised. The door to the first car swung open and another henchmen dropped out, his arm clearly broken and the left side of his face covered in blood.

Sam raised his rifle but quickly dropped it.

The man was no threat.

All threats had been neutralised.

Suddenly, the end of the street burst into flashing blue lights and the sirens wailed a haunting welcome as five police cars swung around the corner. A van followed, undoubtedly filled with highly trained, highly armed officers all with orders to bring him down.

One way or the other.

Sam looped the strap of the rifle over his neck and swung the gun onto his back, the metal was warm against his drenched clothes. As the police drew near, he pulled his Glock from his side holster and raced towards the makeshift High Rise, hoping the mystery man was still alive and knowing that he was quickly running out of time.

As the police cars screeched to a halt and reached the carnage he had left behind, Sam raced full-pelt through the rain, and into the High Rise.

CHAPTER SEVEN

Singh had been sitting at her desk, sleeves rolled up, head rested in one hand staring at some therapy notes about Pope when the call had come in. A young PC, a little portly but incredibly bright, had knocked on her door and told her that there had been reports of multiple gunshots fired in Shepherd's Bush. The reports said that they'd sounded like an automatic weapon.

Despite the terrifying rise in gang and gun crime in London, Singh launched out of her chair instantly. She knew exactly what it meant.

Sam Pope.

As she marched through the office, barking out orders to the team to set up a perimeter and send an Armed Response unit immediately, she felt the adrenaline pump through her veins. Her conversations with Harris and Pearce had threatened to shake her confidence.

All it had done was reinvigorate it.

As she raced down the stairs to the parking lot, Singh thought about the impact stopping Sam Pope would have on her career. After the outrage from the public regarding the bombing at the London Marathon, the Met spin doctors had worked well to shift the focus towards the organised crime and perceived vigilantism that was plaguing the city. As far as the public saw, the police were fighting a losing battle against the likes of Sam Pope.

Bringing him in would make her a hero.

Singh jumped into the passenger seat of a police car, the warmth of the heaters hitting her instantly as the young PC in the driver's seat brought the car to life. The wind was littered with raindrops as it swept by, the freezing night sky was thick with grey clouds. Instantly, the darkness was eradicated by the flashing blue lights of the police car as it shot forward, its siren wailing like a battle cry.

Followed by another three cars, Singh barked her orders across the radio, telling a number of her task force what she expected and where she needed them. An update came through that a civilian had seen a man shooting oncoming vehicles and then unloading on the passengers.

It was Sam Pope.

Armed Response took control of the radio waves, announcing their arrival in less than two minutes, a squadron of ten highly trained, lethally armed officers who would enter the building and bring Sam Pope out at gunpoint.

Singh smirked as she thought about slapping cuffs around his murderous wrists, reading him his rights, and shoving him into the back of the car. She glanced over her shoulder at the empty seat behind the cage and pictured it.

With the chance to end the task force before it had even begun, she demanded her subordinate put his foot down, and as he obliged, the car roared loudly and hurtled through the rain towards the gunfight.

———

As Sam entered the stairwell of the factory, he swept the corridor with the rifle, the stock lodged firmly against his wet chest, his gloved finger wrapped around the trigger. Other than a couple of weak bulbs that flickered, the stairwell was drenched in darkness. A dripping sound filtered through the shadows every ten seconds or so, the upkeep of the building had been abandoned a long time ago. Taking the steps two at a time, Sam approached the door to the first floor, gently pressing it open with his foot before sweeping the corridor.

Nothing.

He marched through the dark corridor, dimly lit from a few swinging, unshaded bulbs. The walls were a depressing grey, severe signs of damp and mould creeping through. What was once a proud office for a large company was nothing more than a damp, desolate shell. Shaking his head, he walked a few steps further, before deciding to ascend further, knowing he needed to find the mystery man who had caused such havoc.

The man had barged into a criminal hideout with a gun, with clearly no idea how to use it.

A man who clearly had nothing left to lose.

As Sam approached the corridor again, he heard a gentle thud behind one of the doors. Raising the rifle once more, he threw his body weight forward, raised his leg and planted a boot against the door.

It swung open.

Originally, the room would have been a bright office, a nice desk in the corner and a few chairs for a chat over coffee. Now, the seedy room was dark, the smell of mould and drugs hit him like a wall and on the floor, was a crumpled, stained mattress. Atop it, a flabby man scrambled in a panic to cover his modesty at Sam's intrusion, fear plastered across his sweaty face.

Laying sprawled on the mattress was a malnourished

woman, her eyes glazed and her body coursing with drugs. The prostitute made no attempt to cover her naked body and didn't even acknowledge Sam at all.

Sam pulled the rifle up, aiming it squarely at the man, who cowered in fear. His thin, wispy hair was slick against his head.

'Please. Don't shoot me,' the man begged, his flabby body reminding him of Chris Morton, a rapist who Sam had battered to a pulp over six months before. Sam eyed the 'customer' once more, noticing the wedding band he was desecrating around his chunky finger.

'Get out,' Sam demanded, shaking his head in disgust. 'Now.'

The man nodded, weeping pathetically as he reached for his clothes which were balled up beside the mattress. Outside, the rain rattled the window, and the sirens grew louder, telling Sam he was rapidly running out of sand in his hour glass. With one final, sympathetic look at the violated woman, Sam stepped back into the corridor.

The fist collided with his cheek instantly, the impact sending him sprawling into the wall and dropping the rifle, the strap causing it to swing wildly.

Sam hit the wall, blood spraying from his mouth and he tried his best to focus. Everything went a bright, painful white for a split second when he suddenly regained control, quick enough to see another fist hurtling towards his nose. Quickly, he dropped to his left, allowing his attacker's knuckles to crack sickeningly against the brick, the large, African man howling pain at the impact. Sam burst forward, ramming his shoulder into the man's solid stomach, before rattling the attacker with a hard right hook. The man reset his footing, his eyes wild with murderous intent, and he pulled a knife from his jeans, slashing wildly as he approached.

Sam weaved like a boxer, watching the blade slice the

air in front of him, before catching a swipe with his forearm and lifting a swift chop of his hand into the man's throat. As his larynx closed, and he gasped for air, the attacker dropped the knife, both hands clutching his neck as he struggled to breathe. Dropping to his knees, the man gasped, and just as a stream of oxygen filtered its way to his lungs, Sam leapt forward, swivelled his hips and planted a ferocious knee into the man's face.

His nose shattered.

A few teeth shot forward like blood-stained missiles.

He was unconscious before he hit the ground.

Sam let out a deep sigh, running his tongue against his quickly swelling cheek and tasting the warm, coppery blood still sloshing in his mouth. Spitting it out onto the filthy hallway floor, he cracked his neck, before pulling his weapon up once more. In the doorway, the plump business man, now dressed, looked on in shock. Sam, seeing the man's fear at his fighting prowess, took a second to point at his eyes, before pointing at the man, mouthing, 'I'm watching you.'

The man cowered, before running to the stairwell, allowing Sam a rare smile.

Following behind, he continued up the staircase, each floor welcoming him with a fresh stench of drugs and desecration. The second floor held no violent attacks, Sam clearing out each room and finding a couple with fresh needle punctures in their arms, vacant faces, and their veins filled with heroin. Shaking his head, he left, knowing that some people were beyond saving. As he continued to the next floor, he wondered what had led those poor people to that moment.

Did they suffer something truly horrific, like he did, and not know how to deal with it?

Or was it just a bad choice?

With a trail of dead bodies, and an even greater list of

those he had injured, Sam was fully aware of the different ways people dealt with their grief. But as he cleared out another building that was a central point of crime that was rotting the country like a cancer, he tried to console himself with the notion that he was helping.

The wailing sirens on the street below laughed in the face of that thought.

Sam pushed the door open to the fourth floor.

Carefully, he swept both sides of the hallway with his gun, on high alert after the previous attack. One wall of the corridor had been stripped down to the bare brickwork, a plastic sheet crudely nailed onto it. The wind, which had crept in through every possible crack in the old building, caused it to flap loudly. There were no makeshift rooms on this floor, the punters not given access to the penthouse.

With reserved steps, Sam approached the open door, a puddle of blood welcoming him at the threshold. The room was bright, the lights burning brightly from the beams above and Sam cast his eye over his handiwork. Tiny, the large enforcer he had disabled at the door, was now unconscious, the pool of blood belonging to the bullet hole in his knee cap. The room was littered with drugs and money, the overturned tables had sent their riches scattering. Among the expensive debris was the motionless body of Riggs, his eyes still open, the side of his skull ripped apart by the impact of the bullet Sam had sent his way.

Another dead body lay among the fifty-pound notes, blood still trickling from the hole in its chest. Sam stopped for a moment and took a deep breath.

'Sorry, Jamie,' he muttered again, his words laced with self-loathing. As the screeching tyres of the police cars rounded the corner of the street, Sam scanned the room and saw the cowering body of the mystery man in the corner of the room, his knees tucked tightly into his chest.

Sam marched purposefully through the carnage and as he approached, the man held his hands up in panic.

'Please, don't hurt me!' he exclaimed, his face stained with tears.

Sam lowered his weapon and held his hands up, listening as a myriad of car doors slammed on the street below, the police surrounding the building and no doubt on the verge of sending an armed team in to drag him out. As the room was bathed in intermittent flashes of blue, Sam took a step closer.

'I'm not going to hurt you,' Sam spoke authoritatively. 'I need to know who the hell you are.'

'It doesn't matter,' the man spat, pushing himself to his feet slowly. He was middle aged; his eyes were red from a mixture of booze and fatigue. The only thing more powerful than the stench of alcohol was the stench of desperation. 'It's done.'

'What's done?' Sam demanded. At that moment, a thud echoed from the other side of the room. Sam spun instinctively, his hand skimming to his waist and retrieving his pistol. Before he spun to a stop, he had it held out, both hands wrapped around it, ready to fire.

The movement had been fluid.

Muscle memory kicking in.

Standing on the other side of the blood-soaked room, with his shattered hand held high in surrender, was Sean Wiseman. Sam held the gun steady but softened his scowl from anger to disappointment.

'Please, don't shoot,' Sean begged, his whole body trembling. Despite his brown skin, Sean looked a deathly pale which Sam quickly attributed to the gunfire and death of Sean's gang. He had seen a number of young soldiers keel over the same way after their first introduction to war.

'Stay where you are,' Sam demanded. 'I told you that your life as a criminal was over.'

'I know.' Sean panicked, his eyes jittering with every flash of the police sirens. 'I was here telling them that. Honest.'

Sam arched an eyebrow and then lowered his gun.

'Stay there. I'm going to need your help.' He turned back to the random intruder, who let out a defeated sigh. 'Now tell me, what's your name?'

'Aaron. Aaron Hill.'

'I'm Sam,' Sam offered, and Aaron looked at him sceptically.

'Sam? As in Sam Pope? Jesus ... you're in the news. You're a killer!'

'A killer who just saved your goddamn life,' Sam retorted. 'Now what the hell are you doing here? Do you know how fucking stupid that was?'

Wiseman had ventured towards the window, peering down onto the street below. Despite the torrential rain, he watched as a ten strong group of heavily armed men made their way to the door, a strict formation and clear instructions.

Aaron took another deep breath and then, fighting back tears, finally spoke.

'My daughter. They took my daughter.'

Sam's eyes narrowed with anger.

'Who did?' Sam asked, but Aaron was shaking his head, tears overflowing through his fingers. 'Who took your daughter?'

Outside, Singh marched through the rain and gave the go ahead for the AR team to enter the building. A few hand signals later, and the team filtered into the building.

They had breached.

Wiseman, without looking back, spoke.

'I hate to interrupt, but I think we have company.'

Sam turned towards the window, watching as the last of the Armed Response entered. He predicted he had two minutes before they reached the top floor. Instantly, he began to unzip his vest, removing the sling that carried his two grenades and then slid his arms out of his jacket. As the excitement built outside the building and the Armed Response team began its clearance, Sam told both Wiseman and Aaron what he needed them to do. As they nodded their understanding, he turned to Aaron, who looked broken. Sam reached into the man's jacket, pulled out his wallet and removed his driving license. Before Aaron could complain, Sam spoke.

'I promise you, when I get out of here, I will come to you and I promise we will find your daughter.'

His words clearly hit home and Aaron's eyes welled up once more. Sam barked his final instructions, and both men went about following them.

By now, the team would be on the first floor. Sam took a deep breath and headed to the stairwell.

Time to go meet them.

CHAPTER EIGHT

Rain clattered against the side of the building, the bitter cold seeping in through the cracks. The building was as depressing as it was broken, a broken relic that had once been a thriving focal point for the community. A memory washed away by the downpour of modern-day progression.

Aaron Hill could relate.

When he and his wife had separated four years previously, his daughter suffered. From the moment Jasmine had been born, they had an unbreakable bond. While he was never the most confident man, he loved his daughter dearly and her smile had brought out a fun-loving side to him that he had never known existed. They would bike ride together most Sunday mornings, he remembered watching with gushing pride as she sped off, whipping through the woodland tracks on their outings.

Then suddenly, his wife, Emma, was diagnosed with breast cancer.

All their smiles faded along with his wife, who deteriorated before their eyes, passing away somewhat peacefully in her sleep over two years ago. It had shattered them both, the pillar of strength of their family had been cruelly taken by the most devastating force.

After that, the smiles stopped altogether.

Jasmine had become distant, her transition into puberty collided with her grief and she began to act out, her grades plummeting and the calls from the school regarding her behaviour had been frequent. Aaron had tried his best but working longer hours to ensure the roof over their head stayed there, meant he felt further from her than ever.

He was a marketing director at an advertising agency.

His life wasn't supposed to be this way.

The previous weekend, he had spent the Saturday evening trying to get Jasmine to pick a film and not watch it from behind her phone screen.

Now he was in one of the most dangerous places in London, having stormed a building full of criminals with an illegally purchased firearm.

As he peered around the room, the chill of the night slithered down his spine and he shuddered.

A beaten, dirty mattress lay against the wall, a couple of used condoms carelessly thrown to the side. Beside them, a pile of needles and some foil.

He thought of his daughter, praying she wasn't held down against her will in this place.

Tears began to fill his eyes and he wiped them with the back his sleeve, taking a deep breath and calming himself down.

His daughter was missing but he had just been promised by the most wanted man in London that he would help him.

Sam Pope.

Now, under his instruction, Aaron was to wait in this room, among the seedy remains of a deplorable evening, and tarnish his name by pretending to be a punter. It made his skin crawl.

But Sam had been adamant that this was the only way Aaron would get out of the building quickly. The police would be too busy focusing on Pope to care about the depraved, middle-aged man who needed to get his jollies from a drug ravaged prostitute.

They would pity him.

As he heard the doors being kicked open on the floor below by the cavalry, he felt bad for the other guy who had certainly drawn the short straw in Sam Pope's plan. Aaron stared out of the window once more, his heart pining for his missing daughter and he hoped beyond hope that Sam Pope was as good as the news reports said he was.

———

Regimented footsteps echoed up the derelict stairwell as the Armed Response unit made their way to the second floor. They would have found the unconscious man from before, but no paramedic would be sent in until they'd given the all clear.

Until they'd neutralised him.

With his back against the grimy wall, Sam leaned forward, peering over the bannister, scanning the stairs between the gaps in the stairwell.

Heavily armed police officers were charging up.

Slipping quickly back through the door into the corridor, he dashed across the corridor and slipped behind the door to one of the vacant rooms, pulling the door to but keeping the handle turned.

He would need to be quick.

Just then, he heard the corridor door burst open and the sound of the tactical unit filtering in, their quiet commands just audible against the crashing rain outside.

With the dim light bathing the grotty corridor in a thick shadow, Sam gently pulled the door open, peeping through the crack. Two officers were a couple of feet ahead of him, bringing up the rear of the group. Their weapons were raised, their steps as measured and as quiet as possible.

The command to stop filtered through the radios, followed by the bellowing voice of the Specialist Firearms Officer who was in charge of the team.

'Down on the ground!'

Through the pathetic, flickering light of the hallway, all ten guns were trained upon the figure at the end of the hall. The man had his back to them, wearing a black jacket, a detail passed on by eyewitnesses who had seen Pope on a few occasions.

The man didn't oblige.

'I said, down on the ground.'

The figure slowly raised his arms, his hands trembling as he held onto the cylinder. Shrouded in darkness, it took the officer in charge a split second too late to realise what it was.

'Grenade!'

A shot fired out, the bullet whipping through the hallway and embedding into the centre of the man's spine. With a cry of anguish, he fell forward, releasing the object and a bright, white flash exploded through the corridor like a tidal wave. As the man collapsed to the floor, the Armed Response team all turned in discomfort, the bright, sudden flash debilitating them for a few moments. Knowing that the visual effects of the grenade would only last seconds, Sam opened the door and rolled the smoke grenade into the centre of the room. As the dizziness of the flash bang pinballed around the room, the smoke began to filter out of the grenade like a genie. A few angry orders were barked, a genuine sense of panic as members of the team spun on the spot, their vision skewed and their senses shaken.

Sam stepped out.

Swiftly, he lunged to the nearest officer, obscured from the rest of the team by the billowing smoke. He expertly wrapped an arm around his throat, blocking his airway and any hope of calling for help. The officer tried to raise his weapon, but Sam latched his other hand onto the man's wrist, squeezing the pressure point and causing his grip to loosen. He spun back towards the door with the flailing officer in tow.

Thirteen seconds was all it took.

The commotion had alerted the rest of the team, the commands coming through on the radio strapped to his captive's chest. With time ticking away, Sam spun the man around, striking the back of the man's leg with his foot, bringing him to his knees. With a silent apology, he removed the gun from the waistband of his jeans and cracked it across the man's head.

Slumping forward, the man was unconscious before he hit the floor.

Nearly a minute.

As the smoke-filled corridor began to regain a sense of a calm despite the thick, unwelcome smoke, Sam quickly stripped the officer of his jacket and helmet, sliding his own, muscular frame into it. A little tight, but it fit. He took the man's face mask, latching it around his face before securing the helmet tightly.

With a mighty heave, he pulled the unconscious man to the corner of the room, picked up the thin, stained sheet from the mattress and draped it over him. In the dark, it could easily be dismissed by a quick search.

It would have to do.

An order crackled from the Kevlar on his chest and Sam slipped on the man's gloves, hoisted the rifle to his waist, and marched to the door. Carefully slipping back into the corridor, he closed the door quietly and assumed the position of the man he had just expertly eliminated.

Ninety-seven seconds.

It's all it had taken.

Now, as the after effects of the flash bang had begun to wear off, the Armed Response team approached the fallen man, the commanding officer instructing two of his officers to check him.

It wasn't Sam Pope.

Sean Wiseman moaned in agony, the bullet colliding with the bulletproof vest and sending a jolt up his spine like a cattle prod. It had sent him sprawling forward, and he could already feel his muscles bruising, the severe ache from the shot causing him to groan.

The order was given to get him out of there, with the two closest officers reaching down with their gloved hands, lifting his limp body to his feet and draping his arms over their shoulders. As they ambled back through the smoke, the commanding officer ordered the two officers nearest to the hallway to provide cover, while he and the final five officers would sweep the top floor.

Sam Pope obliged, following the officers down the stairs, bringing up the rear to stay as far out of their sight as possible. Each second passed like a minute, with Sam expecting them to discover their fallen comrade in moments and then all guns would be trained on him.

They reached the bottom floor, the noise of the outside roaring through the open front door, the rain-soaked street a sea of activity. Several police cars had lined up around the building, the officers all standing to attention, their uniforms covered in see-through plastic to shield them from the freezing downpour.

Three ambulances were set further back, the paramedics tending to the wounded men Sam had left in his wake, and a crew of police officers were searching the two cars they'd arrived in.

The entire street was carnage.

All caused by him.

Sam stepped out onto the street, casually following the two officers as they carried their victim. Wiseman would be badly bruised and would walk with a limp for a few days, but he would be fine. With the original excitement dissipating into disappointment at his disappearance, Sam watched as a petite, pretty officer with a stern demeanour barked orders into a radio, clearly running the show and furious at their lack of progress.

With all eyes on the building, no one had noticed him, the fact that his black trousers and boots were not identical to those of the officers before him.

The rain helped, drenching everyone to their core and providing him with a curtain to hide behind.

He had to move.

Carefully, he followed the officers through the crowded street, nodding casually at a few PCs who looked at his assault rifle with envy. Their attention was suddenly pulled to their radios, the fiery woman he had passed was barking an order and quickly, the officers approached the building. Some punters had been found and needed to be removed from the building, but there were no signs of Pope.

There had been no alarm raised either.

As the rain collided with the fury of the failed raid, the two Armed Response officers carried Wiseman to the back of the ambulance, an overworked paramedic with a thick brow greeting them and helping them with the weight of the limp body. As they handled Wiseman, Sam carefully walked around the side of the ambulance, out of the glare of the police presence and quickly unclipped the helmet and removed it, followed by the mask.

The rain washed across his face and he walked towards

the row of cars ahead, slipping his arms from his jacket and wrapped it around the rifle, sliding it underneath the ambulance.

Behind the cars, lines of civilians waited, all of them watching the action unfold, their phones lifted high in the air, trying their best to capture anything that would grant them any fame online.

None of them noticed the man slip between the cars and join them.

Walking with a purpose into the crowd, eager to disappear, Sam looked back over his shoulder. Two police officers marched Aaron Hill out through the front door, his hands in cuffs and his face wrought with fear. They brought him to a stop in front of their commanding officer, the stern woman he had seen earlier.

Sam pushed on through the crowd and headed into the darkness of the city's alleyways. The final High Rise had been shut down, another criminal enterprise brought to its knees.

He stuffed his hands into his pockets, his fingers running across Aaron Hill's driving licence.

He had made the man a promise.

With the death that he had dealt that night, he knew he had once again broken the promise to his son. Allowing the wet, dark labyrinth of the city to swallow him, Sam Pope vowed that he would not break another promise that night.

CHAPTER NINE

The following morning was mayhem.

The press was having a field day, each paper using the terror of a rampant vigilante to push their own political agenda. The scaremongers questioning the safety of the people and the competence of the senior police figures. The debate about how to tackle gun crime raged on, whereas the number of articles supporting Pope were beginning to, rather worryingly, increase.

People were beginning to show their support.

News had leaked about the task force, with the word 'Watchdog' now being bestowed upon Pope like a well-earned title.

It made Mark Harris's blood boil.

The rain had continued into the following morning, covering the streets surrounding his office in a bright gleam. The sun was threatening to rear its head, occasionally poking a bright beam through the clouds. His large desk was covered in the morning papers, all of them covered in photos of the chaos from Shepherd's Bush the night before, the failure of the police which he knew he could use to his advantage.

Anti-gun crime was one of the pillars of his mayoral campaign.

His entire career had been spent being one of the most trusted and respected MPs, serving his district of London with distinction. The next logical step was to be Mayor of this great city.

It had only been twenty-four hours since he had stood in front of the cameras, proudly launching the task force dedicated to catching Pope.

Now, according to the papers he had spent the morning flicking through, they were already a laughing stock.

Sam Pope needed to be stopped.

Immediately.

Harris glared out of the window, his anger shaking through his arms and balling his hand into a fist. At that moment, the door to his office opened and Burrows, immaculately dressed as ever, entered.

'Sir, I have DI Adrian Pearce as requested.'

'Send him in,' Harris snapped, not even acknowledging his well-mannered assistant.

'Of course.'

Moments later, Adrian Pearce stepped into the office, letting out a whistle of appreciation. Compared to the cramped storage cupboard he was working out of, Harris's office may as well have been the Oval one in Washington DC. The grand bookcase housed several books, many that Pearce had read, and he made a note to test the young politician's knowledge of them. It would help him gauge just how genuine the young man was. Throughout his extensive career, the majority dealing with people with something to hide, Pearce's default mode was to approach everyone with an open mind.

The likelihood they had something to hide was high.

With politicians, almost definitely.

As he crossed the carpet towards the desk, he felt slightly underdressed, his parka coat was soaked through, as were his jeans and black trainers. Harris, turned, dressed in expensive designer clothes that made him look like he had stepped straight off the golf course. He offered the expertly honed smile as he stepped forward, hand outstretched.

'Detective. It's a pleasure to meet you.'

'Likewise,' Pearce said, shaking the hand firmly. Even the man's handshake felt rehearsed. 'Nice office.'

'It's a bit extravagant, but needs must,' Harris replied, gesturing to the seat opposite his desk as he took his own. 'Thank you for coming at such short notice. I trust I haven't kept you from anything?'

'Just sleep.' Adrian smiled.

'Ah yes, you run the Bethnal Green Youth Social every Saturday evening, correct?' Harris said, posing the fact as a question. Pearce nodded. 'It's very commendable. Not a lot of senior officers, especially as distinguished as yourself, give back that much.'

'I have my reasons,' Pearce stated, patiently waiting for the segue into the real reason he was summoned.

'Theo Walker?' Harris said solemnly. 'He used to run that before his unfortunate death earlier this year.'

'He was murdered.'

'Yes, of course. He was a good man who served his country. He died a hero.'

'That we can agree on.' Pearce smiled, the animosity in the room rising slightly. Both men had already realised that they opposed the other and were equally thankful as Burrows opened the door, bringing in two cups of piping hot tea. Pearce accepted his graciously, thanking the senior figure. Harris waited for Burrows to leave and allowed Pearce a satisfying sip. He bridged his fingers together and began.

'We need to stop Sam Pope.'

Pearce took another sip from his mug before leaning forward and carefully placing it on the coaster, not wanting to stain the large oak desk that separated them.

'I agree,' Pearce said calmly. 'That's why you've set up the task force, right?'

'Exactly.' Harris pointed a congratulatory finger at Pearce. 'Some very good officers involved too. DI Singh has made quite the impression.'

'I bet,' Pearce said dryly, raising his eyebrows. As a highly experienced detective, he knew of Harris's reported indiscretions and wondering eyes. 'I've already had the pleasure of meeting her.'

'She is quite something, isn't she?'

'You could say that,' Pearce said diplomatically, his mind returning to the rather heated meeting between them.

'I need you to step up and help her.'

Pearce let out a chuckle, causing Harris to scowl with frustration. As the rain collided with the window behind him, Harris pushed himself from his seat and turned his gaze to the city beyond. The rain-soaked city was still lazily waking up, the combination of the weather, reduced transport services and later opening hours meant the streets were relatively clear. Somewhere nearby, an ambulance wailed loudly, weaving a rapid pathway towards one of the nearby hospitals.

In a months' time, it would be his. Stopping Sam Pope would all but guarantee it. Knowing he needed Pearce onside, he decided to try a different angle.

'I get it. Six months ago, you uncovered a terrible crime perpetrated by one of your own. Now whether that was with or without Sam Pope's help, you need to look at what has happened since then. The man has gone on to terrify this city. He is one of the most dangerous men in the country, trained well beyond the usual gang bangers who are flooding the streets with guns.' Harris noticed the frown on Pearce's face at that comment. 'What I mean is, Sam Pope is a different calibre of criminal. He is highly trained and has left a number of dead bodies in his outrageous quest for justice. Several more have been put in the hospital. It has to stop. *He* has to be stopped.'

Pearce sat contently, one leg draped over the other and took another sip of his tea. Harris clenched his fist in frustration once more.

'Not everyone sees it that way.'

'You condone his actions?' Harris snapped, his short fuse noted by Pearce. Clearing his throat, Pearce calmly responded.

'Not at all. But while yourself, the Met, and even the press are putting Sam front and centre, the real issue of police corruption was glossed over. Howell, despite everything he did, was still seen as a good man who made a mistake. Everything else was kept in-house, swept under the rug, and I was shunted to a goddamn cupboard for 'sticking my nose in'. I was just doing my job. Whilst I don't condone what Sam Pope is doing, I will not toe the line that he is as dangerous as he is being made out to be.'

Harris folded his arms across his chest, his eyes locked on Pearce. The senior officer was formidable, something Harris noted for the future.

'You don't consider a trained vigilante with an arsenal of weapons to be a danger to society? Is that what you're saying?'

'Sir, when senior figures in our own police force are willing to kill their own family to line their own pockets, our society has no idea of how much danger it's in.'

'Those allegations were unfounded…' Harris began, only for Pearce to hold up a hand.

'Just stop.' Pearce pushed himself from his seat, fumbling with the zip of his wet coat. 'Thanks for the tea.'

'Pearce, he needs to be stopped,' Harris blurted out, his composure wobbling. 'Whether you believe me or not, I just want our city to be safe. Now you might believe his intentions are good, but the man is a criminal. No one gets to take the law into their own hands and the longer he is out there putting bullets in criminals, the more terrifying he becomes. He will lose himself to the point of no return and it will only end in one way.'

Pearce extended a hand to Harris, who took a couple of steps forward, frustrated at his lack of influence over the detective. Usually, he had most people eating out of the palm of his hand.

'Good luck with the election,' Pearce offered, leaving his hand in place for a few more moments. Harris just glared at him, the pleasantries clearly gone. Pearce raised his eyebrows and shrugged before turning on his heel and heading towards the door. As he reached for the handle, Harris propped himself against his desk, arms folded.

'When the time comes, and Sam Pope is killed, just know that you could have stopped it from happening.'

Pearce turned the handle and pulled open the door, turning back once more to lock eyes with the cocky politician.

'With all due respect, when it comes to Sam Pope, there isn't anything anyone can do. You'll find that out soon enough.'

With that, Pearce stepped through the door, almost colliding with Burrows who had quietly approached. He apologised and headed to the exit, wanting to distance himself from the situation and return to the warmth of his house.

As Pearce stepped out onto the pavement, Harris stared from the window above. Anger pulsated through his body as the resilient detective headed towards Regent's Park, the rain soaking him in seconds. Watching with fury, Harris wondered if it was the lack of respect for the task force or the man's misguided loyalty to Pope which angered him most. Deep down, he knew it was neither.

It was the fact that the man didn't buckle to him.

Needing his ego massaged, he wondered if bringing in DI Singh and berating her would make him feel better. She would surely be hurting after the extreme failure of her first day in charge of the task force. As he watched Pearce pass the gate and into the park, he heard the shuffling footsteps of Burrows behind him.

He sighed.

'Sir, I trust that didn't go as planned,' Burrows said, pushing his spectacles up his hooked nose.

'No. That man is a pain in the arse.'

Burrows stepped forward, joining his boss by the window and looking out over the city he had served for decades. Pearce was long gone, and the roads were slowly getting busier. A few news vans had appeared on the road, no doubt eager to speak to Harris about the apparent failure of his task force.

Burrows could sense the tension and spoke.

'Sir, redoubling our efforts to catch Sam Pope has to be the number one priority.' Harris turned and glared at him.

'Don't tell me how to do my job,' Harris spat. 'Get me DI Singh in here and get her here now.'

'Very well, sir.' Burrows nodded with respect. 'Just remember, the longer Sam Pope is at large, the sooner some of your biggest backers will get nervous.'

Burrows marched out of the office to call Singh as Harris massaged his temples. Taking a seat, he thought about Burrows' warning. His highly backed campaign was focused on stopping Pope.

It needed to deliver.

It had to.

With a deep sigh, he reached for his cup of tea, the stone-cold cup was just another in a series of kicks in the teeth that the morning had offered.

———

After spending the night in a tiny, concrete cell and an entire morning being treated like a pervert while being interviewed, Aaron Hill was finally released into the freezing afternoon. DI Singh had pulled no punches, labelling him a disgrace for attending the High Rise and asking him a number of personal questions to find the reason for his depravity.

The fact that she didn't recall him from the day before had caused him to keep quiet.

Her focus was so hell bent on finding Sam Pope that she didn't realise he was the desperate father looking for his daughter. Granted, he had been drunk at the time, but she dismissed his pleas then and he was sure she would have that morning.

Pulling the collar up on his coat, he fished his wallet from his pocket to check for cash, remembering his licence being taken by Sam Pope. Judging by the anger of the fiery detective, Pope's plan had worked and both of them had escaped the building alive and well. Aaron had been threatened with further action but didn't care.

He needed to find his daughter.

Rushing home, he walked the seven miles in the bitter cold, trying his best to formulate a better plan. Getting drunk, buying a gun, and storming a known criminal hot spot wasn't the best idea and it was a near miracle he hadn't been killed.

The memory of the evening had flashed in small snippets through his hangover, the vision of being on his knees in front of a large, black man with a gun caused him to go deathly pale, lean over a wall, and empty his guts into a bush. He had come so close to death while his daughter was still missing.

He could have died, leaving her to a fate which he presumed would be worse than that.

Tears filled his eyes as he ran the final few streets, turned onto his road and approached his house.

He pushed open the gate, marched up the garden path and as he pushed his key into the door, he heard the sound of footsteps behind him.

In a blind panic he turned, swinging the key between his fingers and trying his best to blind whoever they'd sent to finish the job.

His wild swing was stopped, a strong grip around his forearm.

As the panic subsided, he opened his eyes, staring straight into the unimpressed face of Sam Pope.

'Careful,' Sam warned. 'You could have someone's eye out.'

A sudden wave of relief flooded through Aaron and despite his best efforts, tears began to stream down his face. Sam gave him a few moments to compose himself, stuffing his hands into his coat pocket as the wind whipped through them.

As he finally calmed, Aaron realised that Sam was being true to his word and offered him a smile.

'I don't know how I can thank you for this.'

Sam smiled back.

'You can open that door and make me a cup of tea.'

CHAPTER TEN

That very morning, Singh had awoken in her bed, her head pounding like a two-day hangover. While the bitter cold day tried its best to creep through the Roman blinds that covered her window, she tried to shut her eyes and force herself back to sleep.

All she could hear were the sirens.

All she could feel was failure.

She had returned home at just after four in the morning, a soul-destroying conversation with Assistant Commissioner Ashton had caused her to pack up her stuff and head home. The task force was less than twenty-four hours old, yet there were two dead, several injured, and no sign of Sam Pope.

Singh clenched her fingers around the duvet and squeezed until her nails dug through into her palm. It was no use and she sat up, her T-shirt hanging loosely from her frame. She lived alone, much to her delight and her parents' chagrin. They were strict Hindus, wanting nothing more for her than to be married to a wealthy man of their choosing. Her trailblazing career through the police, from the Armed Response to dangerous task forces, wasn't exactly what they'd had in mind for their little girl. Still, as the years went by, their sadness at her loneliness was abated by their pride of her achievements.

Amara Singh didn't fail.

The very thought of it drove her from her bed and to the floor where she performed a rigorous press-up and sit-up circuit. Her frame, while small, was lean with muscle and her unbeaten record within the Met boxing club was well known.

And well earned.

After a smoothie, coffee, and a long shower, Singh opened up the folder she'd discarded on the kitchen table the night before. As she roughly attacked her wet hair with a towel, she sat at the table, flicking through the preliminary reports and photos of the crime scene.

The two 4X4 cars destroyed and bullet ridden.

The passengers similar.

Shaking her head in anger, she made a note to read the sergeant in charge of the Armed Response team the riot act. To allow a member of his team to be attacked was one thing. To allow Sam to mimic him and walk out of the front door was another entirely.

Her kitchen opened up onto a modern flat, with rich, wooden floor panels. The furniture was minimalistic, more out of ease than of fashion, and the walls were empty beyond a few framed certificates to honour her sparkling rise through the Met.

The only photos were of her parents.

Singh didn't have the time for a relationship, nor did she harbour any desire for one. It had been a bone of contention for her first few years in the Met, a number of male officers assuming she was a lesbian due to her tough demeanour and lack of reciprocation to their advances. When she made it clear she just found them pathetic, they soon backed off. The married officers, especially the female ones, also looked at her with a raised nose, as if her life choices were selfish.

As a thirty-two-year-old woman, she was just fine on her own.

There had been the odd one-night stand, usually some unsuspecting colleague who thought they'd hit the jackpot. Singh knew she was attractive, her exotic looks complimenting her feisty attitude. But once they realised they were nothing more than a pastime, they soon left.

She didn't need anyone to validate her.

Amara Singh didn't fail.

It was that notion, repeated through her head that had got her through her original training at Hendon Police College. When they'd sprayed her with CS gas to see how she would react, she took long deep breaths through the pain, imploring herself to get through.

When they taught her self-defence, rough handling her to the mat, she told herself to get up.

Then, out on the job, when her and her partner, a PC Jack Wilson, were staring down a seven on two fight with a gang in Hackney, she told herself never to back down.

Every door she broke down, every rifle she'd raised with the intent to fire.

Every pair of handcuffs she'd slapped on a criminal.

Every step of her career.

She had told herself that she would not – could not – fail.

As it echoed in her mind again like a haunting memory, it drove her to change into a pair of jeans and a hoody, wrap up inside her puffer jacket, and head for the front door, car keys in hand and tapping in the address for a youth centre in Bethnal Green on her phone. There were a few missed calls, both of them from Mark Harris's assistant, Carl Burrows.

She ignored them. The last thing she wanted to face

was a smarmy politician leering at her and demanding a report.

In the pocket of her jacket was the device. She had demanded it after yesterday's failure and was pretty sure Assistant Commissioner Ashton would be on-board despite circumventing the usual procedure for checking it out from the surveillance team.

She had a plan.

They needed a result. *She* needed a result.

Amara Singh didn't fail.

It was time to start taking some steps to ensure that remained the case.

———

The front door closed behind them and Aaron shuffled through past Sam, his coat dripping with rain, rushing to the kitchen for a glass of water and a paracetamol. While Aaron scooted by, Sam slowly removed his jacket, droplets of rainwater dotted over the wooden flooring. Sam folded the jacket over his arm and then tucked it over the bannister, the carpeted stairs led to what he assumed was a spacious first floor, which housed three bedrooms and a bathroom.

Taking in the surroundings, he looked over the small hallway table that was decorated with photos. A few of them were of a beautiful woman with olive skin and jet-black hair.

Sam had clocked the ring on Aaron's finger, which led him to believe it was his wife. Small details about people and places leapt out at him. It was what he was trained to do. Assess and store.

He already knew that it would take him twelve steps to reach the front of the garden.

The door had a double lock, which Aaron had neglected to activate.

Aaron himself was just under six feet tall, about thirteen stone of which wasn't muscle, and by the way he opened the door, was left handed.

Sam knew that the majority of those details would be insignificant at that moment in time. He had already scoped the street before blindsiding the terrified dad, ensuring that there was no police tail. But his training was so ingrained in his mind, he was a walking fact finder.

The sound of crockery clinging together and the low gurgle of a kettle filled Sam with warmth, the bitterness of the outside world still drilling through his bones. Careful not to leave any finger prints, he pulled the cuff of his jumper over his hands and picked up a photograph.

Next to the beautiful smile of Aaron's wife, was a smaller, almost identical version of her, her face beaming with innocence and hope. The carefree existence of a young adult.

Sam found himself smiling at the radiant photo, the love that emanated from both sets at eyes at the man with the camera.

A family filled with love.

His mind flashed to a memory, a summer day spent at the park. Lucy, her wedding ring proudly attached to her finger, sat reading, her feet up on the bench as the sun fell upon her. The park was full, families and groups of friends all basking in the sunshine.

Somewhere along the line, the memory had lost any detail, with every face a smooth, blank patch of skin.

Except for Lucy.

Except for Jamie.

Sam stood to the side of his memory, everything tinged with bronze as the colours faded from his subconscious. He watched himself meandering slowly through the throngs of people alongside his son, his three-year-old legs gamely keeping pace as they searched for stones.

It was a cherished memory.

But as the colours of trees and the faces of those around them faded, he realised it was a memory slowly ebbing away from him.

Sam closed his eyes, and a voice brought him back to the hallway of a desperate man's house.

'That's her,' Aaron said, nodding towards the photo in Sam's hand. 'My Jasmine.'

Sam looked at Aaron, his blood-shot eyes a cocktail of hangover, a bad night's sleep, and genuine terror for his daughter's safety.

'She's beautiful,' Sam said. 'They both are.'

'Yeah, her mum was quite the looker. What she ever saw in me, I don't know.'

'Was?' Sam asked, immediately regretting it.

'She, err … she died. A few years back.' Aaron's voice cracked slightly, the painful memory still a gaping wound in his chest. He handed Sam a warm mug, a *Game of Thrones* logo emblazoned on the side. Sam took it carefully, ensuring the sleeve of his jumper still covered his fingers.

'I'm sorry.'

Aaron nodded his appreciation before turning and heading back through to the kitchen, signalling the end of that conversation. Sam understood, following through, past the richly decorated living room and into the large, open-plan kitchen. Scouting the room, Sam couldn't help but be impressed. The room was lined with spotless cabinets, all of them a rustic grey. The marble work tops were also dark, framing the kitchen nicely. In the middle, a large island with an inbuilt sink stood proudly, the rest of the top also marble and a few breakfast stools set up against it.

Despite the gloomy weather, the floor to ceiling

windows that opened onto a large garden bathed the kitchen in light.

It was welcoming.

A home.

'Nice place,' Sam offered, watching with pity as Aaron tried to hide the empty bottle of Jack Daniels from the work top. Sam caught his eye. 'That stuff isn't going to help.'

'I know,' Aaron muttered, shaking his head. 'I just, I didn't know what to do.'

'I'll be honest with you, pal. Running head first into a gun fight with known criminals is probably the last thing you should be doing.'

Sam offered Aaron a smile but received nothing back. The man was clearly hurting, terrified at the thought of what his daughter was going through. If she was even alive?

'I went to the police, but they told me she hadn't been missing long enough for her to be reported missing.' Aaron took a sip of his piping tea, a scowl on his face. 'They said that most teenage girls stay out late.'

'Is it possible she is with a friend?'

'Not without letting me know.'

'Maybe she forgot or she had a drink or…' Sam offered, but Aaron snapped angrily.

'Not my Jasmine.' He shook his head. 'Ever since her mother died, it's been difficult. I mean, she's a teenage girl. Her body is changing and she is experiencing things that she needs her mother for. I try, and my sister is pretty close with her, but she's still hurting. We both are. And while she finds the things we used to do together lame or boring, she has *never* left me in the lurch as to where she is. If she gets stuck or is upset or anything, she calls me. Day or night.'

Aaron's voice trailed off as he choked back tears and Sam finished his tea with a satisfying sigh and placed the mug down on the marble. The kitchen put his grubby little flat to shame.

But then life pulled people in many different directions.

Whatever had driven Aaron to that building, it had caused his path to cross with Sam's.

He couldn't walk away.

He had to help.

Sam looked at Aaron who slowly sipped his tea, his movements were laboured, and the panic had reduced a loving father to a desperate man.

Sam knew desperation.

Throughout his life, through all his tours of Iraq and Afghanistan. When he had faced down several men on his own, bullets spraying around him, he never panicked. When he took down the High Rise six months before, he never questioned himself. Training took over and he became the weapon the UK Government had spent a lot of money turning him into.

But that summer's night over three years before, on his knees in the middle of the road, staring into the lifeless eyes of his son, he had never felt so helpless.

As he watched Aaron fumble with his mug in the sink, dabbing at his eyes with his sleeve, Sam realised that he had a new mission.

He needed to bring Jasmine home.

Stepping forward, Sam placed a reassuring hand on Aaron's shoulder, causing the man to stop dead. It was the feeling of comfort, that he wasn't alone, that suddenly caused the tears to flow fully, drenching his cheeks in seconds.

'I'll bring her home,' Sam said stoically. 'I promise.'

Aaron nodded, refusing to face him. Not wanting anyone to see him cry under the bizarre notion that it would embarrass him. Sam took a deep breath before continuing.

'Why were you at the factory last night?'

'I have an app on my phone that tells me her location.' Aaron spoke with a new-found vigour as he reached into his pocket. 'It tells me how much battery she has, where she is, and so on. The last location it was switched on was the factory. Look.'

Aaron turned the phone to Sam, who stared intently at the bright screen. It was a map of Shepherd's Bush and sure enough, a little photo of Jasmine was pasted over the factory.

'I took a screen shot of it,' Aaron offered. 'I thought it might help.'

'It does,' Sam verified. 'What was she doing there?'

'That's the thing, she wasn't supposed to be there. She was at a friend's party in Perivale, but like I said, she keeps in contact. So I don't know what her phone was doing there.'

'That's what we need to find out,' Sam said, typing his number into Aaron's mobile phone and sending the picture across to himself.

'Find out?' Aaron said in exasperation. 'Last time I saw you, you were armed with a fucking rifle, shooting fucking criminals. You don't need to find out, you need to do what the papers say you do and scare the living shit out of these people.'

'Look, I know you're scared, but I need you to be calm.'

'Calm?'

'Yes.'

'Do you know what it's like to lose a fucking child?' Aaron spat, his face turning red with fury. Sam stared at him before responding calmly.

'Just over three years ago, my son was killed by a drunk driver who got off on a technicality. So yes, I know how it feels to lose a child and to feel like the law isn't on your side.' Sam saw the horror on Aaron's face. 'It's why I do what I do. A sense of justice or whatever the hell people are calling it. I don't know. But all I know is, there are bad things happening to good people and sometimes, they need someone else to stop them.'

Silence hung heavy in the room like a morning fog, Aaron's embarrassment eating at him like a cancer. After a few more beats, he spoke.

'I'm so sorry, I didn't know.'

'You wouldn't have. Don't be sorry, be helpful. And by that, I mean stay calm and don't do anything stupid.'

Aaron took a deep breath and nodded.

'What are you going to do?'

'*We* are going to go and find out why your daughter's phone was at the factory. And I know just where to start. Grab your coat.'

Sam headed back out of the kitchen, back through the well-lit hallway and the shrine to Aaron's wonderful family. He picked his coat from the bannister and smoothly swung it around, his arms sliding into it with ease. The coat hung down below his buttocks, nicely covering the bulge from the back of his jean's waistband.

Aaron hadn't noticed the Glock tucked safely against his spine. He carried it so often that Sam forgot it was there.

It had almost become an extension of him.

As they headed to the door and the teeth-chattering cold of the outside world, Aaron took one more moment in the sanctity of his home to ask a question.

'Why are you doing this, Sam?' he asked thoughtfully. 'Why are you helping me?'

Sam slid a glove over his hand, reached for the door knob, twisted and pulled it open. A blast of cold, wet wind flapped in like a rogue curtain. Sam turned, looking at Aaron and realising he was his only hope.

Jasmine's only hope.

As he answered, he realised it was the same reason for everything meaningful he had ever done in his life. The same reason he was now one of the UK's most wanted men.

He offered Aaron a warm, reassuring smile.

'It's the right thing to do.'

CHAPTER ELEVEN

The thick, grey clouds hung over London, bathing the entire city in a dull shadow. With the continuous downfall of rain, the buildings took on a pitiful, damp look that only added to the depressing weather. Winter had arrived, and as usual, it hadn't entered to a jolly Christmas song or in a picturesque snow storm.

All it had brought was dark clouds and freezing rain.

Pearce looked out of the window, the rain pelting the city and felt its pain. The last six months had been relentless, ever since he had begun to look into Sam Pope. When Chris Morton, a man who was cleared of rape, was found beaten to a bloody and broken pulp, Pearce had delved into all the data. It was what had made him such a revered yet reviled detective.

When it came to investigating their own, most coppers didn't want to delve too deep. There was an unwritten rule.

They were all in it together.

As far as Pearce had been concerned, through his thirty-year career that had seen him run an Armed Response unit, as well as solve over fifty murder cases, the only way you could go into a no-win situation with a fellow officer was if you knew they weren't going to leave you behind.

You had to trust them.

It was that unrelenting commitment to the truth and the justice system that had lead him to becoming an outstanding detective for the Department of Professional Standards and also one of the most hated officers within the Metropolitan Police. But it was also that unrelenting commitment to the truth that caused him to question the justice system. When Sam Pope took a stand against the corrupt police who, along with one of the most fearsome criminals in London, bombed the London Marathon, Pearce soon found himself doing the one thing he swore he wouldn't.

He broke the law.

He allowed Sam Pope access to files while under arrest, aided his escape from custody and then, with the man being held at gunpoint and the net tightening, he allowed a vigilante to disappear, to continue his war against the cancerous crime that was eating the city from the inside.

It had been the right thing to do.

Since then, Pearce had barely slept. The constant, nagging voice questioning his hypocrisy kept him from more than a few stop-start hours every night. When you spend over fifty years of your life, committing yourself so vehemently to an ideal to the point that it costs you your marriage and any chance of a family, but then go against it, it shakes you to your core.

That's why he had taken over running the youth club every weekend. As he stood, staring out of the window of the Bethnal Green Youth Centre, he realised that the young men and women who walked through those doors were the only things keeping him sane.

'Sam. You crazy bastard,' Pearce muttered with a shake

of the head, knowing that the man he had let go now had the whole city in a panic. What Pearce found most amusing was that it wasn't the general public who were scared. By and large, whenever one of the papers went to the people, the general consensus was they were rooting for him. They didn't agree with breaking the law, but the majority saw a capable man fighting for the good of the people.

Like a modern-day Robin Hood.

Their *Watchdog*.

It was the police, being shown up as corrupt and unable to stop a rogue soldier that were panicking most, along with the politicians who claim to back every task force possible just to bring him to his knees. Pearce didn't need to be a detective to know that those who wanted Pope stopped, were undoubtedly the ones with the most skeletons in their closets.

It was why he didn't trust Harris and it was why he wasn't surprised to see a black Audi A3 pull up outside the Youth Centre. Folding his arms across his broad chest, Pearce watched with intrigue as DI Singh stepped out of the driver's side, slammed the door shut and hastily made her way through the gate. Pope was becoming a major priority for more than one party and Pearce actually felt a twinge of sympathy for the young, talented lady.

The pressure being stacked on her slender shoulders was enormous, but Pearce admired how she carried it. Shoulders wide, back straight, she commanded attention as she marched through the gate. Pearce was sure the younger officers also gave her attention for other reasons, but the memory of his marriage still haunted him like an echo. Denise had moved on, but somewhere among his commitment to the job and fear of being hurt again, Pearce hadn't.

Couldn't.

He pulled open the front door and greeted Singh with a warm grin.

'DI Singh. Twice in two days. I am lucky.'

'Pearce.' She offered her hand, which Pearce took. She gave the shake a little extra. It was an old habit.

'Can I get you a drink? Coffee? Tea?' He gestured to the window. 'It's freezing out there.'

'I'm fine, thanks.' She pulled her hood back, allowing her black hair to fall around her shoulders. 'So, this is the place huh?'

Pearce smiled as she looked around the modest room, the wooden floors freshly mopped. Pearce could remember when they were covered in a pool of Andy Devereux's blood.

Yesterday evening's session had been a movie night, with him screening *Iron Man* for the young locals who frequented. Sunday afternoons, he opened the doors from four until eight, offering sandwiches and warm drinks to those who didn't get anything at home. It surprised him how many of the attendees weren't from the council estates or poverty-stricken homes.

Just teenagers and young adults who needed somewhere to go.

Someone to care.

On the far wall, the Theo Walker Memorial plaque was displayed proudly, with nearly a hundred messages pinned to a board beneath. Pearce found himself reading them most days, moved by the number of people who had clung to Theo for hope. For guidance.

Theo had cared about them all. As a former medic, the man had dedicated his life after the army to helping kids from his local community, renovating the Youth Centre and offering some semblance of a safe place to the youth that dominated the gang-heavy borough.

Theo died just as he had lived.

As a hero.

Theo had given his life to save two people who had been wronged by the very organisation that Pearce worked for, and he had taken it as a personal mission to continue Theo's good work. The people who came through those doors had a strong, black role model before and Pearce was determined to continue that idea.

It was as much for him as it was for them. He watched as Singh approached the wall, her eyes taking in some of the warm memories the locals had for Theo.

'He was a good man,' Pearce said, walking slowly behind her, his hands tucked into the pockets of his jeans.

'I heard he gave his life to save Amy Devereux,' Singh spoke, not turning. 'That was very noble.'

'Like I said, he was a good man.' Pearce shrugged. 'Good men sometimes do crazy things.'

Singh turned at the not-so-subtle reference.

'I know we sort of got off on the wrong foot yesterday. I wanted to apologise—' Singh began, but Pearce held up a hand.

'Please. If I took any umbrage against a colleague giving me both barrels, I wouldn't be very good at my job.' He extended his hand again. 'Truce?'

'Truce.' She took it, this time without the extra power.

'So what brings you here?' Pearce said, turning back towards the kitchen which sat just off the main hall. A table was pressed against the far wall near the door, a stack of paper plates and a few bags of groceries on top. Pearce's leather jacket was slung over the chair, a small puddle of rainwater beneath it.

'Last night, there was an incident,' Singh said, then saw Pearce's expression. 'You saw the news, I take it?'

'I did,' Pearce said with a sigh. 'However, I was fully informed by your boss.'

'Assistant Commissioner Ashton?'

'Mark Harris,' Pearce said, with a cheeky grin.

'That man is not my boss,' Singh snapped. 'I'm sorry to hear you've spoken to him. His assistant has been trying to contact me all day.'

'Burrows? He's an odd man, isn't he?'

'Too right.' Singh chuckled. 'Although I'd rather deal with his creepy librarian shtick, than having Harris stare at my tits and pretend he's interested in police work.'

Pearce couldn't help but laugh and realised he was warming to Singh. He was sure that her abruptness would rub a lot of superiors up the wrong way, especially the male officers. But she was tenacious, and it was a characteristic he appreciated.

It was one he possessed himself.

'Well he called me into his office this morning and demanded I help *his* task force.'

'And?' Singh asked, her piercing eyes locking onto his.

'And what?'

'Will you help? That's actually why I came here.'

Pearce stopped just before entering the kitchen and sighed. He turned back to Singh with a resigned look on his face.

'I'm nothing more than a fancy administrator these days. I sit in a cupboard, rifling through paperwork and working dead end cases. The Met don't need or want me as a detective anymore. That's been made perfectly clear.'

'I do,' Singh said, smiling. 'I know that you don't think Sam Pope is as dangerous as we do, but he is still breaking the law. He is still making a mockery of what our badge stands for. We will catch him that much I can promise. But if you help us, then maybe you can help him, too.'

Pearce ran a hand through his grey stubble and took a moment. As much as he believed that Sam Pope was a good person walking a bad but necessary path, there would likely be a time when the net got too tight. When it did, he would need at least one ally on the other side.

One person who cared.

Pearce looked up at Singh, catching her hopeful glance and smiling his warm, pearly white smile.

'Okay. I'm in.'

'Fantastic.' Singh's face cracked a gorgeous smile that could grace any magazine. 'You know what, I will have that tea after all.'

'Sugar?'

'Just dip your finger in it,' Singh joked, getting another chuckle from Pearce. As he wandered into the kitchen, Singh could understand why he was so revered at one point of his career. The man was as charming as he was authoritative and Singh felt a kinship with a man who wanted nothing more than to see the law used for good. It saddened her that she believed he had aided Sam Pope, but she knew that as a Detective Inspector, you were always swimming upstream.

Having an ally, especially one as experienced as Pearce to offer a branch was like gold dust.

As he returned with two mugs of piping hot tea, Singh sat down and allowed the natural conversation to flow, hoping that any insight he could offer, would be useful.

She had to catch Sam Pope.

She knew it.

Pearce knew it.

She hated the idea of putting him in an uncomfortable position, but she would test his loyalty to see which direction it pointed in.

Pope or the badge.

As the rain drummed against the window like impatient fingers, they began to chat.

———

Just under nine miles away, the same relentless rain had cleared the streets of Neasden. The roads that framed the estate like a moat were usually alive with activity, with large numbers of youths congregating in their gangs, grime music playing and a sense of menace hanging around them like a bad smell. On average, there was at least one stabbing a week within the square mile around the large estate, with unfortunate people being caught in the wrong place at the wrong time, or a casualty in a rivalry over being born in a different postcode.

It was all becoming senseless to Sean Wiseman.

As he walked with his head down, the rain slapping the back of his neck, he relived the last few evenings in his mind.

The attack on his car near Holborn.

The gun pressed against his head before Sam Pope put a bullet through his hand.

Weeping in the corner as people he had grown up with were shot dead through the window of their High Rise penthouse.

The lifeless eyes of Elmore.

The whole lifestyle had begun to feel worthless, a pathetic reason to live like gangsters to rally against a system that was built to keep them down. Wiseman agreed with some of the racist barriers his friend spouted about, but he never went as far as to kill to break them down. Whenever he questioned the methods, or the criminal activity, he was just dismissed as a half-breed.

Elmore used to point to his white mother as a sign of Wiseman's weakness. Wiseman knew he was weak, but it wasn't because of his mother's ethnicity.

He just wasn't a criminal.

He was good with data and money and was able to build a system for his childhood friend who wanted to live like Tony Montana.

Everything about the lifestyle had sickened him then. Now, it terrified him.

The guns. The drugs. The killings.

Looking around at the drenched estate, he saw the desperation of the area. The usual hot spots were vacant, but once the rain relented, they would soon be filled by young gang members, all treading the same path as Elmore.

All willing to kill to get there.

All likely to die trying.

Wiseman held his injured hand in his other, gently massaging the palm of it. He needed to change the bandages, which were now red with blood. His back ached from the bullet which had sent him sprawling as it lodged itself in the lining of the bulletproof vest Pope had given him.

A thick, purple bruise was already reaching up his spine like an errant vine.

They had carted him to an ambulance and taken him to hospital. They had treated him for shock, but once the nurses had finished, a couple of police officers read him the riot act in a desperate attempt at intimidation. They leaned heavily on his links to Riggs and told him that he would be needed for more questioning.

They hadn't even offered him a lift home.

Home.

He looked up at the building that included his modest, but expensively decked out flat and made a decision to move away. To find something better to do with his life.

Sean Wiseman was a lot of things, but he wasn't a criminal.

Not anymore.

Thanking his lucky stars that there were no gang members polluting the stair well, he made his way up the heavily graffitied steps, ignoring the stale smell of piss. As he approached the fifth floor, he began to think of how much money he had saved, how much more he could get, and how quickly he could move out of the gang infested mile that had tried its best to drag him under.

As he stepped out onto the walkway that wrapped around the building to his flat, he was accosted by two figures who stepped in front of him.

Rain hit his panic-stricken face.

Standing in front of him was the terrified man from the High Rise, his coat zipped up to the top and a nervous look on his face.

The man next to him made Wiseman wish he had just walked into two rival gang members. He felt his entire body stiffen with fear. The pain in his hand echoed through his body.

The other man was Sam Pope.

CHAPTER TWELVE

The gold-plated handle of the boning knife was weighty as Andrei Kovalenko gently tossed it, allowing the heavy grip to slap against his palm. Sure, it was extravagant, but a man who ran the London side of a multi-million-pound operation was allowed certain privileges.

It was certainly more aesthetically pleasing than the rusty knife he had used to murder his father back in Donetsk over twenty years ago. Igor Kovalenko had been a brute of a man, working as a bouncer for their uncle, Sergei, at his nightclub, The Red Room. When he was home, he flitted between drunk and high, assaulting their mother to the point that she left.

Andrei had heard she'd gone on the game somewhere in Kiev.

He couldn't have cared less.

Not when that anger was directed at him and his siblings. Their father would mercilessly beat them due to his own inadequacies, and as the oldest, Andrei took the brunt of it. He had been acquainted with his father's leather belt on an almost daily basis, especially when he stood up for his brother, Oleg. Despite his hulking size,

Oleg suffered with mental disabilities, something their father would not accept.

It was when his sister, Dana, began to flourish into a beautiful young woman, and he noticed his father's leering glances, that he decided to take action. That fateful night, as the derelict street they lived on twinkled under the stars, a thin layer of snow frosting the entire street, he murdered their father.

Igor Kovalenko had entered his daughter's room with the sole intent of raping her. Andrei had entered behind him with the largest knife he could find and slit the man's throat without a moment's hesitation.

He had then called his uncle, who swiftly arrived to his three kin sitting in the snow, their bloodstained clothes contrasting with the snowfall.

He told them it would be okay.

Uncle Sergei would look after them.

The man had been good on his word, and soon, his nightclubs evolved into something beyond the law, where any drug or woman was available for the right price. The police took their cut and looked the other way. Andrei manned the doors for a while, just like his father, but Andrei soon saw the business opportunity every time he saw a group of beautiful English girls, all of them strapped up with backpacks and innocent hopes of a magical journey of self-discovery through Europe.

When Andrei turned twenty-five, Sergei sent him and his siblings to England, to set up a similar club and experiment with a new clientele and a new type of merchandise.

Seventeen years later, as he held the gold-plated knife, Andrei knew that he had exceeded even his own expectations. They had given up the night club game a long time ago. Now they were the ones in charge of what came in and out of the city, previously supplying Frank Jackson with the materials he needed to run his High Rise.

The business was lucrative.

It paid for the fancy knife and the Versace suit he was about to ruin.

It paid for the phenomenal penthouse suite in Kensington, with its five bedrooms and exquisite views of the city.

It had turned him and his siblings into some of the richest and most feared people walking the city.

But it hadn't changed him.

As he held the knife limply in his hand, he caught a glimpse of himself in the mirror. His early forties had seen his hair begin to thin, the blonde waves cut shorter and into a neat side parting. His skin, freshly shaved, was now wrinkled around the edges, his pale blue eyes as cold and as lifeless as the severed head of his father.

It hadn't changed him.

He knew it. His siblings, watching with quiet respect knew it.

Malcolm Peterson knew it. With his hands tied behind his back and his mouth taped shut, he tried in vain to beg for mercy. Oleg stood quietly, his six feet five inch frame of pure muscle looming over him like a tidal wave of fury. He had already roughed up Peterson, the pathetic sales exec who had decided he would treat one of their girls to some rough stuff.

When she'd returned from her night's work with a split lip and a black eye, Oleg had kicked down the door to Peterson's marital home, pulled him from his bed in the middle of the night and dragged him to the car, the man's wife screaming in terror and begging for help.

Peterson was beyond help now.

The puddle of urine around his knees was a sign that he knew what the outcome was.

The large, plastic sheet that covered the floor was a hell of a giveaway.

Andrei squatted down in front of the man, shaking his head with pity. It took a weak man to pay for sex.

A weaker man to pay to hit a woman.

But Andrei knew that most men didn't go through what he had.

What Oleg had.

What Dana had.

Men were weak. And weakness was where the profit was.

With a deep sigh, he locked his icy stare onto the quivering man before him. The man noticed the skull tattoo on Andrei's neck, before looking away with fear.

'Mr Peterson,' Andrei begun, his Ukrainian accent thick with menace. 'You made a very big mistake.'

Andrei raised his eyebrows to Oleg, who stomped forward, reached out with his mighty, war-weathered hand and gripped Peterson's hair and yanked it back. Forcing him backwards, his throat shot invitingly forward and Andrei plunged the boning knife directly into the Adam's apple. An immediate burst of blood shot forward, the deep red creeping from the man's throat like a ghostly shadow. Peterson fell forward, the blade lodged in his trachea and he wheezed pathetically, flopping onto his front. As the life drained from him and began to pool around his twitching body, Andrei motioned for Oleg to begin the clean-up.

Silently, his dim-witted brother went to work. As big and as powerful as he was, Andrei knew that Oleg's greatest strength was his loyalty. He had shown it during his seven years serving the Ukrainian Special Forces. A brutal and efficient killer, Oleg had been captured and tortured, the left side of his face brutally burnt with a blow torch.

He had not said a word.

While Andrei knew that any adversary looked at Oleg's face with fear, he himself looked at it with pride. His family were tough and they were loyal. And as he watched his brother begin to clean up the blood-soaked mess, he felt that pride stronger than ever.

On the far side of the room, Dana, dressed elegantly in a black, figure hugging dress, stared malevolently as the final gasps of life escaped Peterson's body. Ever since that glorious night where he had beheaded their father, Dana had developed a penchant for violence despite never perpetrating it herself.

She was a voyeur.

She was his little sister and he loved her dearly.

'Brother,' she spoke in Ukrainian, her English too broken for a full conversation. 'It seems Elmore Riggs' operation was just hit.'

'Hit?' Andrei raised an eyebrow, a few drops of blood splattered across his face like a mask. 'Cops?'

'No. They believe it's the vigilante?'

'The Watchdog?' Andrei chuckled. 'Pope?'

'Yes. Riggs is dead. Two others.'

'I don't give a shit about a useless black fuck being killed.' Andrei turned to his brother. 'Oleg, go and find out from Riggs's lap dog what the hell happened.'

Oleg looked at Andrei, his good eye vacantly looking for an explanation that never came. Dana walked towards him, a gentle smile across her striking face. Her painted lips twisted upwards.

'Brother, go to the address and ask the following questions.'

As Dana began to run through the necessary instructions, Andrei took one final look at the dead body and felt a surge of power rush through him. He didn't care that Riggs was dead, but he did care that someone dared to step into his world and not kiss his ring.

If Pope wanted to be involved in his business, then Andrei was adamant it would be by his invitation only.

Stepping towards his drink cabinet to fix himself a drink, Andrei lit a cigar to remove the coppery smell of blood that clung to his expensive suit. It would be burnt.

It was okay.

His murderous stranglehold over the city of London ensured that he had a selection of replacements hanging in his wardrobe.

———

Standing on the walkway, exposed to the elements, Sam stuffed his hands into his pockets for warmth. Icy rain danced along the wind as it crashed into them and he stared at the young man before him. Wiseman was clearly terrified, his dark eyes shifting from Aaron to Sam. Now that Wiseman was clearly no threat, Aaron's posture had changed and the anger and desperation to find his daughter were dancing dangerously close to the surface.

'That's all I know.' Wiseman shrugged, pulling his jacket tighter to his body.

'He's fucking lying,' Aaron spat, gesticulating wildly.

'I'm not. Seriously, we don't really have much dealing with that side of things.'

'Think, Sean. Think back a couple of evenings. Who was there?' Sam spoke calmly, stepping forward gently to provide a blockade between the cowering young man and the furious father. 'Jasmine Hill went missing nearly two days ago. In this city that means we have a few more days tops before her life and her future disappear like that.'

Sam snapped his fingers, causing both Wiseman and Aaron to shudder. Her fate wouldn't be worth contemplating. Sam continued.

'I'm not saying you did this, Sean. But you have done some bad things for worse people. This girl is only fifteen years old. You can help her.'

Wiseman swallowed, his eyes watering and he looked out over the balcony to the estate below. The rain was thrashing the gloomy streets and old, damaged cars. Aaron took a deep breath, shaking his head with anger.

'He's wasting our time, Sam. Do your thing and make him talk.'

'My thing?' Sam turned, an eyebrow raised.

'Yeah, do what you do. Hurt him or whatever.'

'He's already done that,' Wiseman barked, raising the bloodstained bandages that were strapped to his hand.

'Then I'll do it,' Aaron snapped, lurching forward and gripping the wounded hand in his own. Squeezing with all his might, he crushed down on the fresh bullet wound, causing Wiseman to squeal with pain and buckle loosely. With his other hand, Aaron grabbed the lapel of his coat, forcing Wiseman back and rocking him over the edge of the balcony. 'Where the fuck is my daughter you piece of shit?'

'Easy,' Sam muttered, placing a hand on Aaron's shoulder and gently pulling him back. Aaron brushed him off, roughly shoving a terrified Wiseman back further, one of his feet coming off the concrete walkway as gravity threatened to take control of the situation.

'Please, help me,' Wiseman begged, tears streaming down his rain-stricken face.

'Tell me where she is,' Aaron spat venomously, his own tears drawn by rage. 'Tell me.'

Sam reached out again, firmly pulling both Aaron and Wiseman back. Instantly, Aaron slapped Sam's hand away and stormed back towards the stairwell, his rage pouring out of him. Sam watched him leave, annoyed by his lack of composure, but he understood.

A father's drive to protect his child is something he understood.

Something he had failed at.

Wiseman fell forward onto his knees, gingerly massaging his injured hand with the other and holding back his tears. Having grown up on the estate, he knew better than to show weakness, but the gravity of the whole situation had got to him.

He had been shot twice in the last two days.

He had seen his lifelong friend killed.

A young girl was now missing and most likely facing a fate worse than death. Despite turning a blind eye to Riggs's dealings in women, Wiseman knew the operation. They got the girls young, they hooked them on drugs and then they sold them overseas to dangerous men with worse intentions.

The thought of it broke the barrier, and Wiseman began to weep.

'Sean.' Sam broke the silence, his arms folded. 'Sean, you need to tell me what you know.'

'I don't want this.' Wiseman's words were quiet and feeble. 'I never wanted this.'

Sam squatted down to face him, his hair slick with rain.

'Look, Sean. I have about two days, tops, to help this man find his daughter. It doesn't take a genius to figure out what happens when young girls go missing with guys from your gang. So I'm asking you, if you don't want this … help me.'

Wiseman took a couple of deep breaths before wiping his eyes with his drenched sleeve. Sam extended a hand which he gratefully took and he pulled himself up, groaning slightly as he wiped away the final tears. A couple of his neighbours were loitering in front of one of the doors further up the walk way, carefully eyeing up Sam Pope. Wiseman shook his head to signal it was okay, but it was more for their safety than Sam's.

Wiseman looked out over the drab surroundings, the gritty world that had encompassed his life so far. Although he had never pulled a trigger or sold any of the product, he had enabled others to do so. He was just as big a monster as they were, if not worse.

It was time to do the right thing.

'That evening, we had a couple of new members of the NW Acid Gang with us.'

'Acid Gang?' Sam's eyes narrowed with anger.

'Yeah.' Wiseman looked away with shame. 'They work for some big people. I'm talking dangerous, paid-up people. The people who have connections, you know?'

Wiseman's lip wobbled with sadness as Sam pulled his focus back.

'What do they do? For these people?'

'The gang? They are the takers.' Wiseman's voice cracked again. 'They take the girls to sell on…'

'You're doing great,' Sam said, swallowing his own disgust. 'Where can I find them?'

'Stonebridge Estate,' Wiseman said, taking a deep breath. 'It's in Harlesden and…'

'I know where it is.'

'A couple of their younger members were with us that night, but there was no girl.' Wiseman had stopped crying, but his body shivered in the cold. The temperature was dropping as the city lashed its freezing power on its inhabitants. 'That's all I know, I swear.'

'Thanks. It's a big help.' Sam offered a smile, which soon dissipated. 'One last thing, why do they call them the Acid Gang?'

Wiseman rocked nervously from one foot to the other.

'Because they have to perform an acid attack as initiation.'

Sam nodded, his fists clenching in anger at the senseless violence deemed necessary for acceptance. The newspapers were rife with innocent people being blinded, scarred, or even killed by someone throwing acid in their face. It was cowardly and it was vicious.

It was wrong.

It made doing things the hard way a little more appealing. As the silence grew between them, Wiseman took one last glance towards the stairwell, but Aaron was gone. He offered Sam a meek smile, before walking past him, headed towards his flat.

'Sean,' Sam called after him, taking a few steps towards him. 'Did you mean what you said? About wanting out?'

Wiseman nodded. Sam asked for the young man's phone, and he reluctantly handed it over. He tapped in an address and handed it back, smiling at Wiseman's confusion.

'When you realise you really want to help, go there. And Sean…' Wiseman looked up from the screen to Sam's smiling face. 'I hope I never see you again.'

Wiseman finally cracked a smile and Sam nodded his thanks, stuffed his hands in his pockets, and marched back down the walkway with a renewed purpose.

A new target.

As the rain lashed the poverty-stricken estate like a cat-o'-nine-tails, Sam disappeared into the stair well to tell a desperate dad that he may have some hope after all.

CHAPTER THIRTEEN

'I don't believe in no-win situations, sir.'

Sam Pope spoke proudly, his back straight, chest out. His jaw was set, a thin layer of stubble an indication of the three-day hike he and his squadron had taken. The relentless heat poured from the sun, bathing Sudan in a scorching glow. The African country, home to over thirty-eight million people, sat just below Egypt, with the town of Wadi Halfa situated just over twenty kilometres from the border. With the rocky, desolate plain that they were walking, it had taken the troop just over a day, and as they reached the border with Egypt, Sergeant Carl Marsden had called them to a halt. He had asked his squadron to lie low, set up base camp, and for them to keep an eye out for Egyptian patrols. When questioned, he had responded with the notion that being spotted would end in defeat. It had been Corporal Sam Pope who had responded with his usual lack of fear.

'Every situation is a no-win situation, Corporal. It's just you are trained to not lose.'

Pope smiled, his white skin clearly sun-kissed and sweat dripped from his forehead. As a man whose parents had emigrated from the very continent they were standing on, Marsden's skin showed less evidence of the heat. He wiped his brow with the back of his forearm and looked around at the five-man team. Corporal Simon Murray, as loyal as he was intimidating, who had proven himself to be an exceptional leader of men. Theo Walker, calm, well-educated, and one of the finest young medics within the armed forces. Private Lawrence Griffin, the youngest of the group, a little scrawny and his ginger complexion was providing a lot of entertainment for the rest of the crew, especially in the relentless heat. Corporal Paul Etheridge, a bomb disposal expert and one of the most intelligent men Marsden knew, if maybe a little too smug for his own good.

And Sam Pope. The man was by far the finest sniper he had ever witnessed in his twenty-two years serving his country. With over fifty confirmed kills, he had been the first name on the sheet that Marsden's superior had given him for the mission.

General Ervin Wallace.

Marsden knew that there was a specialist unit being put together under the notorious General, one that would exist so far off the books they were out of the library.

Project Hailstorm

Marsden knew he was too old for such an elite team, his years of combat were weighing heavily on his body, despite the lengths he took to maintain his physique. He still ran an extra mile every morning, more than even the youngest recruits, but his wisdom and experience was best served in putting together the team.

Not leading it.

This exercise would be a simple in and out job, with the team expected to infiltrate a jihadi base just past the Egyptian border and neutralise the threat. Intelligence had strong suspicions that a bomb factory was hidden behind the ancient, rural ruins that housed a small terrorist cell and Marsden was to deploy the team at midnight.

Pope would cover from the rocks. Murray and Griffin would accompany Etheridge in, eliminate any hostiles and decommission any explosives. Etheridge would do the technical parts.

Murray and Griffin the grunt work.

A simple job.

As the men checked their weapons, Marsden tried to radio back to base, his signal hitting nothing but a high-pitch block. Angered by the uselessness of his equipment, Marsden turned to Etheridge expectantly, the man's reputation with technology preceded him. Etheridge gladly took it and began twisting the frequency knob, staring intently at the device, his attention focused on the task and not on his feet. With the rocky terrain alienating them from existence, Etheridge took a few steps to the right side of a large boulder, lost his footing and found himself tumbling down a twenty-foot slope. His body bounced and collided with a few rocks, his femur shattering in an instant.

His cry of pain alerted his squadron to his dilemma.

It also drew immediate fire from a three-man patrol that was circling the area in a roofless jeep.

Etheridge closed his eyes and accepted his fate.

Three shots echoed through the caves in quick succession.

When he opened his eyes again, Etheridge saw the last of his attacker's slump forward from the vehicle and hit the dusty track, a bloody hole in his forehead. He assumed the other two motionless bodies bore the same injury.

As he peered back up the slope, he could see Theo Walker carefully abseiling down towards him, the beefy Murray holding the other end of the rope and gently feeding it to Griffin who steadied it as best he could. Marsden stood beside them, offering his expert hand and still considerable strength to the task.

Beyond them, Sam Pope stood, the rifle still in his hands, his eye at the scope, ready to lay down covering fire. As the sun began to set beyond the rocky vista, Etheridge took a deep breath. Although his left leg was shattered, his pride hurt more.

He wasn't seen as a soldier. He had been trained as they all had, knew how to handle a gun and himself in hand to hand, but his strengths were in strategy and the equipment.

The man was a genius.

He was a thinker. Not a fighter.

Tumbling down a mountain, exposing the mission, and sending three men to their graves would give the guys no end of material.

He would never hear the end of it.

Theo fashioned a makeshift splint and with careful, measured steps, the two of them ascended the incline, hand over hand as they made their way back to base. After a gentle ribbing by his team, Etheridge thanked them from the bottom of his heart for saving his life.

Marsden watched on with pride.

Wallace was right.

This squadron was something special.

As the men made their way back through the rocky path to their base camp to collect their stuff, Murray and Griffin began plotting a new location to set up as their position had been compromised. Etheridge took a seat on a dusty rock, the pain of his broken body bouncing through him like an echo. Theo began packing away the gear, updating Marsden on the condition of their fallen comrade. As the first stars began to emerge like blossoming flowers in the navy skyline, Sam Pope stood, one foot rested on a rock, his rifle resting against his chest, the barrel aiming at the wondrous twilight above. The evening soon turned chilly and as the night sky lit up with a thousand more stars, Etheridge felt a chill run through him.

'Thank you, Sam.'

Sam smiled, nodding his acceptance to his friend and looked out into the dark, rocky surroundings.

'No problem, bud.' He offered him his hand, to help him limp through the base. 'Although for someone with a high IQ, you have pretty shit vision.'

The two men laughed and Sam's attention turned to Marsden, who beckoned him to the side. Sam smiled at Etheridge, before walking across the dusty gravel path to his superior.

'That was some good shooting, Sam,' Marsden said admiringly.

'It's what I'm here for, sir.'

'Quite.' Marsden smiled. 'Tell me, Sam, you have a family, don't you?'

'Yes, sir,' Sam said with respect. 'My wife, Lucy, is expecting our first child.'

'Fantastic.' Marsden genuinely beamed. 'Etheridge also has a wife who, because of you, will be seeing him again.'

They both let the importance of his actions sit silently between them like an ugly secret. Sam glanced back to Etheridge, who was trying his best to get the radio to work.

Despite the horrendous fall and injury, he was still following orders.

They all were.

Sam took a deep breath, his chest filling with fresh, humid air and swelling with pride.

'Like you said, we are trained not to lose.'

'That maybe so.' Marsden chuckled. 'But we are also trained not to put ourselves in those situations to begin with.'

Sam could sense Marsden's frustration and offered him another smile.

'With all due respect, sir, he fell. It's not like he ran head first into a gun fight.'

Marsden shook his head.

'What he did was reckless. We are trained to win, Sam. But we are also trained not to put ourselves needlessly in danger.' Both of them could see an embarrassed Etheridge arch his head round. He had obviously heard, but Marsden ignored it. He rested a reassuring hand on Sam's shoulder. 'Because if we do, regardless of whether we walk out alive, we still lose a piece of ourselves if we go looking for it.'

Sam watched as Theo finished packing up and called their superior down the final few rocks and into the group which had begun to regroup, their packs strapped to their backs. A glum, humiliated Etheridge pushed himself to his feet, waiting patiently as the always attentive Theo scurried to help.

The mission would need to be re-evaluated and most likely postponed for the night.

As another brisk chill danced along the night sky, Sam climbed down to the rest of the group and followed his orders.

———

Sam sat in the passenger seat of Aaron Hill's black Ford Mondeo and thought about no-win situations. Everything since the High Rise six months before had been meticulously planned. Every attack on a safe house, every ambush of a criminal's hide out. Sam had scoped and planned it to the finest detail.

There were no surprises.

No blind spots.

There was always a chance of winning.

This … this was different.

Sam stared out of the rain-covered windscreen at the towering concrete block before them. Similar to the urban pillar that they'd confronted Wiseman on, the Acid Gang were a notorious stain on the map of Wembley. Despite its connections to the national football team, the town of Wembley had decayed badly. While the modern, gentrified streets that surrounded the stadium gave off the scent of money, the poverty rippled outwards from it, as if the stadium was a huge, expensive rock dropped in a sea of suffering.

'So … what's the plan?' Aaron asked, his brow furrowed and his fingers nervously drumming the leather steering wheel.

'Plan is, I go into that building and try to find out where the hell they took your daughter.'

'And how are you going to do that, huh?' Aaron's words were laced with agitation. 'You've never been here before.'

'Look, you need to calm down,' Sam said sternly. 'What you did back there, to Wiseman. You can't lose your mind like that.'

'Fuck him.'

'Say you had pushed him over the top of that balcony? Say you painted the pavement with his blood. Then what?'

'Then I would say good riddance. Another scumbag

off the streets,' Aaron spat, shaking his head. 'I'll be just like you.'

'You're nothing like me.'

'What? Because you don't kill criminals?'

'I've only killed the ones I've had to. And believe me, Aaron, it isn't easy. None of it is easy and I wish I didn't have to do it.'

'Then why do it then?'

'Because...' Sam sighed. 'Look, bottom line is, if you had killed him, we wouldn't have known to come here, would we? That kid is just that. A kid. He grew up in a world that you and I will never understand and has had to do things just to survive. That isn't a reason to take the law into our own hands. You want to do that, then at least do it for the right reason and aim higher.'

Aaron scoffed, shaking his head and peering angrily out of the window. A group of black youths were gathered in a doorway to one of the buildings, their hoods up, their eyes focused fully on the car.

They were not welcome there.

Aaron knew that and despite the fury, Sam could tell the man was nervous. A few droplets of sweat were forming around his hair line, his eyes flickered from side to side.

Sam watched, took it all in.

Every detail.

He may not have had a plan, but he had a gun.

He had training.

And he had a rapidly declining window.

Calmly, he reached a gloved hand to the door handle and flicked it, the door popping open slightly and an immediate blast of cold air violated the vehicle. Aaron turned uncomfortably.

'Wait here. Don't do anything stupid,' Sam ordered. 'If

I'm not back in five minutes, go. Okay? You do not wait for me. Do you understand?'

'Yes,' Aaron stammered. 'B-but…'

'Do you understand?' Sam barked firmly, causing the driver to jolt with apprehension.

'Yes.'

'Good.' Sam kicked open the door and stepped out, feeling the eyes of the gang lock on to him like an eagle swooping over a field mouse. He casually eased a hand to the base of his spine and felt the pistol wedged in the band of his jeans. He lowered his head back into the car as Aaron spoke.

'What are you going to do?' Aaron asked, his eyes wide with fear.

Sam offered his reassuring smile.

He was headed into a no-win situation.

As rogue rain drops infiltrated the back of his neck and slid down his spine, he replied, 'Something stupid.'

Slamming the door shut, Sam stepped around the car, headed towards the building and the eagerly awaiting gang, as the arch of Wembley Stadium cut through the dark, grey sky above. As he approached the doorway, the first hooded figure moved forward, his head low, a bandana pulled across his face.

'Yo, what you doing here, cuz?' the young man said coldly, his arms out as if he was offering a hug. Despite the boy's intentions, Sam felt no intimidation.

Just pity.

The gang consisted of teenage boys, all of them besotted with the gangster lifestyle. All of them dealt horrible hands by society and gang culture which had undoubtedly run rife through this part of London.

The parts that are not just forgotten about.

The parts people didn't even know existed.

Sam knew the young man would have a blade on him,

the rules of the street pretty much necessitated these gangs were armed. In a different scenario, he would want to help them all. Talk to them. Try to put them on a better path.

But somewhere, Jasmine Hill was terrified and facing a life worse than the ones they'd chosen.

There was no time.

As the thug reached towards the pocket of his hoody, Sam thrust his arm forwards, connecting with a hard uppercut right to the diaphragm. Despite the tight muscles of the gangster's stomach, he felt the air rush out, winding him instantly. As the thug hunched over, gasping for air, Sam expertly drove his knee into the side of his skull.

The thug crumpled to the floor, unconscious.

The next hooded guard dog was on him within seconds, wildly slashing at him with a crude knife, the blade slicing through the rain drops as Sam arched his neck back, evading each murderous swipe. On the fourth one, he threw up his arm, connecting his elbow viciously with the attacker's frail forearm.

He heard it snap.

The knife fell to the floor.

The attacker stumbled back, and Sam took a two-step run up, leapt upwards and caught him with a punch which cracked his jaw and shut his lights out.

The two remaining gang members were fumbling in their pockets, one of them desperately trying to find his weapon while the other flicked through his phone in terror.

Sam whipped the gun out from the back of his jeans with a fluid motion, bringing it up with both hands until the chamber was at eye level.

He couldn't miss.

'Stop. Both of you,' Sam demanded.

The two gang members did as they were told and Sam approached them both slowly, the rain crashing against the metal of his Glock. With their hoods up and faces covered, it was hard to identify them, but Sam could see from their eyes that they were terrified. He needed them that way.

'Hoods down, now,' Sam ordered, knowing that there would be no chance of a police intervention. Not in this estate. Both of them obliged, their hoods sliding backwards and their bandanas pulled down.

They were so young.

Sam's knuckles whitened with fury at the lives these young men were exposed to. They couldn't have been older than eighteen years old. The two unconscious members who were motionless in the rain behind him couldn't have been either.

Sam knew he had a mission, one that was rapidly running out of time. He knew that he needed the head of the gang, the person who put all this into action.

The man who had orchestrated the kidnapping of Jasmine. Knowing he was the same man who encouraged these young men to strive for this lifestyle, who demanded they use acid to disfigure and destroy to prove their 'worth' to him made this even more necessary.

Sam needed to get to him. Now.

With regret, he looked at the two frightened young men before him. They were drenched, the relentless rain soaking them through. He marched towards the one to his left and before the thug could react, Sam swung the gun and crashed the hard, metal handle against the side of his head.

The young man crumpled into the puddles surrounding them.

Sam spun on his heel, aiming the gun at the final member who swallowed hard and was shaking more out of fear than the cold. Sam was sure, that despite all the tough talk and the gangster lifestyle, the young man had never looked down the barrel of a gun before.

If he had, Sam was sure it wasn't attached to someone as deadly as he was.

With brisk steps he approached, pressing the gun to the young man's chest.

'How many?' he demanded, looking up at the dour building and trying to think back to a time where he wasn't about to storm a building full of criminals.

'Eight. Including us.' The words were dripping with fear.

'Is he armed?'

'No. He's with his yat.' Sam arched an eyebrow. 'His girl.'

'Take me to him.'

'The boss don't like being disturbed when he's getting fresh, you know what I'm saying?'

Sam pressed the gun to the young man's forehead. The colour fell from his face, his eyes widening in genuine terror.

'I do know what you're saying and I don't give a damn.' Sam nodded to the door. 'Let's go.'

Slowly, the boy turned and walked calmly back towards the door of the building, the cold metal of Sam Pope's gun pressed to his forehead. Behind him, three gang members were sprawled across the concrete in an unconscious tribute to his abilities.

In the Ford Mondeo parked at the side of the road, Aaron Hill stared, mouth open, at the sheer brutality of the man he had put his faith in.

CHAPTER FOURTEEN

Pearce let out a deep sigh as he pulled up to the estate, the streets a beehive of activity as police officers battled tirelessly against the elements and the growing crowd. Police tape framed the crime scene in front of the run-down estate and the groups of locals were angrily gesticulating that the law wasn't welcome on this turf. Considering what Pearce had been told by Singh when the radio call had come in, it seemed like a bigger police presence in this area was exactly what was needed.

It would stop young adults falling in with the wrong crowd.

It could have stopped Sam Pope dismantling them in broad daylight.

Pearce and Singh had been in the Bethnal Green Youth Centre, discussing previous cases and war stories like old friends. As their tea got colder, Pearce found himself warming to the ambitious young lady, recognising a tenacity that many would mistake for rudeness. She was a serial winner, determined to make the streets a safer place, and he admired her for it.

Sure, she was curt, but she cared.

Which made it difficult when it came to her priority.

Despite spending his entire life upholding the law, Pearce felt a kinship with Sam Pope. The man was a vigilante, taking the law into his own hands and representing everything Pearce had dedicated his career to stop. But somewhere along the line, Sam had shown him the clear fractures in the very system he served, exposing crime and corruption on a level that Pearce never could. Since then, he had taken down more criminal safe houses in six months than the entire Metropolitan Police had in six years.

Good and bad used to be black and white.

Sam Pope had painted it grey.

As Pearce stuffed his bearded chin into the collar of his coat, the wind slapped a frozen hand across his face, coating his dark skin with icy drizzle. The estate was a depressing collection of dirty, decrepit buildings, all shooting out from the earth like jagged teeth. The narrow balconies spiralled around the building and Pearce could see eager faces peering over the edges, members of gangs all wishing ill upon the unwelcome police force.

He didn't blame them.

It wasn't as if the Met had forgotten about this place.

It was as if they never knew it existed.

As he thought of the kids who walked through the doors to the Youth Centre, he looked over at the stern, wrinkle free face of DI Singh. Her dark eyes were wide with interest as a SOCO pointed to an area on the floor where they'd removed a young man with a broken arm and a shattered jaw.

Pearce could feel the ferocity emanating from her as she turned away and marched back towards him. The rain seemed to bounce off her like bullets off of Superman.

'This is a lovely way to spend a Sunday, eh?' She offered with a smile, looking around at the dreary estate.

'It could be worse. I could be watching *X Factor*.'

Singh chuckled.

'Well there goes my suggestion for this evening.'

Pearce smiled, annoyed at the inner conflict he was experiencing. He stuffed his hands in his pockets, gently rocked on his heels and looked around at the mayhem.

'So, how many?' Pearce eventually asked.

'Eight in the hospital. No casualties,' Singh stated coldly. 'Seems your boy is showing some mercy.'

'Firstly, he isn't my boy, Detective Inspector,' Pearce corrected with an authoritative tone. 'And second, this doesn't feel right does it?'

'What do you mean?' Singh raised her thin, dark eyebrows and turned to him. Pearce pulled his lips into a thin line, his eyes darting around the crime scene.

'This. Last night. It doesn't fit his routine.'

'So he decided to beat eight men half to death instead of kill them. So what?'

'But that's just it. Six months ago, Sam wiped out an entire crime gang, killing thirteen men in the process. Since then, nothing. Sure, he's put over forty people in the hospital and a number into wheel chairs, but he steered off the executions. But last night ... last night was different.'

Pearce stepped forward, looking around the crime scene, imagining a rain-soaked Sam disarming and demo-bilising the look-outs. The young men who knew all the right words and stringently followed orders. Any normal man would have either turned and run as fast as they could or would have been found dead in a bin behind the stadium.

But Sam took them apart quicker than he could dismantle a handgun.

Why?

Singh stepped forward, her hair flat and soaked through. Behind her, a few police men in high-vis jackets spoke to an agitated group of locals, all of them decrying a 'white man beating up black kids.'

'So what the hell is going on?'

'Something's changed. Pope isn't just on a quest for justice anymore. He's too careful to be this reckless.' Pearce shook his head. 'Think about it. Yesterday, he only killed a few of the men in that High Rise. Riggs and a couple of his lackeys. The others … the guys in the street. He put them down with leg shots. So why did he kill the others?'

'He had no choice?' Singh offered, realisation creeping into her voice. 'He was protecting someone?'

'That's my guess. When Amy Devereux was being held at gun point, Sam acted. It's second nature to him. He's a born and bred soldier. He serves. He protects.'

'We need to go back through the people who walked out of that building. Lean on them … see who Sam was actually protecting.'

Pearce sighed, realising that he had just set a very tenacious dog after a potentially delicious bone. While he respected Sam Pope, he also respected the badge.

The justice system.

If Sam was as good as he had seen, then he would still be ahead of them. But Singh wouldn't stop. Pearce knew it because the same tenacity had rocked through him like a hurricane throughout his entire career. Singh barked orders at a few officers and then turned back to Pearce, her face resigned to having to go back to work. There was also a sadness hidden behind her eyes.

As if she felt guilty.

She cleared her throat and smiled at Pearce through the rain.

'Thanks for your help today, sir.'

'Please.' He smiled. 'Call me Adrian.'

'Adrian.' She returned a smile in kind. 'It appears the leader of the gang, a Leon Barnett, is missing. Apparently,

Sam pulled him out of bed while he was mid-romp with one of his lovers.'

'Talk about a mood killer.'

'Quite.' Singh looked back up to the top floor of the building, imagining the sight of Sam marching a naked man through the dangerous stairwell at gunpoint. The man was fearless, she would give him that. 'We are putting out a BOLO as soon as possible.'

'I wouldn't bother,' Pearce said, as he approached his car. He shook his head, dismissing the 'be on the lookout' order.

'How come?' Singh said, watching in disappointment as Pearce slid into the driver's seat of his car. The door slammed shut, and with a low hum, the rain drop covered window slid down, welcoming a blast of wet air to assault the leather interior. Pearce looked up at Singh, noticing that sadness once more.

'Because if he took him with him, then it means Sam needs something from him.'

'Do you think he will get it?'

Pearce raised his eyebrows and turned his attention to the road, turning the key and letting the engine roar to life.

'I'd bet this car on it. And I'll bet, considering the mess he has left behind, he won't do it nicely.'

————

Sean Wiseman took a deep breath before lifting the photo frame from his bedside table. It had been three hours since he had been confronted on his balcony by Sam Pope and Aaron Hill, and as soon as they'd left, he had marched to his door, entered his flat, slammed it shut, and fell to the floor in floods of tears. The last few days had been a war zone, where he had been shot through the hand, shot in the back, seen his childhood friend die, and realised how their way of life impacted the unde-serving.

Jasmine Hill didn't deserve what would happen to her.

The Acid Gang would take her to their employer, and she would be sent abroad, to a dusty, derelict village in Eastern Europe where she would likely be raped, forced into a drug addiction, and then sold to the highest bidder for a lifetime of sex slavery.

She was just a teenage girl.

After he had thrown up twice, he had lit a spliff, allowing the calming effects of the marijuana to filter through his body and his worries momentarily melted. The pain in his hand subsided.

The guilt of the broken family.

He faded…

After awaking a few hours later on the floor of his bathroom, Wiseman brushed his teeth and whilst staring into the mirror, a revelation hit him.

He wanted out.

With no idea how or where, he was determined to pack anything of value into a bag, strap it to his back, and leave the godforsaken estate behind. The guns, the drugs, the life of crime.

The constant looking over the shoulder.

It was all going in the rear view.

At any moment, he was expecting a message to ping through on his phone, telling him that someone had burnt the estate to the ground with the Acid Gang in it. He had unleashed Sam Pope on them like a rabid dog, and if it ever came back to them that he was the one who provided the road map, they wouldn't chuck acid at him.

They would submerge him in it until he disintegrated alive.

Rapidly pulling his room apart, he soon found it depressing how little he cared for the material items that cluttered his home. All the pain they'd caused and the laws they'd broken, all for the glamourous life and a stock piling of artefacts he couldn't give a shit about.

Leaving now felt so right.

After stuffing a couple of sets of fresh clothes into his bag, he pulled up the picture frame.

It was of him and Elmore, back in their high school days. Shirts untucked, ties ridiculously short, gangster poses. They had thought they were so cool but Wiseman had always expected them to grow up, to move on and make something of themselves. He was smart, which was why Elmore kept him around.

But Elmore wasn't around anymore.

He was dead.

Sam Pope had removed the contents of Elmore's skull with a well-placed bullet.

The horror of the previous night suddenly rushed to the forefront of his mind and a wave of nausea crashed over him. His knees buckled, and he dropped the treasured photo, his vision going blurry as he stumbled to the bathroom again, his body arching over the toilet as he dry heaved, wishing more vomit forward.

He was empty.

He dryly smiled at how apt that was.

As Wiseman reached out for the grey towel that hung from the rail affixed to the wall, the room shook as a violent knock echoed through the house. Startled, he fell back against the wall, wrapping his injured hand around his shins and pulling them towards him. A bead of sweat slithered down his neck and his heart raced.

Was it Pope? Had he changed his mind?

Was it the police?

His old crew?

Taking deep, concentrated breaths, Wiseman remained

perfectly still, ignoring the thunderous hammering on his door.

As suddenly as it had begun, it stopped.

The flat went silent.

Wiseman took a few more moments before he slowly began to push himself forward when the terrifying crash accompanied the door flying from its hinges. He saw it hit the floor of the hallway, a barrage of splinters burst off upwards like fireworks. Heavy footsteps echoed across the hallway and Wiseman began to feel nauseous again.

The steps drew closer.

Wanting to remain as silent as possible, Wiseman felt his body betray him.

The fear rose up in him, manifesting as another bout of vomit, this time a pale-yellow liquid that splashed into the toilet below.

It drew the intruder to the door.

As Wiseman tried to calm himself, he looked through watery eyes at the thick, black boots at the threshold pointed in his direction. A voice, weighed down by a thick, European accent, followed. The softness of the words took Wiseman by surprise, as if a child was speaking.

'You like glass of water?'

Surprised by the offer of kindness, Wiseman helplessly nodded, listening vaguely as the boots trudged back through the flat, a brief clatter in the kitchen and then the water bursting from the tap. He tried to reclaim his bearings, the panic and lack of hydration keeping him grounded. As he rocked back onto his knees, he finally wiped his eyes, just as the intruder reappeared.

Wiseman felt like he was in a horror film.

The man filled the entire doorway, his huge frame causing him to arch his neck slightly forward so he didn't catch his scalp on the frame. The man was a stack of muscle, his arms and chest looked like they were made of stone, even through his jacket.

It was his face that scared Wiseman most of all.

The entire left side was hideously scarred, the eye entirely white, useless. It looked like a ping-pong ball stuffed into a rotten peach.

The man's hair was cropped, the stubble fading at the charred skin.

His granite-esque hand shot forward, handing Wiseman a glass of water.

'Here.' His voice was soft. 'You drink.'

Wiseman did as he was told, eagerly chugging the water. He was confused, having no idea who the gigantic stranger was or why he was being kind. Without taking his eyes from the gentle gaze of the giant man, Wiseman cautiously handed back the glass. The man took it.

In a flash, the large man swung it forward, slamming the glass into the side of Wiseman's head. The glass shattered, the shards spraying across the bathroom and Wiseman slumped forward, blood trickling from the blow and his thoughts as scattered as the glass.

He tried to murmur for mercy, but realised it was useless.

Behind him, the attacker removed his jacket, his giant frame stretching his black T-shirt to its limit.

It wasn't the only resolve he was there to test.

He stepped further into the bathroom, his boots crunching over the shattered glass that covered the floor like a litter box. Wiseman reached his bandaged hand out towards a shard of glass, a useless attempt to protect himself.

The boot slowly lowered down on his forearm, the edge of the leather touching the band aid.

Wiseman went rigid with fear.

'My name is Oleg.' The man's voice sent a chill down

Wiseman's spine. He spoke with the simplicity of a child. 'I have to ask you some questions.'

'Please,' Wiseman sobbed. 'Please don't kill me.'

'I will not kill you.'

Wiseman burst into tears, a mixture of pain and relief at the man's reassuring words.

It was short lived after the following seven.

'But I will have to hurt you.'

CHAPTER FIFTEEN

The shrill beeping of a heavy-duty vehicle echoed through the metal walls and caused Jasmine Hill to open her eyes. They were sore, the last two days had been spent in a terrified panic and she couldn't force another tear from her eyes if she tried.

She had never known fear before.

Neither had the three other girls sharing the metal chamber.

The confines of the metal room were narrow and under furnished, with three rough mattresses thrown lazily onto the unforgiving iron floor. In the far corner, a bucket had been placed, which was now overflowing with human waste and causing a toxic aroma to fill the dark prison. Drifting in and out of sleep, there had been a number of occasions where the smell had invaded Jasmine's nostrils and caused her to roll to her side and retch at the stench.

She was weak.

The other girls were too.

All of them were in their mid to late teens, with two of them staying deathly silent, rocking back and forth in the dark and resigned to a fate that Jasmine was beginning to realise was worse than death. The only one of the girls to speak back, Hannah, had agreed with her that if they were going to be killed, they wouldn't have been fed. While that was a generous word for the loaf of bread that was thrown into the room with them, it did make sense.

They were wanted alive.

Jasmine pushed herself from the battered mattress and sat with her back against the metal wall. There was the odd sound from the outside world, one which made Jasmine want to bang against the wall and beg for freedom. However, one of the girls that lay a mere two feet from her had done just that.

Within two minutes, the door had opened, a blinding sheet of light causing them all to turn away. Two gruff men, both with heavy accents and high-vis jackets demanded to know who it was or all of them would be punished.

The girl bravely raised her hand.

The man cowardly raised his own.

Jasmine had shuddered with horror as the fully grown man clobbered the young girl in the face, reducing her mouth to a washing machine filled with blood and loose teeth.

An hour or so after the brutal beating, the door had opened again, the light dimmed by the emerging twilight and a striking woman with dark hair entered, her accent as thick as the previous attacker's but with enough allure to bend any man to her will. She calmly introduced herself as Dana, telling the girls that drawing attention to themselves would not be tolerated. She explained that while they were staying with her, they would not be subjected to any further harm as long as they behaved. Jasmine couldn't believe the woman's turn of phrase, as if they'd booked a few nights through Air BnB.

They had been kidnapped.

One of them had been beaten.

She had heard the men who had taken her, referring to her as a 'high grade', with one of the boys gloating that she would be passed around more times than a bong at a Reggae party. She had cried, realising that Tyrone, the boy she'd grown fond of at school and who had garnered her attention with his 'bad boy' attitude, had tricked her to going to that party in Shepherd's Bush.

She was fresh.

A virgin.

Tyrone's boss, a terrifying man called Leon, had congratulated him on bringing her in, telling him that he could join the main crew soon as long as he went through initiation.

A chloroform-soaked rag was soon pressed to her face and she never got to hear what that process would be.

But now, as the outside world roared around them, the four girls sat silently in the metal room, all of them lost.

All of them helpless.

Jasmine thought about her dad, how he had tried so hard to connect with her when her mother had died. How he had been overbearing, always calling, and always checking in. It had driven her mad at the time, but now she felt a lump forming in her throat as she longed for her father's embrace.

He would keep her safe.

He had always tried to.

She recalled heading for the door, rudely telling him that she was going to the party whether he liked it or not. She could see the hurt in his face, the futile attempts to act as both of her parents.

She sobbed.

Her tear ducts dry, she felt the salty sting of an absent tear as she pulled her knees towards her, cowering in the dark of a foreign room in an unknown place, with a life-time of sexual abuse ahead of her.

She closed her eyes, wishing that somewhere, someone was looking for them.

Jasmine took a deep breath, fully aware that despite her private pleas of rescue, her situation was nigh on hopeless.

———

'Wake up.'

The gruff voice filtered through Leon Barnett's wooziness, and he slowly began to regain consciousness. As the light burrowed into his eyes, he squinted, his surroundings blurred like a camera out of focus. His head hurt, a throbbing pain roaring like a siren. Fragments of his memory began to whirl around his mind, the blow to his head making it harder to piece them together. Very slowly, clarity began to ease its way into his line of sight, the edges of the furniture becoming clearer.

He was in a kitchen.

It was one he had never seen before and one he ventured hadn't been used properly for a long time. The tiles were plagued with grime, the whiteness faded and smeared with a brown sheen. The sink was a bowl of rust, somehow still attached to pipes that were on the verge of collapse.

The sharp pain in his head caused him to grit his teeth and he reached his hand to his head. Or at least tried...

Leon looked down and found his arms strapped to the metal chair, his naked body locked in place. A muscular man with a body covered in tattoos, he was used to being in full control of every situation; his very presence a cause of great fear throughout not just his estate, but most of London.

Here he was trapped, naked, and vulnerable.

Behind him he heard the sound of water being poured into a jug, accompanied by a satisfying fizzing noise. He tried desperately to turn his head, to find the source of the voice that had woken him from his fragile state and the man responsible for his abduction.

'Do you have any idea how fucked you are?' Leon spat, trying his hardest to lace the words with venom. 'You got any idea what my boys are gonna do to you? To your family?'

The only response he received was silence, as he heard the man open a plastic wrapper, and then the snap of rubber gloves. Leon felt his heart begin to beat faster, a strange feeling that he never had to feel.

Fear.

Swallowing hard, he tried to counteract it.

'This is a bad idea, bruv.' Leon tried to sound nonchalant as he tried to rack his brain for what had happened. 'You know who I am, right? What I can do?'

Again, nothing but more liquid being pumped into a jug, the hissing sound as the contents fizzed filled the awkward silence. A horrible smell began to filter around the room, like an unwelcome fart in an elevator.

It smelt toxic.

Leon flexed his considerable bulk, trying to free himself from his restraints. It was no good, the plastic of the cable ties pinched into his dark skin, threatening to draw blood at any moment. Gaffer tape locked his abdomen to the back of the chair and further cable ties secured him by the ankles. A towel had been generously donated to cover his modesty.

He racked his brain, the memory of one of his skanks bent over while he went to town on her filtered back when he remembered the door bursting open, causing her to scream and him to stumble naked to the floor of his flat. The young drug runner, usually situated out on the steps, got halfway through an apology before a sickening clunk rendered him unconscious. The man who held the gun stepped into the room, aiming it squarely at Leon. The naked woman begged for mercy on the bed as Leon told her to keep quiet.

The man was white, mid-thirties with a soldier's physique, the stance of a fighter and, judging by the fact he had gone through roughly eight of his crew to get to him, Leon assumed was a dangerous motherfucker.

He had marched him out of the flat as naked as the day he was born, stripping him of his masculinity, pride, and fear factor for anyone who was watching.

They stepped over the unconscious bodies of his crew members.

The man had stuffed Leon into the boot of a waiting car and as he turned to ask why, Leon saw the man swing the gun and that was it. The next part of his memory was waking up in this room, with no clue of where he was, what the man wanted, or what was going on behind him.

But Leon felt that fear again.

Whatever it was, it wasn't going to be good.

As the toxicity began to tickle the back of his throat, Leon coughed violently, the sting in the air causing his eyes to water, the need to rub them almost as unbearable as the chemical aroma wafting around them.

He shook violently, trying to loosen his grip.

It was hopeless.

Panic began to settle in.

'Fuck, man, just let me go, aight?' he begged, feeling as pathetic as he looked. 'Please, this shit is burning.'

At that moment, Sam turned from his makeshift lab table and stepped across the grotty kitchen, hoisting a plastic box from the stained, cracked tiles that zigzagged the floor in no discernible pattern. He walked to the other side of the small table, Leon's eyes locking onto him with a mixture of resentment and fear.

It didn't matter.

With a casual sigh, he offered Leon a smile before reaching into the box with his gloved hand and pulled out a pair of protective goggles, followed swiftly by a face mask.

'What the fuck is this, bruv?' Leon pleaded, shunting his body violently in the chair, causing the towel to drop and take away his final modicum of modesty.

'You're going to tell me where you've taken the girls your crew snatched,' Sam said calmly, looking beyond Leon to the plastic vat sat on the counter. The kitchen was tacked onto a bare living room, one of the few safe houses Sam had acquired over the previous six months. While each criminal hideout was brought down brick by brick, he took a slice of their money to purchase small safe sites around the city for refuge. Each one was stocked with a couple of automatic rifles, pistols, grenades, and enough money to disappear. He had no intention of doing so, his war on the organised crime that was rotting the city like a decaying tooth was just beginning.

But this small property sat above a back-alley repair garage just outside of Harlesden, where people looked the other way and didn't come running when people screamed for help.

Which, judging by the terror on his face, Leon was fully aware of.

Sam could only smirk as the man tried to cover his fear with false bravado.

'You're a dead man, you hear me. My boys will be here soon and they gonna take you apart. Then find your wife or your gal and gonna tear that ass up!' Leon kissed his teeth, his lip lifting to reveal a gold tooth. Sam allowed the empty threat to sit for a moment, before pulling his mask over his airways and stepping back across the small kitchen, returning quickly with a large container. The container was made of Teflon and inside it, the steam slithered upwards, a cloud of toxic gas. Leon struggled for breath as Sam placed it on the table before speaking through his mask.

'Leon, this here is a vat of strong, hydrochloric acid. It's incredible what you can pick up from B&Q if you know what you're looking for. Now a concentrated dose of that, mixed with bleach, makes this an extremely toxic and harmful acid. You would know … you have your crew throw it at people just to get into your inner circle, right?'

Sam took the silence as Leon's acceptance of that fact. The tear rolling down his stubble covered cheek was his appreciation of how much trouble he was in. Sam didn't have time to play games.

'Now I know you arrange to have girls taken and you took one two nights ago. Fifteen, brown hair.'

'I don't know any young bitch,' Leon offered meekly. Sam rocked him with a hard right, the impact causing his jaw to shake like a maraca.

'Her name is Jasmine,' Sam said sternly. 'Now I don't have time to mess about here, Leon. So you're going to tell me where I can find her otherwise I'm going to put you through more pain than you have ever thought possible.'

Leon looked at the murderous vat of acid before a treacherous moment of machismo filtered through. The pointless display of power from someone used to being in control.

'Fuck you.' The following ball of saliva he spat in Sam's direction was the exclamation point. Sam didn't hesitate. Using a small, Teflon jug with a spout, he carefully dipped the edge into the makeshift tub and pulled it back, his jug heavier.

He gently trickled it over Leon's naked thigh.

As he roared with pain, the skin instantly began to sizzle, the acid burrowing its ferocious path through the protective layers as it tried its best to pass through him. The smell of burning flesh began to overpower the heavy smell of chemicals and Leon shook in agony as the muscle of his leg began to reveal itself, the skin disintegrating like a burnt piece of paper.

The pain was unbearable.

Sam added to it with a hard slap to the face.

'Where is she?'

'I don't know.'

'Where?' Sam slapped him again.

'I don't fucking know, blad,' Leon spat.

Sam trickled another few droplets onto his other thigh, the same cries of pain accompanied the same smell of burning flesh. The chair rocked back and gravity took over, welcoming the squirming, naked man with a hard thud. As Leon squirmed in agony, Sam stepped forward, roughly pushing a boot down on the man's tattooed chest and squatting down, calmly looking into the terrified eyes of his prisoner.

'Please. Please stop,' Leon begged, his eyes full of tears, the skin of his thighs burnt clean off.

Any power the man had once held was gone.

Beaten.

Naked.

Begging for his life.

Sam had come to realise that every criminal, when pushed to their limit, when just dangled over the edge of their pain threshold, always begged. The odd few, like the Mitchell Brothers, he had faced in hand to hand combat six months before, were titans, willing to fight until the last of their life was forced from them.

But the ones sat in the thrones, they were the ones who begged once everything had been stripped away.

Leon was begging now.

Which meant he would talk.

Sam lowered his face so it was a few feet from Leon's, his unblinking stare causing Leon to blink nervously. More tears slid down his face.

'Leon, you need to tell me how I can find her, or this is really going to hurt.'

Sam held up the small receptacle that held the acid and motioned to pour it on his chest. Leon instantly squirmed and cried out through his tears.

'We never meet them. Okay?' he spoke through sharp, panicked breaths.

'Who?'

'I don't know. Some Ukrainian family. Three of them. Two brothers and a mighty fine bitch. They came to me a few years back and since then we been doing jobs for them.' Leon spoke hurriedly. 'They want young English girls. Virgins go for more money. We collect and they pay.'

Sam turned away, his mouth curling into a snarl under his mask. His knuckles whitened around the acid container.

'How do they pay?'

'We get a bank transfer after every drop. We put the girls in a van that they park on one of three streets every week and on that Friday we get paid.'

'How much?'

'Sorry?'

'You're not sorry,' Sam spat angrily. 'How much do they pay you? Huh? How much is the life of an innocent girl worth?'

Leon looked away, the shame causing more tears to form. The burning had stopped and his thighs were now numb, the acid having eaten away at the layers of muscle like bacteria.

'Answer me!' Sam yelled.

142

'Five grand,' Leon said, shaking his head and choking back more tears. 'It's worth five grand.'

'Which street was the van on?'

'I don't know, I didn't do the drop…'

Leon was cut out as Sam reached back with his gloved hand and pushed two knuckles deep into the exposed muscle of his burnt leg. Leon howled in agony.

'My boy, Curtis, he said it was by KFC. Down by the stadium.'

Sam made a note, the possible location of that vehicle could lead to an address. It was a door Sam very much wanted to knock on. He stood up once more, allowing Leon a moment to catch his breath. Beneath his boot, the feared and respected leader of the Acid Gang was a quivering, naked wreck who had cracked and begged.

'Where does the money go?'

'It goes into an account under the name of a shell company.' Leon didn't even try to hold back the information. 'Burn Group Inc. That's all I know, man.'

Sam shook his head, the man openly mocking the severity of his crimes with the name of his corporation. But he had an account and a possible vehicle location. He believed Leon knew little else and finally stepped back, relinquishing the gangster from under his boot. Still strapped to the chair, Leon looked on helplessly.

'I helped you, right?' Leon questioned. 'We cool, yeah?'

Sam begged himself to walk away, to head out the door and spend every precious moment ripping the under belly of the city apart to find Jasmine and any of the other missing girls.

But this man made maiming people an entry fee to his crew. The willingness to ruin lives, be it through the acid attacks, the abduction of innocent girls to be sold into a life of sex slavery, or just the fear with which he had run his estate.

They were not cool.

He turned, his eyes burning deeper into Leon than the acid he had subjected him to earlier and he stepped forward. Leon squirmed, realising the imminent danger.

'You have taken so much from so many people. You have snatched them from their lives all to make money. How many girls have you sent into the back streets of Europe? How many people have gone through hours of surgery in the faint hope of restructuring their face after you ordered an acid attack?'

Leon turned away, not wanting to meet the furious glare from Sam.

Not wanting to face the truth.

Eventually, he mustered up the courage to utter two words.

'I'm sorry.'

Sam closed his eyes, sending a silent apology to Jamie. He thought of all the young girls being pushed into rooms in foreign countries, while hungry men subjected them to a horrifying awakening.

How they had no way out.

All thanks to the man lying before him.

He took one more breath before reply.

'Me too.'

Sam overturned the cup of acid, dropping it all over Leon's right arm. The instant sizzling of his skin caused him to scream, the pain shooting through his body and overwhelming his brain. As Leon passed out through shock, Sam watched, his fists clenched, knowing that extreme crimes call for extreme measures.

Within two minutes, the room was cleared and empty, with nothing but bloodstains and acid burns adorning the tiles like a sickening rug.

Time was running out.

CHAPTER SIXTEEN

The following morning was one of the worst days of Mark Harris's career.

Since he burst onto the political scene as a twenty-three old prodigy in Croydon, he had been presented by the press as a new hope. The chiselled features, the well-groomed hair, the muscular physique. It all blended with his 'voice of the people' shtick that had been rehearsed and fine-tuned into a tremendous symphony. In front of the cameras he was a natural, always ready with a tasty soundbite or a charming quip.

The smile was a mixture of reassurance and desire, his handsome features going a long way to building his popularity.

When he finally took the seat of his political party at the tender age of twenty-six, he quickly became the media darling they'd been hoping for, and as the public latched onto him, so did the party themselves. He was pushed to the front of the queue, the future power of the current regime trying their very best to cling to his coattails.

Ten years on, he was waiting to ascend the throne of

London, where he would be Mayor of the city that had moulded him.

With crime at an all-time high, the terror alert dangling precariously like the sword of Damocles, and the public screaming for the country to fight back, Harris could almost touch the seat with his fingertips.

Destiny was so close to proclaiming him the white knight of London.

But now, with Sam Pope raging a one-man war against every crime syndicate in the city, the press were having a field day. Especially since it had only been two days since he had officially backed the task force as a sure-fire step on his way to the top.

They would bring an end to a dangerous vigilante.

He would get the credit.

Probably even a couple of rounds with the attractive Singh once she relaxed her obvious guard.

But as he stepped back into his office, he felt deflated. Suddenly, the panache with which he tackled every task had been sapped from him, replaced with hunched shoulders and tired, heavy eyes. He stomped around the large oak desk, unbuttoned the expensive grey suit and slumped into his chair, his eyes vacantly scanning the useless artefacts on his desk.

He looked at the picture of his wife, her smiling face full of joy and love. A look she hadn't given him for over five years, not since she'd found out about his indiscretions. It didn't stop him, and she was fond of the lifestyle.

But separate beds and the odd, disgusted glance only caused his body to yearn for Singh.

The press had been unrelenting, all of them querying the effectiveness not just of the Sam Pope Task Force, but of Harris's ability to lead a full-scale project against crime. It was the life force of his entire campaign and it was starting to unravel, each journalist pulling on a separate thread. Although flustered, Harris was able to deflect a lot of the negativity, a skill he had acquired through years of schmoozing the public, offering them hard quotes that would likely make the paper.

Then the press conference turned in the direction he had been terrified of.

A young woman he didn't recognise raised her hand, claiming to be from an online paper he had never heard of. He had almost pitied her from her introduction. Then, when she spoke, he found himself loathing her. The lady, who he had since demanded that Burrows have banned from future events, had suggested that Sam Pope was in fact doing the very job that Harris himself had claimed to be doing.

That Sam Pope was doing more to tackle crime than Harris or the entirety of the Metropolitan Police Service. Rattled, Harris had snapped back, belittling her as nothing more than a blogger who believed the whispers of desperate people, obsessed with the notion of heroic justice.

Then she read out the facts. The laundry list of hits that Sam Pope had been responsible for in the last six months.

Frank Jackson and the High Rise.

Four safe houses.

The makeshift High Rise in Shepherd's Bush, with over eleven wanted criminals arrested.

The uncovering of corrupt, senior police officials.

And in the late hours of the night, Leon Barnett, who had since been identified as the head of the notorious Acid Gang, had been found naked, beaten and tortured, with his entire right arm mutilated to the point of amputation.

All from a highly decorated soldier who had fought valiantly for his country.

The room turned soon after, with many other journalists jumping on the bandwagon, all of them probing Harris for a response to the notion that Sam Pope was what was best for the city.

Sam Pope.

A highly trained, dangerous vigilante with a death wish.

Harris had never felt lower.

The sound of the door clicking shut snapped him back into the room, his gaze falling upon the neatly groomed Burrows as he shuffled towards his desk. Harris sighed, turning slowly in his chair until he faced the window, the depressing grey sky once again covering the city below with rain. The traffic was gridlocked on Marylebone Road, with car horns polluting the air with their impatience. Unfortunate pedestrians ran, many of them holding the Metro over their heads for shelter, the free paper finally offering something of use to commuters.

'Now is not the time to sulk, sir.'

Burrows spoke confidently, his back straight. He had served as an assistant to a number of party leaders and was respected throughout the political world as a man of unshakable loyalty. Harris knew he was lucky to have him, so allowed the jab at his maturity to slide.

'What a fucking mess,' Harris eventually mumbled, glumly staring out at the horrible weather.

'Every mess can be cleaned, sir.'

'The man is essentially shitting on our door step.' Harris gestured angrily. 'Less than ten miles from this fucking door step.'

Burrows allowed a moment to pass, for Harris to regain his usual composure. Harris was grateful.

'I spoke to Detective Inspector Singh this morning, she said they are following up on a lead from the attack on the second High Rise. She sounded positive.'

Harris shrugged.

'Until she gets me a result, she's got nothing,' Harris barked. 'Is there anything else, Carl?'

Burrows seemed slightly awkward at the informality of being addressed by his first name. He smiled, the wrinkles dominating his face and offering a fatherly warmth.

'The usual, sir. A few emails regarding your investments, but nothing that I cannot handle if you would like.'

'You always do,' Harris said numbly, the anger still gripping him in a bear hug.

'Quite, sir.' Burrows turned on his heel to leave but then stopped. Harris spun the chair back around to face him.

'Yes, Carl?'

'I know it may be stating the obvious, but you cannot afford Sam Pope to continue on his rampage too much longer.' Before Harris could angrily react, Carl raised a calming hand. 'Not only would it jeopardise your campaign, but these investments you have made will also be affected.'

'Thanks, Carl,' Harris snapped. 'Why don't you go make me a cup of tea?'

'Yes, sir.'

Burrows hurried to the door, feeling the glare that Harris had aimed at the centre of his spine. Despite the fury he felt, Harris knew that his trusted aide was right. He slumped back in his chair and gently massaged his temples.

Sam Pope needed to be stopped.

———

That same morning, Aaron Hill stood in his kitchen, the kettle boiling when he caught a glimpse of himself in the window. With the sun hiding for the majority of the morning, the orange glow of the street lights outside his house caused his window to double as a mirror.

A week ago, he would have been faced with a smartly-dressed, middle-aged man who was making a packed lunch for his beloved daughter. Clean shaven, thinning blond hair neatly brushed to a more flattering style.

Not fat, but years of living well had given him what the magazines had recently labelled the 'dad bod.'

The reflection staring back at him was unrecognisable.

His skin was grey, the bags under his eyes were dark and heavy, a memento for another sleepless night.

His chin was covered in a dark, grey stubble and his hair shot off in wild directions like he had been electrocuted.

His body craved sleep, but Aaron knew his brain wouldn't shut off.

Not while she was still out there.

Not while there was still a chance.

As the kettle rumbled to a bubbly conclusion, he slowly raised his skinny hand to the top of it, gently holding it above the spout. A barrage of piping hot steam filtered out, enveloping his hand and instantly burning him.

He held it for a few more seconds.

Then, with a yelp of pain, he retracted it, using the jolt of anguish to snap him back to the current world, awakening him enough to make a cup of coffee and face another hopeless day. Aaron flicked on the cold tap and held the palm of his hand underneath it, the skin turning a shade of raw pink and the freezing water instantly cooled it. After a few more moments, he turned back to the kettle, pouring the water into a mug, watching as the coffee granules swirled like dirt in a tornado.

He stirred and just as he raised the mug to his lips, a firm hand slammed against the front door.

Startled, he placed the mug down on the side and instantly felt terrified. The world had recently shown him just what lived in its dark shadows and in all likelihood, his daughter would spend the rest of her life in them.

He pulled his dressing gown tight against his belly and shuffled towards the door.

Another firm knock. Then a voice.

'Mr Hill.' It belonged to a female. 'My name is Detective Inspector Singh. I'm with the Metropolitan Police.'

Aaron shuffled closer, unlocking the door and pulling back, allowing the chain to catch and a crack, large enough for him to peer through to emerge.

A striking woman was stood on the doorstep, her dark hair pulled back, her brown skin as clear as a summer's sky. She offered him a friendly smile before holding up her badge.

'Can I come in, please?'

'What's this about?' he asked, feeling his knees weaken.

'I think it would be best to do this inside,' she said, looking around at the neighbouring houses as if to suggest they may be listening.

Aaron closed the door and took a breath. The afternoon before, he had watched as Sam Pope, the most wanted man in London, easily took apart four youths before swarming one of the most dangerous estates in Wembley. Minutes later, he had stuffed a naked man into the boot of the car and demanded Aaron drive. They stopped at the B&Q near Park Royal Station where Sam told him he needed the car. Aaron made his way home via the London Underground and Sam drove away with a gangster and a number of bottles of liquid.

Aaron had no idea what Sam had planned, but he was sure it wasn't a cocktail evening.

'Mr Hill, please,' Singh spoke through the door, a hint of frustration in her voice. With a trembling hand, Aaron removed the chain and pulled the door open, welcoming the DI and a gust of freezing, wet wind with one of his best smiles.

'Please, come in.' He stepped aside, ushering the law into his house. Singh obliged. 'I just made some coffee, if you would like?'

'No thanks,' Singh responded, looking around the house as she stepped through the hall way. Aaron closed the door and sheepishly made his way back to the kitchen, focusing on his coffee as the Detective Inspector stared at him.

'Mr Hill, I know you came to the station a few days ago to report your daughter missing. I believe you had been drinking at the time and I think it was myself who asked you to leave.'

Aaron squinted, trying hard to locate the memory as if he was searching for a door on his advent calendar. Singh continued.

'Now since then, you happened to be at the High Rise in Shepherd's Bush the night Sam Pope took out a dozen men and your car was discovered late yesterday in Wembley, not far from where reports say Sam Pope attacked another gang.'

Aaron looked at her blankly.

'My car was stolen and…'

'Stolen?' Singh raised her finely plucked eyebrows. 'Right. Well you see, Mr Hill, I'm in charge of a specialist task force put in place to ensure that Sam Pope is taken off the streets immediately. Yesterday evening, Pope committed two more acts of violence that the media are now spinning into something heroic.'

'He's taking down criminals, isn't he?' Hill asked, sipping his coffee.

'That's what we are for. The police. We abide by the same laws that we hold everyone else to and we uphold them with respect and dignity. Last night, Sam Pope tortured a known gang leader with acid to the extent where the man has had his arm amputated. Is that justice?'

Aaron felt woozy as a sudden rush of vomit threatened to explode out of him like a fountain. The sudden colour drain in his face wasn't lost on Singh, who recognised a terrified man when she saw one. Usually, it was after they'd realised how head strong and career driven she was after they'd slept together. Singh assessed the mild-mannered man before her and reached into her pocket, removing an envelope.

Time to hammer the point home.

She slid out four mug shot photos, all of them of young, black youths. All looked angry, all of them sporting facial wounds.

'These four boys were also assaulted yesterday, before Sam took their leader. The youngest, this one here...' She tapped the photo. 'He's only sixteen years old. Sam Pope broke his jaw yesterday. Tell me, is that justice?'

Aaron stared at the photo, a light bulb threatening to go off in his mind. Singh re-shuffled the photos before stuffing them into her jacket.

'Look, Mr Hill. If you can give us any information, anything we can do to stop this man, you need to help us. If you're holding onto a shred of hope that this man is going to help you and find your daughter, just remember these photos as to just how far he will go for what he calls justice. Your daughter isn't going to matter to him if there is a bigger prize on the table.'

The sudden mention of his daughter caused Aaron's eyes to open with fury.

'I think you should leave now,' Aaron suggested, ensuring he kept his tone unthreatening.

'Absolutely,' Singh agreed. 'I know this is a hard time for you, Mr Hill and I'm personally going to ensure our missing person's unit do all they can to find your daughter.

But if you can think of anything, or need to tell me anything that can help, here is my card. You can call anytime.'

She held the card out for a few moments, but eventually placed it gently on the table as Aaron glared at her. She nodded at him.

'Thank you for your time. I'll see myself out.'

Singh marched to the door, hating herself for goading the man regarding his daughter but she was sure he had made contact with Pope. While she would honour her promise to help find his daughter, her entire focus was on finding Pope.

She needed to. It was her neck on the line and the stern words of Carl Burrows that morning had reiterated the impact a public failure would have not just on her career, but on Mark Harris's too.

While he was a creep, he was a powerful ally.

She closed the door behind her and marched back to her car, looking back once at Aaron Hill who stood in the bay window of the front room. Watching her briskly walk through the rain, Aaron waited for her to approach her car. As soon as she slid into the driver's seat, he shot upstairs, the realisation that he himself may be able to find his daughter becoming very real.

Bursting into his daughter's room, he swept his gaze around the room, dismissing the piles of clothing that had sprung up in the corner, or the posters of Hollywood heart throbs. He approached her book case, moving past the *Twilight* and *Hunger Games* novels until he pulled out her year book.

Yet another Americanisation that had filtered into British society but one he was eternally grateful for.

He flicked through the book until he came to Jasmine's class.

Her beautiful face smiled back at him.

But it wasn't her face he was looking for.

On the bottom left corner of the page, he saw the familiar face. Only this time, it wasn't sporting a bruised jaw and a freshly blackened eye.

Tyrone Clark.

The member of the Acid Gang that was in Jasmine's class.

Hill shook with excitement as he raced to his bedroom to get ready, with his own ideas of justice racing through his mind.

CHAPTER SEVENTEEN

Sam Pope shot upright, his eyes darting around the dark room. His breathing was erratic, and his body was encased in a cold sweat. After a few moments, he recognised the sparse room that had been his bedroom for the last few months and his pulse slowed.

It was just a nightmare.

He collapsed back onto his damp sheets, the springs from the cheap camp bed poking through the thin mattress and pressing into his spine like a cheap massage.

It wasn't the "Jamie Nightmare". The usual haunting image of his dead son, lying crumpled and motionless in the middle of the street, his hands inches away from saving him. Ever since that fateful night over three years ago, Sam had blamed himself.

He could have stopped the drunk driver who had killed his son.

Miles Willock.

This was a different nightmare.

This was him, surrounded by darkness, out in the sand-covered wasteland of Afghanistan. Under strict orders to eliminate the entire enemy squadron, Sam had ventured into their compound, finding it surprisingly empty. As the roar of gunfire echoed around the building, he made his way further in, the memory fading fast.

Two bullets ripped through his chest.

The life began to seep from him as he collapsed to the stone floor, his eyes wide and trying hard to focus on the boxes piled on the table before him.

He heard his superior officer's voice, echoing over the radio.

A man with a balaclava stepped past him.

That was when he had woken.

Glimpsing at the time on his phone that lay on the floor next to the bed, he also lifted the loaded handgun beside it. Instinctively sliding the cartridge and checking the ammunition, he placed the gun back down and swung his legs over the side of the bed. Despite only wearing his boxer shorts, Sam was sweating like a whore in church. He slid them off, walked across his cramped apartment and entered the grimy bathroom.

He had worked diligently with a scrubbing brush to remove the thick layer of limescale that had covered the wall like a grim paint job. It would have been enough for the past few months and Sam didn't even give the growing mould in the corner of the room a second glance.

He turned on the taps, the water eventually trickling out into a steady stream.

Allowing a few minutes for the water to rise above a temperature that would chill him to the bone, Sam turned to the smeared mirror on the wall. He wiped it with a towel and caught a glimpse of his face. The eyes were soulless, two dark balls of pure vengeance. They sat back in his world-weary face, the handsome smile faded and replaced with a hard jawline covered in stubble. His muscular body was covered in thick, purple blotches, reminders of the brawls he had been in and the increasing punishment he was putting himself through. His nose was sore from the attacker in the second High Rise and adorning his sculpted chest were the two white circles.

The bullet holes from yesteryear.

The end of his career.

Staring back at him like lifeless eyes, Sam ran a finger gently over them, the skin a rough tissue against his fingertip. Lucy had called them his lucky spots as both of them had been a mere inch away from ending his life.

He felt a twinge of pain in his chest, the usual response his heart gave when his mind drifted to his ex-wife. Lucy had been everything he had ever wanted, and she beamed with pride every time he returned home from a tour.

She understood his desire to serve his country, stemming from the military childhood he had but never revisited. Sam knew that his mother's death at a young age caused him to latch onto his father, who served with distinction in the army until he was killed on his final tour when Sam was just fifteen.

There was never any other choice.

Sam was always going to be a soldier and Lucy understood that every shot he fired from his rifle, every terrorist he eliminated, and every person he saved was what he was born to do.

Then Jamie came along, and he promised he wouldn't kill anymore.

Two bullets to the chest evicted him from the army.

The want to be with his family kept him from returning.

But that was all taken away on that haunting summer evening, when he crumpled to his knees in Hendon, just outside of the Metropolitan Police College where he was top of his class.

The flashing blue lights.

The shimmering pool of blood.

His wife's agonised cries of pain.

His dead son.

Fury rocked Sam's body like a cattle prod and he drove his fist into the mirror, the glass shattering and two shards ripping into the flesh of his battered knuckles. That was why he had mutilated Leon Barnett. To help a man who was as helpless as he had been.

Aaron Hill had no chance of saving his daughter. Not on his own.

That's why Sam had tortured Leon. It was why he had attacked that gang.

It was why he had waged his one-man war on the entire crime empire that pulsed through the underbelly of London like a heartbeat.

Because he had been helpless.

As he stepped into the bath tub and allowed the steam of the shower to envelope him, he dipped his head under the boiling water.

As it crashed against his face, his mind raced back to one memory over three years before and one name.

Miles Hillock.

––––––

Sam had been sitting in the car for over fifteen hours. Parked on the side of the street in Edgware, he stared out onto the road. The pavement was lined with shops, a number of low market supply stores and cheap takeaways. The Broadwalk Shopping Centre had long since closed, the employees of JD Sports and Boots shutting up shop and heading up the road to the local pubs.

As the clock ventured closer to midnight, Sam's focus never shifted.

It was locked upon the small flat above the Dallas Fried Chicken shop. A small, pokey residence, with just enough dark corners for somebody to fade away.

Sam ran a hand through his overgrown hair, the brown locks flopping over his ears. It had been months since he had had a haircut.

Since he had cared.

The hair flopped down the side of his gaunt face, his appetite disappearing the moment he stared into the dead eyes of his son. His eyes, vacant and cried dry, sat back into his pale face which was framed by a scraggy beard.

Sam had stopped shaving when Lucy left.

For the first two months, they had grieved together. Each day melted into the next, the absence of their son weighing heavily on them both. Somehow, hand in hand, they had made it through his funeral, the room a chamber of broken hearts and shattered souls. As the weeks went by, Lucy decided to push forward, honouring the boundless energy of their son by trying to get their life back on track.

Sam just couldn't do it.

He found himself sitting on the floor of his son's room, thumbing through the books that adorned the neat book case. Tears fell freely as he remembered his son's love of books, the polar opposite to himself.

His son was a bookworm.

As he tried to digest the words that accompanied the colourful caterpillar before him, he broke down. Time after time.

He could have stopped it.

Sam had spent his entire life as a soldier, protecting the freedom of those under the relentless, oppressive boot of terrorism.

But he couldn't protect his son.

He had failed in his one duty as a father.

After those two months turned to six, Lucy soon packed her bags, refusing to watch as the man she loved allowed the guilt to swallow him. He had dropped out of the police, the idea that he was capable of protecting the public seemed almost cruel.

Soon, Sam was left in an empty house with the request for divorce written before him.

He granted it to her, his heart breaking when he realised that she was better off without him.

It had been just over ten months since his son's broken body lay *before him, the bright lights of the smashed car illuminating him like a museum show piece.*

It was an image that would stay with him forever.

As would the name.

Miles Hillock.

Twenty years old, Miles had been drunk behind the wheel when he had veered off the road and snatched Sam's son from him. Sam had known because he had watched the man exceed the limit at the very pub he had been attending. But circumstances beyond his under-standing saw the sentence reduced to a measly eighteen months.

That was what his son's life had been worth.

Eighteen months.

After nine, Miles walked with good behaviour, emerging from the prison a different man. The handsome face had been replaced by one that had experienced horrors. His previous calmness replaced with a skittishness that betrayed the abuse a pretty boy like him had suffered. Horrified with the crime he had committed, Miles had moved into the very flat Sam was staring at, spending his days drinking in the empty hope that it would erase his memories.

Theo had begged Sam not to do this.

But he understood.

Sam slid open the glove compartment and removed the eight-inch serrated blade, the knife that had been strapped to his boot for a number of miles in the deserts of Afghanistan. A knife he had used to remove the innards of a violent terrorist who was about to unload his gun on Theo during Project Hailstorm.

It seemed a lifetime ago.

The scars that stained his shrinking chest were a memento to the times where he was part of society. A weapon for the same country that valued his son's life at less than two years.

At that moment, the cracked, white door that sat between the chicken shop and a closed estate agents opened, and Sam felt his heart stop. Miles Hillock stepped out into the flicking glow of the lamp post, the brightness revealing him to Sam like a prize on the world's cruellest game show.

The man seemed smaller than when he had been sent to prison, the nine-month stint clearly breaking him and he walked with his arms crossed against his chest, literally holding himself together. The wind swept by, causing some of the blossom on the trees to filter through the cool evening sky. Sam had been waiting nearly a year to be this close to the man who took his son, and as he watched him meekly walk up the street towards the newsagents, he felt a surge race through his body.

It wasn't of anger.

It wasn't of vengeance.

It was guilt.

Guilt that this was what his life had become. That he had let his son only spend five years on the earth before letting fate lead him away. That he had sat helplessly, staring into the abyss whilst his wife begged him for his support.

Guilt that he had let her leave.

Guilt that he would never have asked her to stay.

Not when he knew what the future held. A lifetime in prison didn't scare Sam. He had stared down the barrel of enough guns and had been under heavy fire in the treacherous mountains of Iraq. Coming face to face with a murderer or a corrupt prison guard would carry the same amount of threat as a bubble-wrapped marshmallow.

Sam felt guilty for the life he had worked hard for and the family he had literally walked through a war zone to return to. It had all crumbled to ash.

All at the hands of the man emerging from the off-licence. A blue plastic bag hung from his hands, the plastic wrapped tightly around numerous cans of cheap alcohol. With quick steps and frightened glances over his shoulder, Miles Hillock made his way back to the door of his flat, for another evening of guilt-ridden solitude, endless tears, and the mind-numbing power of alcohol. He shut the door behind him and headed up to his flat, already cracking open a can and guzzling its contents.

He was going to drink himself to death.

Outside on the street, Sam pushed open the car door and stepped out onto the empty High Street that ran through Edgware like a concrete vein.

With the knife hidden inside his jacket, he headed towards the door, hell bent on helping Miles succeed.

———

Sam stared into the mirror, the cheap Braun beard trimmer had been surprisingly strong against his thicker, longer hair. The sink was now filled with clumps of his brown hair, entwined with the cheeky grey ones that were becoming more regular. In the army, the boys would quickly buzz each other's hair, the sweltering heat soon made a fool of those who relented. Sam wasn't exactly a stylist, but he had a steady hand and was able to trim his hair down to a passable level, with a shorter grade around the sides. The grade four on top left just enough hair to look presentable and his hair line and natural curl to the front gave it the hint of style.

He kept the beard, enjoying the thickness of the brown and grey coating for his strong jaw. It wasn't scraggly, but it was enough to hide his skin from the bitter cold.

For the first time in a few days he felt refreshed.

The evening before had been difficult, the torture of that man, no matter how horrifying his actions had been, had wiped Sam out. Now, with a good night's sleep, he felt refreshed.

He also had the information the man had spat out as he begged for his life before Sam had melted his arm with acid. Sam had taken the man to Northwick Park Hospital just outside of Harrow and dumped him on the steps of A&E, his brutalised arm wrapped in a blood-soaked blanket with no hope of being saved.

Sam didn't care.

The man was a monster and removing his right hand would hinder his reign of terror.

People couldn't kiss the ring if the hand didn't exist.

As the world around him echoed through the thin windows and the rain clattered against the glass, Sam slid his gun into the back of his jeans and then pulled his long-sleeved top over it. He slid into his bomber jacket, pulled on a baseball cap, and headed to the door with Leon's confession fresh in his mind.

He had a potential van location and a fake company's bank account.

It was enough.

The memories of Jamie had added fuel to the fire inside of Sam to ensure another child wasn't lost to the cruel world.

Armed with a handgun and enough information to start bringing down another criminal empire, Sam headed for the front door, knowing exactly who he needed to see for help.

CHAPTER EIGHTEEN

Adrian Pearce sat at his desk, staring at the blank screen of his computer. From the glare he could make out his vague reflection, the dark skin trimmed with grey tinted hair cut close to the scalp. His beard, also frosted with age, ran neatly across his jaw. Despite reaching a half century, Pearce was in good shape and regularly passed gentlemen half his age on the local running track.

Within the Met, he was known as a tenacious detective, willing to bring down his fellow officer in the name of the law. It had earned him a fearful reputation but also had ostracised him. He didn't care, as far as he was concerned, he would rather not make friends with bent coppers.

The small, cramped office mockingly enveloped him, a reminder for what happened last time he rattled the wrong cage. When several convicted criminals had turned up beaten half to death, it took Pearce a little over three hours to piece together the common denominator.

Sam Pope.

It was what made Pearce such a valuable asset to the Met, but such a terrifying prospect for any police officer on the take. Not only could he find discrepancies, but he noticed patterns, could decipher facial tics, and was biologically programmed to ask the most infuriatingly intrusive question at the optimum moment.

When Pearce sat opposite Sam Pope over six months ago, he couldn't have imagined how drastically his life was about to change. Bit by bit, Sam Pope began to uncover irregularities in the supposed terrorist bombing that had shattered the London Marathon earlier that year. The loss of five civilians and a young police officer had hurt the city, with the Met promising to bring those responsible to justice.

Sam made the same promise and soon uncovered an inside job, led by superior officers with superior greed. With those in charge of the police in bed with those they were trying to stop, it put the lives of Adrian, Sam, and an innocent psychiatrist and her husband in jeopardy. Pearce had made brief contact with Amy Devereux after she'd moved away from London, wishing her well and telling her he was always free for a coffee should she ever return to the city.

He had never received a call.

Now, glancing into the blank screen, Pearce recounted how he had placed his faith in Sam Pope, stepping beyond the line he had stuck to like glue. Willingly leading Sam into the station and assisting his escape was bad enough but allowing him to walk free after he had unloaded an entire gun into one of London's most notorious criminals would be the straw that broke the camel's back. It had been a whirlwind few days back in spring, ending with Pearce holding Sam at gun point in a tower block in London, with a police inspector begging for his life.

Now, as Pearce glanced around his tiny, hidden office, he realised it was worth it. He may have earnt even more disdain from his colleagues, but he took heart that he, like Sam Pope, knew why they'd acted the way they had done.

Why they'd ventured down the unreturnable pathways. It was the right thing to do.

Pearce sighed, giving his stretched, vague reflection one final glance before pushing himself from his desk and headed towards the door. He chuckled, realising that the only use he had for his computer was for a dodgy mirror. Throughout the years, Pearce had preferred to do things the old-fashioned way, ignoring the digital world as it slowly seeped into the Met. Then, out of nowhere, technology leapt forward and suddenly Pearce was being asked questions about cloud storage and online records.

He wasn't much of a computer person. And he preferred it that way. As far as he was concerned, the world was so entrenched in the internet nowadays, that a one-day outage would bring half the city to a standstill. He had read recently that the bus stop time tables ran off an internet source provided by a leading phone company.

The thought of that terrified him, especially if the phone company went the way of the train companies and decided to hold the city to ransom whenever they wanted a pay rise.

Meandering through the corridors, Pearce soon pushed the doors open to the Scotland Yard building, the rain instantly slapping him in the face with a cruel, freezing hand and he pulled his coat tight to his body. He passed the iconic spinning logo and headed across the street to the local Starbucks, the idea of piping hot caffeine had assumed dominance over his brain.

The past few days had been a blur. Sam Pope had been working diligently for the last six months, knocking off known criminal safe houses and sending a number of the police's most wanted to hospital. From there, it was a relatively easy process to steer them towards a prison cell. But over the past few days, something had changed and attacking these gangs had led to killing, with three confirmed kills in the abandoned factory in Shepherd's Bush and the brutal torture of Leon Barnett.

As Pearce had suggested to Singh, it appeared that Sam Pope now had a time limit.

Singh had agreed, and Pearce found himself thinking of the young DI. She had made quite the impression the first time she'd barged into his office, making wild demands and treating him with the same lack of respect as her peers. But, as the scope of her task became clear, she'd humbly asked for his help and as far as Pearce could tell, had begun a friendship with him.

As far as he was concerned, if anyone could stop Pope, it was probably her.

What concerned him more, was he wasn't sure if he wanted her to.

Pearce ordered his double-shot latte and waited to the side of the counter, wondering what bizarre way they would try to spell his name on the cup. He enjoyed a Starbucks coffee, but their nonsensical way of marking up orders always baffled him. Pearce stood still, his eyes closed, taking in the hustle and bustle around him, the hum of the machines, and the gossip of the young women behind him.

The rich smell of coffee filled his nose.

Pearce felt, for a moment, at peace.

'Aidan?' The barista called out, her impatient eyes scanning the room. Pearce, realising their mistake smiled warmly and took the cup, the piping hot coffee instantly warming his hand. He strode to the small unit that held the sugar sachets and as he selected two small packs of brown sugar, he felt the presence behind him.

A recognisable voice quickly invaded his ears.

'I never pegged you as a sugar man.'

Pearce's entire body tightened. His spine stiffened as if an ice cube had just been slid down the back of his crisply ironed shirt. His hand tightened around the Styrofoam cup, threatening to crush it entirely and spray the coffee shop in its own juices. It wasn't the voice itself that had caused the shock. In some ways, he had been expecting it for a while now.

It was because it was in the coffee shop opposite the busiest police building in London. The same building that was the headquarters for the task force set up in the man's honour. Pearce took a moment, gathered his thoughts, and recomposed. Then, with a wry smile across his face, he turned and faced Sam Pope.

Pearce couldn't help but offer a warm smile.

'Why? Am I sweet enough?'

Sam nodded and his lips quivered, threatening to break into a smile of their own. Pearce admired how casually Sam stood, a stone's throw away from the building that he once worked in.

That now offered him nothing but confinement.

Sam sipped from his own coffee, his leather bomber jacket still slick from rain and the hood of his under layer flapping over the collar. His hair was cut shorter than six months ago, but Pearce doubted that regular trips to a hairdresser were top of Sam's to-do list.

The man was a soldier.

Fashion wasn't a priority. Only the mission. Pearce quickly glanced around, looking for any colleagues. Sam noticed, leaning forward for a napkin.

'Relax, I'm just a handsome man getting some coffee.'

Pearce smirked.

'Same here.' He turned to the stand, reaching for a stirrer and swirled it into his coffee. He scouted the place once more, refusing to look at the most wanted man in the City. 'It's good to see you, Sam.'

'Likewise,' Sam said, taking a sip. 'I hear they didn't promote you after you brought in the head of the snake.'

'Well, not exactly,' Pearce replied dryly. 'I did get a new office.'

Sam nodded, his trained eyes flicking around the Starbucks, taking in every detail for the umpteenth time. There were seventeen customers seated around the premises, three of which could potentially be police officers based on their disposition. There were eight steps to the front door, a further fifteen to the back. Four members of staff on shift and a cleaner currently in the disabled toilets.

It would be an easy escape if he needed to.

But he needed something else. Sam took another sip, waited for Pearce to stop stirring his coffee and give him his attention.

'I need your help.'

Pearce took his own sip, deliberately swashing the coffee in his mouth.

'Last time you asked for my help, you ended up thumping me in the face and diving into that river over there.' Pearce nodded through the rain-soaked window to the restless Thames beyond. 'I'm in.'

'Good.'

'But…' Pearce turned to Sam, locking onto him with his dark eyes. 'You need to tell me what the hell is going on.'

'I don't have time, I need…'

'Make time,' Pearce demanded. 'You went from delivering criminals on a silver platter to sticking them in the goddamn morgue. They have an entire task force up there, dedicated to bringing you in. Hell, they have even given you a nickname. Do you know what that is? It's the Watchdog!'

Sam scoffed, mulling it over.

'I like it.'

'Yeah, well you won't like the woman in charge. DI Singh.

She's a storm in a tea cup and she's got a real hard on for you. If she knew I was talking to you, she'd throw us both in a hole for the rest of our lives. So if you want me to go further down this rabbit hole with you, then I deserve the goddamn truth.'

Sam knew he was right. He sighed, turning so he and Pearce both leant against the stand, both of them facing the large counter, where two Japanese tourists were ordering their lunch.

'Just before I took down Elmore Riggs, a man was brought in at gunpoint. He had no business being in that room with those men. Turns out, he's a dad whose daughter went missing and that was her last known location.'

'Jesus.' Pearce was already stroking his beard in frustration.

'The guys who took her, they snatch teenage girls off of our streets, dump them in a truck, and get paid five fucking thousand pounds.' Sam gritted his teeth in anger, his fists clenching. 'The name Leon Barnett mean anything to you?'

'You mean the mutilated man you sent our way this morning? Yeah, he was the head of The Acid Gang.'

'That was them. The people who took her. Who take all of them,' Sam spat. 'But who pays them, that's where I need your help.'

Pearce stared vacantly ahead, a blur of shoes passed his vision as customers passed his line of sight. He took a final swig of his coffee and thought about the choice he had to make. He was already being managed towards the exit, that much was obvious. The police couldn't sack him for bringing down a superior officer. He should have received a medal. But the 'rich boys' club' that scratched each other's backs with fifty-pound notes had made it quite clear he would never get a sniff of their arses again. Tucked away in a cupboard and given busy work until a mind as capable as his couldn't take it anymore.

They had pushed him into a corner.

Literally and figuratively.

If his access to police resources was dwindling, then he was going to use it to do some good.

'What do you need?' he finally said with a sigh.

'Leon told me everything he knew. I didn't really give him much choice,' Sam said coldly. 'He didn't do the snatch or drop himself, but he said that she was dumped in a van behind KFC by the stadium. So any access you can get to CCTV would be…'

'That's going to take at least two days to get the clearance to footage and…'

'Pull some strings,' Sam demanded, frowning.

'Listen, son, I don't have strings to pull anymore. Do you understand? Ever since you cleaned up the High Rise and put Howell behind bars, I've been shunted so far down the fucking ladder I need a whole new one just to reach the first rung.'

'I have a bank account too,' Sam said hopefully.

'Now that, I can run with,' Pearce said, appreciating Sam's frustration. The man was hard wired to protect people and the idea of a teenage girl being sold into European sex slavery made his stomach flip. Pearce had never been a father, but he knew how personal this would be for Sam.

Protecting a child from harm.

Sam's horrible past came back to Pearce and he looked at the man before him. Despite his tough exterior and deadly training, Pearce knew that Sam was broken. The loss of his son had caused him to withdraw from the world, losing his wife and eventually the line between right and wrong. But since he had embarked on his quest for justice against organised crime, Pearce could appreciate how easy that line was to blur.

The right thing to do wasn't always the lawful thing to do.

That much was becoming clear.

'What's the account?' Pearce finally asked.

'Burn Group Inc.' Sam shook his head in disgust. 'They get payments of five grand into that account. Whatever you can find, whatever you can trace.'

'Okay. Wait … how do I contact you?'

'You don't.' Sam quickly glanced around ensuring no one was in earshot. 'Tomorrow. The one place I'll never be scared to go.'

Pearce nodded his understanding and Sam reciprocated. Sam looked around once more before pulling his hood over his head and stuffing his hands into his pockets. He offered a friendly smile as he headed for the door.

'Thank you, Pearce. I owe you one.'

'Don't mention it,' Pearce muttered. 'What about the CCTV?'

'Don't worry,' Sam said, not turning back. 'I know a guy.'

CHAPTER NINETEEN

The sterilised aroma of the hospital bought back horrible memories for Singh as she charged through the corridor, remembering watching her dying grandad fade away from her when she was sixteen years old. Despite her strict Hindu upbringing, Singh's grandfather had always told her to follow her own path in life. He used to tell her that fate held something else for her, something which she would be able to wear with pride.

Her Metropolitan Police Badge was testament to that.

Once he had died, she felt even more pressure from her family to fall in line with the life they'd chosen for her, which caused her throw herself into Mixed Martial Arts and a career on the front lines.

Singh was tough. Physically, mentally, and emotionally.

But as she stepped through another set of doors, she couldn't help but feel a slight flicker of pain, remembering the sixteen-year-old girl who held onto her grandfather as he slipped away from the world, tears rapidly sliding down her cheeks.

She could be whoever she wanted to be.

Do whatever she wanted to do.

That's what he had told her.

Now, as she barged her way towards the nurse's station on the fourth floor of Central Middlesex Hospital and with the pressure of Sam Pope's one-man crusade against every gang in London, she wanted to speak to the one man who might be able to make sense of it.

As she knocked impatiently on the desk, a senior nurse scowled over the top of glasses, her Irish accent as thick as her ginger bob that framed a wrinkled face.

'Manners don't cost you a penny, my dear.'

Singh held up her badge.

'Detective Inspector Singh, Metropolitan Police.'

'Ma'am.' The nurse stepped forward, clearly regretting her curtness earlier. 'I'm Sister Conway. How can I help?'

'Thank you, sister.' Singh noted the smile from the woman who clearly believed in respect. 'A young man was brought in here not too long ago, I believe. Severe injuries to his hands and face.'

'Ah, the poor young man.'

'I need to speak with him.'

'Follow me.'

The sister stepped out from behind the desk, beckoning Singh to follow. As they stepped through the ward, Singh noticed the plethora of rotas and signs adorning the walls, each one of them filled with countless pieces of information. The corridors were filled with trolleys of medicines and supplies, the nurses working at double speed to get round to all of their patients. Each room was split into four, each one containing a bed and an unfortunate occupant. Their only sliver of privacy was a thin, blue curtain affixed to a curved rail that slithered across the ceiling.

One man was hunched forward, coughing violently while a nurse rubbed his back. A few others lay motionless, staring numbly into space.

As they passed another room, Singh was treated to the

same view, watching as one nurse scurried between beds to helpless patients, understanding the charts that sat at the end of their beds and the notices placed on the walls above. Singh watched with admiration as the young nurse smiled a beautiful smile at a cantankerous old man and calmly approached him.

The NHS had been fighting a losing battle for years, the government doing its best to bleed it dry before Americanising the healthcare system. Until then, Singh could only applaud the people keeping it ticking over, despite the barriers in their way.

They were heroes.

It angered her that some people were using that label for Sam Pope. Ex-forces or not, criminals or not, the man was taking the law into his own hands.

He was not a hero. He was a criminal.

And she needed to stop him.

As her thoughts drifted to slapping a pair of cuffs around Pope's wrists, she nearly collided with the stern sister who had come to an abrupt halt. She turned, her weary face etched in a wrinkly smile as she nodded towards the open door before them. The room was well lit, with one of the blue curtains pulled out from the wall, containing the bed within. Through the gap, Singh caught a glimpse of a Nike trainer.

'He's in there.' Sister Conway shook her head. 'Poor soul. They really did a number on him.'

She nodded to Singh and stepped away, marching back towards the nurse's station and an undoubted mountain of paperwork.

Singh could relate.

With a deep sigh, she stepped into the room and pulled back the curtain. Sister Conway wasn't lying. Resting on the bed was the young man she'd seen at the High Rise.

Sean Wiseman.

Although he had been the right-hand man to one of the most ambitious criminals in London, Singh had never got a sense of evil from the boy. He was intelligent, too intelligent to be running drugs on an estate, but he had been able to help his childhood friend ascend through the criminal ranks. Wiseman, despite his frailties, had drastically improved Elmore Riggs's criminal operation and put a lot of drugs into a lot of desperate hands.

As she thought about Riggs now being off the street due to a bullet through the skull, she refused to credit Pope with making the streets safer. Likewise, as her eyes scanned the brutal, purple swelling around the eyes of Wiseman, she held little sympathy for the pain he was in.

'Mr Wiseman, it's Detective Inspector Amara Singh from the Metropolitan Police.' She noticed his head turn. 'Can you hear me?'

The young man nodded. Singh had been informed by her colleagues that he had been found in the bathroom of his flat when a neighbour noticed his door open. His already injured hand had been mutilated with a screwdriver, the metal tip had been driven into the bullet wound Sam Pope had drilled through it a few nights earlier. The hand lay in a new cast which hung in a sling, the attacker breaking his arm in two places. Both of Wiseman's eyes were swollen shut, evidence of pummelling fists battering him black and blue. One of his cheekbones was cracked. The opposite eye socket shattered.

The boy wept quietly on the bed, his lifestyle finally catching up with him.

'I know you must be very scared right now and we are here to help you, okay? I'm the head of a task force set up specifically to stop Sam Pope.' Singh spoke assertively. 'You're safe now.'

Wiseman murmured but Singh couldn't understand it.

Two of the young man's teeth were missing. Three separate scars crossed his lips. Singh continued.

'You were in the High Rise the night Sam Pope attacked, weren't you? One of my team interviewed you about Sam Pope using you as live bait so he could escape. Is that correct?'

Wiseman smacked his tongue against his broken lips and stirred and Singh lifted a glass of water from the bed stand and lifted it towards him. He feebly sipped and then fell back to the blood encrusted pillow.

'I interviewed Aaron Hill earlier today, who was also found at the High Rise that night. If there is any information you can give me about why Sam Pope is helping him or what they are planning to do, just remember you are safe. Pope cannot get you in here.'

'He didn't,' Wiseman finally croaked.

'What was that?' Singh said, stepping closer, head cocked.

'Pope … didn't … do this,' Wiseman spluttered, the pain of every word hurting his battered jaw.

'He can't hurt you now,' Singh reassured. 'We have eyewitnesses saying they saw him and another man at your estate.'

'He is helping him.' Wiseman struggled, trying to sit up. 'Pope is helping that man. His kid is missing.'

'Aaron Hill?'

'I think so. My head's a little fuzzy,' Wiseman hissed in pain. 'They need to find someone from that gang. I told them where to go.'

'You sent Pope to Leon Barnett?' Singh spat accusingly. 'Do you know that he tortured him to the point that he had his arm amputated?'

'The fuck I care. The man was a monster.'

'Pope is a monster!' Singh yelled, realising her personal need to catch him was living dangerously close to the fore.

'He kills your best friend, leaves you to die, and tortures a man.'

'Pope saved me,' Wiseman interjected. 'He got me out of that building without a bullet in my head. The man who did this to me wasn't English. He had a strong accent, Russian, Polish, Ukraine … something like that. You should be looking for him.'

'Why? Because he beat up a scum bag drug dealer? Isn't that what Sam Pope does?'

Wiseman smirked and then winced in pain.

'You're right, I am a scum bag. I've done bad things to make bad people richer and I've paid the price. But Sam Pope isn't doing this for himself. He's doing it to find a young girl who only has a slim chance because he is out there.'

Singh stepped forward, her face a few inches away from the battered remains of Wiseman's.

'We will find Jasmine Hill, because we are damn good at our jobs. And I will personally bring Pope in myself.' Singh stepped back, looking at the brutal beating the young man had taken. 'Why are you protecting Pope, anyway?'

Wiseman turned his head away from her, surprising a tear that was struggling to make it through the broken remains of his eyes.

'Because he didn't turn his back on me. He tried to get me out of it.'

Wiseman thought about the card Sam had given him, the idea of a safe haven, a sanctuary that may be able to save him. Pull him back from the life he had always feared, that had finally caught up to him. The pain was agonising, his face was a battered mess and he was doubtful he would ever have a functioning hand again. Singh didn't care, he knew that. Neither did the Met. He was just another criminal who had received a well-earned comeuppance.

But Sam Pope, despite his extreme measures, had given Wiseman the opportunity to step away. Had offered to help him.

Had cared.

Now, as the pain of his injuries threatened to overwhelm him and the angry Detective berated him, he refused to accept that Sam Pope was a danger to anyone other than criminals. He was far from a hero, but at least Sam Pope was doing things for the right reasons.

Unimpressed, Singh turned on her heel and stomped away from the brutalised young man, marching back down the corridor towards the elevator. She grunted a goodbye to the sister, who returned in kind.

They were both busy, the weight of expectation that rested upon their shoulders made them kindred spirits. As the elevator door pinged open and Singh stepped inside, she thought back to her grandfather, his words pushing her to do what she needed to.

Catch Sam Pope.

At all costs.

———

As the rain collided against the steel door of his garage, Aaron Hill took a deep breath. Sitting in the driver's seat of the hired car, he still had his fingers gripped around the wheel. His knuckles were white and a blister was threatening to form on the palms of his hands.

He felt sick.

Desperation had taken a hold of him, the anger of being so impotent. Sam Pope had dragged a naked gang leader into the boot of his car and got in, demanding he drive immediately. Aaron had panicked, stalled the car and had felt his breath quicken. Behind them, a gang of locals was gathering, all of them angry that a white man had stormed their estate and beaten the living hell out of a group of youths.

Things would turn even uglier very quickly.

Eventually, he had started the car and pulled away, just as a brick had crashed against the rear window, cracking the glass into a tremendous pattern. They had sped through the busy streets until Sam finally got him to pull over, demanding he take deep breaths. Shaking, Sam had told him to get out, that he would take the car and handle it from there. Aaron, fear threatening to choke him, obliged, stepped out into the rainy streets of Sudbury and walked aimlessly away. Sam assured him he would see him tomorrow; that he would find out where his daughter was and get her back.

That had been nearly twenty-four hours ago. Since then, he had been visited by DI Singh and passively threatened as an accomplice.

He didn't care.

All he cared about was getting his daughter back.

Anger jolted through his body once more and he took another deep breath. Seeing those photos earlier had lit a fuse and with Sam nowhere to be seen, Aaron had let it explode within him. He knew he was in too deep. He had known that when he approached the estate on his own, passing the discarded police crime scene tape that had been mockingly tossed to the ground. The same group of boys had been huddled around the door, a slight look of trepidation in their stance after yesterday's humbling.

As Aaron had approached, one of them had stepped forward, just as they had done to Sam Pope the day before.

This time, however, they were not greeted by extensive hand to hand skills and a highly trained soldier on a mission. They were confronted by a desperate father who had seen red, and the oncoming youth was greeted with a gun barrel.

Aaron screamed at him to get on the ground, which the young man did instantly. Before the rest of the gang could hightail it, Aaron screamed at them to stop, marching through the rain, the gun pointed at them and his heart beating like a pneumatic drill. They stopped and he approached, demanding they remove their hoods. As the third member of the gang did, Aaron felt the flame reach the end of the fuse and he lunged forward, cracking Tyrone Clark with the handle of the gun. As he dropped to the ground, the rest of the gang ran in any direction they could, racing as far away as they could from the mad man with the gun.

Aaron, still seething, reached down and slid his hands under the lifeless arms of Tyrone and for the second day in succession, passers-by witnessed a man dump a gang member into the boot of a car and speed off.

Now, as he sat in his garage, a moment of calm wrested control of his body and the gravity of what he had done hit him.

Aaron pushed open the door of the hire car, ignoring the collision with the wall of his garage, hunched over and vomited onto the concrete below. As he emptied his stomach, he fell to his knees, catching himself with his outstretched arms before he plummeted into the pile of puke. The sour smell attacked his nostrils and he pushed himself back, falling back against the wall and tried to calm himself down.

In the boot of the car was a teenage boy, beaten and kidnapped.

That wasn't what worried him.

What worried him, was what he intended to do.

CHAPTER TWENTY

It had been a frustratingly busy Monday, with the monthly board meeting overrunning by an hour due to the HR Director's insistence on a new sickness absence policy, but Paul Etheridge was still smiling. As he approached the gated border at the end of the private road he lived on, he slowed his Porsche 911 Carrera GTS to a stop. Leaning out of the window, he held out his fob to the receiver, triggering a loud groan as the metal gates began to slide open. The weather was relentless, the winter paying the country back for a hot summer and it upset him that he couldn't roll the roof back and feel the wind rush through his hair.

He chuckled at the thought, especially as the final strands of his hair had abandoned him long before his forty-second birthday.

As the gate slid wide enough for him to move forward, he felt his blazer pocket rumble against his chest. His work phone was always on and constantly buzzing even though he had a PA. As the founder of BlackOut Software, he was in demand. The revolutionary data security software had made waves in the last five years, a pet project he had undertaken when he left the army. As a computer whiz, he was never cut out as a soldier, but his sharp intellect and ability to navigate systems had made him a useful weapon. As he pressed down on the clutch to shift gear, he felt a sharp pain, the remnants of the shattered leg he had suffered all those years ago. It was what had spurred him on to make such a success of his life, knowing that he tumbled down a mountain side into a terrorist outpost and only the sharp shooting and pinpoint accuracy of his friend had saved his life.

Sam Pope.

His life had flashed before his eyes, but was returned to him thanks to his friend.

Paul Etheridge was given the gift of life and he wasn't going to waste a moment of it ever again.

As he glided down the road, passing opulent houses that celebrated money, he thought back to those cold nights under the stars, discussing their tactics as they marched to the border of Sudan with blood-thirsty intentions and cut-throat orders. It was a world away from the multi-million-pound company he had founded and grandiose lifestyle that his second wife had been attracted to. Kayleigh was twenty years his junior and an aspiring model and although he was hardly the Elephant Man, Etheridge knew it wasn't his shiny bald head and slightly tubby stomach she was attracted to.

As he pulled onto the immaculate driveway, he parked his Porsche next to the pristine Range Rover that he used as his 'weekend car' and he chortled.

The papers were saying that Sam Pope was waging war on the London underworld, murdering criminals and shutting down their supply lines. In the same papers, they were lauding Etheridge as an entrepreneur and his six-bedroom mansion, forty-six miles out of London in the picturesque Farnham was testament to that.

Life took people down some strange paths.

Whatever path he was led down, considering the man had saved his life, there was no way that Etheridge would ever see Sam Pope as anything other than a hero. With a deep sigh, he pushed open the door of his car and gingerly pushed himself from it, his leg stiffening, the bones creaking as the cold wrapped around his long-standing injury like a python. The large house was a brilliant white, with floor to ceiling windows across the entire front of the house. Kayleigh appreciated the modern décor, but Etheridge was sure she wanted them simply to boast. To show off their leather corner sofa and matching recliner chairs. The marble fire place, the open kitchen with stain-less-steel work tops.

It was all extravagant.

All a world away from the gravel paths he had trudged with his fellow soldiers, backpacks full and guns loaded.

As his expensive, Italian shoes navigated around the puddles forming on the driveway, he looked across at the Kayleigh's Aston Martin Vanquish, its custom paint job a brilliant yellow.

What startled him most was the hooded man leaning against it.

Etheridge dropped his satchel, the documents fanning out into the water and rapidly decreasing in importance.

'Sam?'

'Evening, Paul. Long time.' Sam Pope flashed him a welcoming smile as he pushed himself off of the bonnet, his drenched hood stuck to his head, and his leather jacket soaked through. Etheridge stood still, the shock rooting him to the ground. Eventually, he reached out and took Sam's outstretched hand and smiled, blinking a couple of times.

'Jesus. It has been. Come in, you must be freezing.'

Etheridge scurried towards the front door, his limp visible to Sam who absorbed details like a sponge. Just as the memory stayed with Etheridge and spurred him to make the most of his life, Sam had never forgotten that moment in the northern plains of Sudan, watching his good friend tumble to a likely death. Sam had acted instinctively, rushing to the edge and whipping his rifle to his eye, discharging three bullets in quick succession that ripped through the skulls of the approaching enemy.

He had saved Etheridge's life.

It was a selfless act, but one he knew carried an unwritten debt.

As he stepped in through the grand front door, he slowly lowered his hood and looked around. The welcoming hallway was white, with a black, tiled floor. A large piece of art adorned the wall, a bizarre structure of colour that Sam speculated was incredibly expensive. The hallway led on to the spacious living room, the large sofa the centrepiece that faced the magnificent fire place. A TV the size of Sam's bedroom wall stood on a white stand, the shelves filled with video game consoles and TV provider boxes. The far wall was also a floor to ceiling window, offering a view of a garden ravaged by the power of winter. Empty flower beds framed a vast, well-trimmed lawn that Sam would confidently bet his entire life savings hadn't been cut by Etheridge.

The man lived a life of luxury.

He was the head of a multi-million-pound company and was making money hand over fist. He wasn't going to mow his own lawn.

'Can I get you a drink?' Etheridge offered, walking through the archway to the right and into the pristine kitchen Sam had seen through the window. 'Beer? Gin?'

'Water is fine,' Sam responded as he followed.

'You sure?'

Sam nodded. Etheridge reached out and tugged at a huge handle, the gigantic fridge opening and bathing him in a halogen glow. He pulled out a bottle of mineral water and a bottle of Peroni, pinging the lid off on the bottle opener affixed to the metal door. He handed the bottle to Sam.

'Cheers.'

'It's bad luck to cheers with water.' Etheridge smirked, taking a swig. 'It's good to see you, Sam.'

'You too, Paul. You've got a lovely house.'

'Meh, the wife loves it. It's a little big for just the two of us but it's unlikely we'll have anyone else joining us anytime soon.'

Sam detected the noticeable disappointment in his friend's voice and decided to side step that avenue of conversation. Some parts of a marriage are best kept behind closed doors.

'Fucking awful what happened to Theo.' Etheridge took another sip, leaning against the metal counter. 'We missed you at the funeral.'

'I was there,' Sam said proudly.

'Well you were always able to blend into the surroundings. It's what made you so damn good.' Etheridge finished the bottle and quickly replenished it with another. He looked embarrassed as he sipped it, worried that Sam would disapprove of a man who had everything clearly needing alcohol to get by. Sam didn't pass any judgment.

Everyone had their demons.

He knew that more than anyone.

Before Sam could speak, the clicking of heels echoed through the house and Kayleigh stepped into the kitchen. Wearing a white blouse, designer black jeans, and heels, she marched into the conversation, her heavily made-up face scowling below an expensive haircut. Etheridge stepped forward to embrace her, receiving a cold glance and offering Sam another insight into a life that was only luxurious to the outside world.

'Honey, this is my old friend, Sam.'

'I know who he is,' Kayleigh snapped, her stern words betraying her upper-class lifestyle. 'He's the one from the telly. The one the police are after.'

Etheridge looked at Sam apologetically, but before he could respond, Sam spoke.

'You're right. I'm sorry to turn up here at your lovely home but I need Paul's help.'

'You need to leave,' Kayleigh barked, before turning to her husband, a look of disdain wrestling her make-up for domination of her face. 'Get him out of here or I'm calling the police.'

Both men watched her stomp back towards the archway, her outfit hugging her tremendous figure. Sam could see why she would make the perfect trophy wife for a middle-aged entrepreneur, but Sam didn't put his stock in beauty only being skin deep. Terrible people tend to show themselves to be unattractive, regardless of how much they spend to look 'pretty'. Etheridge's shoulders slumped and he turned back to Sam.

'What do you need?'

'I should go,' Sam offered, resealing his water bottle and placing it on the side.

'Nonsense. This is my house.' Etheridge stated, more for himself than Sam. 'Besides, I owe you.'

'That's not why I came.'

'I know.' Etheridge finished his second beer. 'But none of this would have been possible without you. I don't give a shit what they say on the news. We're brothers and it's going to take more than you killing some drug dealers for me to turn you away.'

Sam smiled and patted Etheridge on the arm.

'Thanks, Paul.'

'Don't mention it.' Etheridge opened the fridge and retrieved another cold beer. 'Besides, it might be fun.'

Two hours later and Etheridge was sitting in his loft converted office, the entire floor adapted into a slick, all white room with a large desk, four monitors, and enough computer power to send a rocket into space. The barrel of Sam's gun was pressed against the back of his head, a bruise forming from the pressure. Sam had kept his finger off the trigger but insisted on holding a gun to Etheridge's head. When the police inevitably questioned him, he could at least say that he was forced at gun point. A forensic specialist would be able to corroborate it and Etheridge would have been acting to preserve his life. Sam's arms ached, but it was a small price to pay to keep his friend out of the firing line, the irony not lost on either of them as he held the gun to Etheridge's skull. The air conditioning units controlled the temperature, the large shelves of data intimidated Sam, the clear glass giving him a view of a world he would never understand. It had taken Etheridge half an hour to hack into the London Borough of Brent's CCTV network, the man throwing out terms like 'worm-holes' and 'data access channels' like they would mean something.

Sam trusted him.

Etheridge may have shown himself to be locked in a loveless marriage, but the one thing he knew was how to hack into a system. It was what he did for his country out in the war zones he was sent to.

It was how he had built his fortune when he returned.

As Sam watched, equal parts impressed and baffled, Etheridge navigated through a number of secure files, using a separate program to generate a passcode that allowed him to circumvent their security protocols and access their files undetected. When Sam queried how Etheridge even knew to do that, the response came with a victorious grin.

'Because I fucking built it for them.'

Soon they were looking at a video feed from the night Jasmine went missing, with the four monitors all split into eight different cameras giving them thirty-two different streets around Wembley Stadium. Sure enough, on the road positioned behind the nearby KFC, a white van pulled up, a large white man at the wheel. They watched, the man sitting statue-esque in the driver's seat, his large hands gripping the wheel. Etheridge made a couple of clicks of the mouse and the footage sped up, blurs of people zipping past and then Sam spoke up.

'Slow it down.'

His words were cold, and Etheridge obliged. Sam's eyes narrowed with anger as he watched a car pull up next to the van and two black youths spill out of the back, both of them grabbing at the terrified girl in the backseat, who swung her feet and clawed for freedom.

No one was coming to help her.

Not in that area.

Sam watched as one of the young men lunged into the back seat, throwing a violent fist and the kicking stopped. Quickly and with little regard for her safety, they hauled her out, roughly grabbing her arms and legs before the side panel of the van slid open, another unknown man waiting inside. With the same amount of care as a baggage handler at an airport, the two youths tossed Jasmine Hill into the back of the van.

The door slid shut.

Both vehicles sped off in different directions.

'Run the plates,' Sam demanded.

'Already on it,' Etheridge responded, his eyes glued to the screen. 'The van is registered to a Vaneheim Building Solutions. It's a dud. A shell company.'

'Damn it.'

'Hang on.' Etheridge's fingers clicked along the keys. 'Checking the government records and the company was set up a week ago as a subsidiary to a larger company known as Red Room Inc., a property management company. One that has set up separate shell companies every two weeks for the last few years.'

Etheridge rolled the screen, the information whizzing by and Sam watched, impressed as his genius friend began to connect the dots. The screen stopped and he placed a finger on the screen.

'Red Room Inc. has a controlling stake in a small shipping firm, with weekly shipments heading out to Europe from the Docklands in South London.'

'That's them.' Sam stood, his eyes wide with fury. 'The guy I spoke to, he told me he worked for some guys with thick accents.'

'Spoke to?' Etheridge smiled. 'He just offered that information did him?'

'I can be persuasive if I have to.'

'Well, they have another shipment heading out tomorrow. Scheduled in.'

'That's her. I need that crate number.'

Before Etheridge could respond, a shrill alarm erupted in the corner of the room, a red light flashing into life. Both men looked at each other and Etheridge made a couple of clicks of his mouse and the perimeter of his expensive house filled the screen. A man who spent his life securing the online world made sure he had top of the line security for his own.

A large police van was parked to the side of the gate and Sam watched as six men with tactical vests and rifles quietly and carefully filtered out of the van, lining up against the wall.

Sam saw the same woman he'd seen at Shepherd's Bush, the lady who had grilled Aaron Hill and was clearly in charge of the task force set up to catch him. She was standing, hands on hips, talking to Kayleigh.

Sam glanced at Etheridge, who remorsefully looked away.

Both men knew that marriage had an expiry date.

They also knew they didn't have much time.

'Paul, I need that crate number and location.'

'It's going to take some time, they're covering their tracks well with an ever-changing manifest working off a two-minute algorithm.'

'English?'

'They are doing a good fucking job covering their tracks.' Etheridge scanned the screen, which was filled with numbers and symbols that may as well have been Russian to Sam. 'I don't have time to decipher it. We need to go.'

'Find it and call me. You still good with numbers?'

Etheridge raised his eyebrows and committed to memory the mobile number Sam gave him. On the left-hand screen, they watched as four of the armed men approached the patio door in the back garden. Two stood guard at the front gate, rifles clutched to their bodies. Sam stepped away from the computer, walking with purpose towards the stairs.

The power died in the house.

Emergency lighting filtered through, enough to light the way.

'Where are you going, Sam?'

Sam didn't look back as he approached the stairs to the first floor of the mansion.

'To buy you some time.'

On the ground floor below, the panel to the patio door shattered and the SWAT team breached the house.

As Sam disappeared into the darkness of the stairwell, Etheridge turned back to his screen, cracked his knuckles, and hoped like hell he could find what they needed.

CHAPTER TWENTY-ONE

When the call had come through that Sam Pope was holed up in a luxurious mansion forty miles from London, Singh had been in the incident room, her eyes firmly on the wall of evidence before her. The pyramid of photos all led to a smart photo of Sam Pope, his military issued beret inch-perfect on his shaven head. The scattered photos below all presented bullet-ridden bodies, broken buildings, and the devastation he left in his wake. A picture of Aaron Hill was pinned to the side, along with Sean Wiseman.

Both men were protecting Pope.

It made her blood boil.

As her fists clenched with anger, a young officer had knocked on the door, her eyes full of admiration for the strong woman leading the task force.

'Ma'am,' she muttered nervously. 'It's Sam Pope. We have him.'

Singh burst through the door and into the corridor, the young officer struggling to keep up. As they entered the office, a gathering crowd quietened down as Singh snatched up the phone and curtly demanded information from the Farnham police department.

The wife of an old army acquaintance confirmed that Sam Pope was in her house and was working with her husband. She had recognised him from the TV, even argued with her husband about the merits of such a man.

Her husband thought he was a hero.

Singh had taken an instant disliking to him.

Due to a nationwide request that any information for Sam Pope be run through this channel, the officer awaited further instruction.

Singh told him to sit tight, put two squad cars either side of the house, and wait for them to get there. It would take just over forty minutes with the blues and twos going.

As soon as she'd slammed down the phone, she gave the order for a small Armed Response unit to mobilise, following them to the armoury with every intention going with them. After what had happened in Shepherd's Bush, she was adamant she would bring Sam Pope through the doors herself.

'Singh,' a stern voice called out. 'A word.'

Singh angrily stopped in her tracks, her face relaxing with respect as Assistant Commissioner Ashton approached. Other officers stood to attention, their senior nodding her approval.

'Yes, Ma'am?'

'What's the commotion?'

'We have him, Ma'am. Pope. He's at an acquaintance's house in Farnham. I've deployed an AR unit and we are heading there now.'

'Hmm.' Ashton rubbed her chin. 'It's risky. The man is smart and heavily trained in the art of disappearing. Surely he won't stay in one place for long enough for you to reach him.'

'It's not a social call, Ma'am. I have reason to believe that he is investigating a missing person and...'

'How have you come across this information?' Ashton

could sense Singh's impatience and decided to take a menacing step closer, underlining her authority. 'Is this a new line of enquiry?'

'Yes, Ma'am. I had to act quickly and DI Pearce theorised that…'

'Pearce? Don't make me laugh,' Ashton spat. 'The man is a busted flush on borrowed time. When I told you to use every resource available, Singh, I didn't mean for you to waste your time.'

Singh scowled. The van was ready to go and she wanted to be in it. She glanced towards the window, the darkness falling over the city earlier than ever. Regardless of the time of day, the rain continued to batter the city.

'I haven't been wasting my time,' Singh insisted. 'I've been doing what you asked me to. Bring in Sam Pope. Now if you don't mind, Ma'am, that's what I intend to do.'

Ashton glowered at Singh, her opinion of the ambitious DI flipping back and forth like an acrobat. After a few more moments, she slowly stood to the side.

'Then get it done,' Ashton said coldly. 'Otherwise the next time we talk, I won't be so polite.'

Singh stormed past her superior, instantly regretting the animosity between the two of them. As a high-ranking female, Ashton was someone she'd looked up to as a mentor. It was Ashton who had pushed for Singh to be put in charge of this task force and had been a guiding presence in her career for many years.

But Singh knew how the game was played.

If the task force failed, it wouldn't be Ashton who'd be thrown under the bus.

It would be her.

Sam Pope was the key to her career growing or dying. Her mission was slowly becoming an obsession which was pushing her to breaking point.

So, as she stood outside the mansion in Farnham, the

rain slapping her face with mocking repetition, she jostled impatiently from foot to foot.

The lights in the house died.

Word came through on the radio that they'd breached.

Moments later, a gunshot echoed throughout the house.

Followed by another.

The two other armed officers abandoned their posts at the gate and hurried towards the building as a panicked voice crackled through the radio. Kayleigh Etheridge, the helpful trophy wife who watched from the van, looked terrified.

Singh's eyes narrowed, her hand snapping to the holster on her belt, the handle of her gun brushing against her handcuffs.

When a third gunshot rang out into the torrential rain, Singh's resolve broke. Allowing her obsession to catch Sam Pope to take the wheel, she darted through the gate, towards the war erupting in the house.

———

As the shadows of the stairwell engulfed him, Sam slowly removed his Glock from the back of his jeans and held it loosely in his hand. He reached the first floor, listening carefully as the muffled steps of the armed team tried to carefully navigate the ground floor layout.

Sam had committed it to memory. The placement of furniture. The number of steps from the kitchen to the stairs. He counted backwards from three and sure enough, a beam of light filtered up the stairs. Sam took a deep breath. The last thing he wanted was another altercation with the police, but with the idea of Jasmine Hill being violated by an angry, drunk customer rattling around in his head, he swallowed his reservations.

These men were good men. Following orders and upholding the law.

He was the criminal here.

As he waited in the darkness, that sobering thought washed over him. In the eyes of the justice system, he was deemed a bigger monster than those responsible for the capture and trafficking of teenage girls.

Sam Pope was the bogeyman.

The men who were approaching the stairs, they were the heroes. Sam wasn't going to kill them. Despite the recent evidence to the contrary, he wanted to uphold his promise to his son. These men were just following orders.

Upholding the law.

But sometimes, the lawful thing wasn't always the right thing.

As the first footsteps began to ascend the stairs towards him, Sam took a few steps back into one of the darkened doorways, the room opening out into a large dance studio that Kayleigh obviously frequented. Through the darkness of the corridor, Sam watched as the first armoured man stepped by, his entire body clad in uniform, the issued rifle held expertly to his shoulder. A torch was strapped to the bottom, illuminating the corridor.

A second followed, sweeping the surrounding room with his rifle. Sam ducked back, evading detection by a millisecond.

They both walked beyond, the captain at the front signalling for the following two men to sweep the rest of the floor as they continued their search. The magnificent house provided plenty of space, for which Sam was eternally grateful. As two men searched the bedrooms further down the hall, Sam waited for the third officer to reach the landing.

Sam stepped out.

Cloaked by the darkness, he swung the gun towards the

officer, the butt of the handle colliding with the man's skull with a sickening thud, shaking his brain like a maraca. As the officer slumped unconscious, his partner turned, raised his rifle, casting them both in a magnificent glare.

Sam grabbed hold of the falling officer, holding him upright and protecting him from the scope of the rifle.

The officer demanded Sam raise his hands but refused to fire. With his human shield in front of him, Sam reluctantly lifted his pistol and pulled the trigger, shattering the officer's shin bone with a precise shot. The armed officer instantly fell to the floor, roaring in pain and clutching the broken leg, blood pumping from the wound and ruining the soft, white carpet below. The noise instantly drew the attention of the two other officers, both flashlights landing on the chaos before them.

'Drop your weapon,' a voice called out, Sam unable to place it due to the glare of the torches. He spun the unconscious body around before dropping to the ground, tugging the motionless body on top of him. As the two bodies crumpled to the ground, Sam's vision fell out of the torch's blinding radius and instantly zoned in on the legs of the officers.

Two shots.

Two more broken legs.

Sam knew that they would survive, he had delivered enough killer shots in his time to know that. But it had immobilised them sufficiently and they would soon pass out due to either shock or blood loss. Either way, he had less than a minute before the final two armed officers were on him, and he angrily shoved the unconscious officer to the side and rolled back into the studio, away from any potential shots from the recently wounded.

Two footsteps pounded through the kitchen.

The cavalry had arrived.

Sam pushed himself to his feet and scanned the studio.

A few comfy chairs, some yoga mats, and a full-length mirror embedded in an antique wooden stand. Judging by the effort Kayleigh had put into her appearance when he had met her, Sam wasn't surprised. Vanity wasn't a trait he found attractive, but he had enough character defects to keep him off a high horse.

As the footsteps approached the stairs, with a voice barking out an alarmed warning, Sam grabbed the mirror. He walked quickly to the doorway, positioning it in his place before stepping into the doorway to the left, a lovely white, tiled bathroom greeting him.

The first officer stepped onto the landing, sweeping light across the floor and gasping at the blood-drenched carpet and the pain-filled moans of his fallen comrades.

The second officer joined him, his torch frantically panning the hallway.

It landed on the mirror.

The light rebounded back, flashing in both of their eyes and momentarily blinding them.

Sam pulled the door back and launched out, one foot forward and delivered a hard Teep Kick, a brutal Muay Thai move used in Mixed Martial Arts, into the centre of the second officer's chest. With a shriek of panic, the officer fell back down the stairs, crunching hard against the steps as he crumpled to the bottom. Sam prayed the man wasn't dead but wasted little time in grabbing the stock of the final officer's rifle and twisted it, whipping it from the man's hands and tightening the strap around his neck. As the man gasped for air and batted at his neck with gloved hands, Sam took a step to the side and in one fluid motion, yanked the gun over his shoulder, flipping the man over and sending him crashing to the floor.

As he tried to struggle, Sam brought his own pistol down hard into the man's temple, the blow striking the man instantly unconscious. Footsteps echoed from above and Etheridge appeared at the other end of the corridor, torch in hand and a look of disbelief on his face.

'Fucking hell, Sam.' He shook his head, his mouth agape. 'Look at my carpet.'

'Stick it on the tab,' Sam retorted before nodding his goodbye and darting down the stairs. As he reached the bottom his memory kicked in, guiding him through the house and towards the shattered patio window and into the dark downpour beyond.

He stepped out into the rain, his highly trained ears picking up the sound of the raindrops splashing against the metal of a gun.

The sound was rapidly approaching his head.

With his eyes adjusted to the dark, Sam turned and saw the gun. In one swift movement he shot a hand forward through the rain, gripped the barrel and pushed it upwards. Gripping the handle was the woman he had seen on the camera, her face distorted in a hateful scowl.

Singh shook with adrenaline as she locked eyes with Sam Pope.

She tried to wrestle back control of the gun, but Sam used his considerable strength to wrench her arm to the side, her shoulder tweaking slightly. She swung a vicious kick to the side of Sam's leg, his knee buckling slightly. She swung another, but as she took her foot off the concrete, Sam stepped inwards, leant into her, and used her momentum against her. The world whizzed by as Singh flipped over Sam's shoulder, colliding hard with the soaking pavement. The air drove out of her body on impact.

'Stop,' Sam demanded.

Singh scrambled onto all fours and realised the gun was pointed directly at her. Sam stood five feet away, his arm outstretched with his fingers expertly wrapped around the pistol.

'Drop the weapon,' Singh demanded, slowly pushing herself back to her feet, her clothes soaked through.

'I can't do that,' Sam responded. 'You need to step away.'

'I need to bring you in.' Singh got to her feet, trying her best to slow her breathing. The moonlight bathed Sam in a white glow, his face dripping wet. His piercing dark eyes bored through her. She shot a nervous glance to the house above.

'Singh, right?' Sam said, recognising her from the brief description Pearce had given. She certainly was tenacious. But even in the darkness and the rain, there was a powerful beauty behind her scowl.

'How the hell do you know my name?' she barked.

'It doesn't matter.'

'It does. Especially when you have just unloaded a gun at my team.'

'I didn't kill any of them.'

'You shot them though?' Singh spat furiously.

'Flesh wounds. They'll live.' Sam motioned with the gun towards the door. 'Move.'

Singh held up her hands and obliged, but then launched forward for the gun. Sam stepped to the side, wrapping an arm around Singh's neck and pulling her forwards. Her feet slipped on the rain-soaked concrete and Sam held her upright, their faces a few inches apart. Sam quickly swung Singh up, pinned an arm behind her back and pressed her against the wall. She grunted on impact and Sam quickly released the handcuffs from her belt and slid one through the door handle before slapping the other around her wrist.

It clicked.

Sam stepped back, lowering the gun.

'I'm sorry,' he offered. 'But I have to go.'

'I'll get you. I promise you that much.'

'Give me twenty-four hours and I will give you the people responsible for all of this.'

'For all the killing?' Singh yelled over the thrashing rain. 'For all the crimes you have committed? Whatever you think you're doing, Sam, you're a criminal. Do you hear me? You're responsible for the people you have killed, and I will hold you to account for every single one of them. You're not a hero, Sam. You haven't been for a long time.'

Sam slowly laid the gun on the ground, out of reach of the volatile Singh and then solemnly looked her in the eye.

'I know.'

'Then why do it? Why bring all this on your shoulders?'

'Because someone has to.' Sam shook his head dismissively. 'Someone has to fight back.'

Singh angrily pulled at her cuffs, the shattered frame of the patio door rattled in its fixture. Sam took a step back towards the darkness of the garden.

'I will get you, Sam. Do you hear me?'

'Loud and clear.'

With that, Sam turned and disappeared into the darkness surrounding the house. Singh pressed her foot against the other door, wrenching as hard as she could until she felt the cold metal begin to cut into her skin. Knowing she'd been inches from Sam Pope had made her blood boil and as the weight of failure crashed onto her like the unrelenting rain, she let out a thunderous roar of fury into the night sky.

CHAPTER TWENTY-TWO

As the incident room filled up with eager officers, Pearce took up his position at the back of the room, his arms folded across his pristine blazer and his memory taking him back to that previous spring. He could see Detective Sergeant Colin Mayer standing at the front, the arrogant officer who had been in bed with the wrong people. Pearce himself had stood next to him, listening as he gave a passionate speech about the importance of safety during the London Marathon.

He had headed up the Counter Terrorism Unit, yet had worked diligently with some of the city's most dangerous criminals to orchestrate an attack.

It had claimed the lives of several people, including a young officer.

It had piqued the interest of Sam Pope, who Pearce had been investigating at the time. So much had changed in the months since then and now Pearce stood at the back of the room where Pope had, an outsider to the rest of the Force. Since Sam had audaciously reached out to him in a coffee shop across the street, Pearce had been like a dog with a bone. With his current reputation in tatters, it was hard to call in favours with any department and he was damned if he was going to figure out how to use his computer to hunt for the account.

Instead, he had called in a favour with a former colleague he had busted for computer fraud, who now made a living hacking bank accounts and syphoning funds from large corporations who failed to pay their tax bills. The young man went by the name TERA, and he thought of himself as a Robin Hood for the millennial generation. Pearce often reminded him he was a thief and a criminal and if Pearce put the correct calls in, the young man would know the true spelling and meaning of his name.

TERA obliged and was currently doing his level best to trace the payments being made to the bank account Sam had provided. He also reminded Pearce that what he had requested was illegal.

It was becoming an increasingly frequent warning.

Pearce knew his decisions had put him on a path of no return, but hearing that Sam Pope had once again evaded capture, with six officers injured, he knew he had to listen in.

Especially when DI Singh stormed in, bringing the entire room to a hush with a furious glare.

Behind her, Assistant Commissioner Ashton strode in, the entire room rising to their feet in respect. Ashton nodded and the room sat down in unison, apart from Pearce and a few late comers at the back. Singh stood against the wall, arms folded and a look of sorrow across her face.

'Let me begin by saying that up to this point, the Watchdog Task Force has worked diligently to apprehend Sam Pope. As you know, after the events earlier this year, bringing an end to this vigilante's reign of terror on this city has become a priority.' Ashton scanned the room and continued, 'Despite recent efforts to ensure his capture,

Sam Pope is still at large and for the second time this week, he has assaulted members of this police service.'

A wave of angry murmurs rose up among the seated officers. Pearce shifted uncomfortably. Ashton was rallying them well and she continued.

'As this task force is very much in the public eye, it's imperative that no information regarding these failures leak to the media.' Ashton shot Singh a glance, underlining her point. 'In the meantime, it has been requested that I step in and assume command over the task force to bring it to a successful conclusion.'

A few murmurs echoed through the room and Pearce watched as Singh pushed herself from the wall and marched to the door, leaving the room to a flurry of whispers. Shaking his head with disgust, Pearce opened the door at the back of the room and walked into the corridor, wanting to console his new-found friend. As he turned the corner, he collided with a sturdy man in an expensive suit.

Mark Harris.

Pearce raised a surprised eyebrow, his startled expression obviously causing the smarmy politician amusement judging by the well-practised grin.

'Adrian Pearce.' He reached in double handed, grip and shake. The handshake of a champion. 'Good to see you.'

'Mr Harris.' He looked over Harris's shoulder at the emotionless Burrows standing a few feet back, his immaculate suit hugging his chubby frame. 'Burrows.'

The executive assistant nodded. Harris stepped back into Pearce's eye line, his white teeth displayed in a wide grin.

'I take it you're here for my speech,' Harris said confidently.

'Speech?' Pearce shrugged.

'To the task force. I called in a favour with Ruth,

Assistant Commissioner to you.' Harris spoke with an air of undeserved superiority. 'Thought it would be good for morale and my campaign when I personally showed up to push us on to finally catch that bastard.'

'Well it sounds riveting, but I have actual police work to do so if you'll excuse me.'

'Of course. Also, if you see DI Singh, please tell her this wasn't a personal decision. We just felt it would be better for Ruth and me to take things from here.'

Pearce chuckled and took the extended hand from Harris. He squeezed it, catching Harris by surprise with the power of his grip and he stepped in close.

'Typical. Let the real police do the work and then have Ruth cross the finish line from a yard away.' Harris went to speak but Pearce squeezed again. 'I'm sorry, I meant Assistant Commissioner.'

'Quite,' Harris barked, pulling back his hand and nervously running it through his well-combed hair. 'Well, if you don't mind, Pearce. Some of us have criminals to catch.'

Harris stepped away, heading towards the door to the meeting room just as Pearce heard AC Ashton make the announcement, a round of applause greeted Harris as he stepped into the room. Pearce stood, his brow furrowed and fists clenching.

'Apologies, DI Pearce, but it's imperative for Harris's mayoral campaign that Sam Pope be brought in as soon as possible. An awful lot hinges on it.'

Burrows moved alongside Pearce, his hands behind his stiff back.

'It's imperative for his ego.'

'We have a vested interest from many private companies and businesses, some of whom are reliant on Pope being stopped.' Pearce raised an eyebrow as Burrows continued, 'A vigilante in the city isn't good for business.'

'What business is that then?'

'Their business. Our business.' Burrows grinned, his smile lacking the panache of his bosses. 'Certainly not yours. You see, Pearce, despite your clear abilities as a detective, your inability to see the bigger picture is what sets you apart from great men like Mark Harris.'

'Is that so?' Pearce asked dryly, rolling his eyes.

'Yes. While you make decisions that have blacklisted you and, if you don't mind me saying, sabotaged your own career, Mark strives for perfection. For greatness. Sam Pope is a slap in the face of his campaign, of the badge you wear, and the very basis of this entire legal system. Mark wishes to eradicate it and use it to push him to office where he will finally be able to change things.'

'So he can feed his superiority complex?' Pearce offered, agitated by the nerve of the condescending man before him.

'No complex, Pearce.' Burrows met his eyes, his stare as intense as his words. 'It is transcendence.'

With that, Burrows turned and marched emphatically towards the open doors to the meeting room, leaving Pearce alone in the corridor. He could hear the eager voice of Mark Harris, rolling out his well-rehearsed speech like a modern-day Mark Antony. He stuffed his hands in his pockets and turned on his heel, willing himself to go and find Singh and ensure she was okay. If anyone knew what it was like to be side-lined, it was him.

But his mind had triggered. Something wasn't right. As he slowly ambled down the corridor, the dots began to connect.

Something Burrows had said.

'Shit,' Pearce muttered, and two seconds later, was running as fast as he could back to his office.

———

As he flicked the indicator down and turned onto Aaron Hill's road, Sam Pope took a sip of his coffee. The lukewarm caffeine sloshed down his throat and he willed himself awake.

It had been a long night.

After escaping through the gardens, he emerged through an alleyway two streets from the gated road that housed his friend. He felt bad for Etheridge, the impact of his shoot-out with the police would undoubtedly have repercussions for him. The unhappy marriage would surely hit breaking point, not to mention the devastating effect it could have on his business if it became public knowledge that Etheridge had aided and abetted a wanted fugitive.

Especially one that opened fire on the police.

But Etheridge was a good man. Sam knew that Etheridge was never a soldier at heart, he was a mastermind with the will to do good. Knowing he was helping Sam to rescue a teenage girl would be more than enough to balance the scales.

As he steered the stolen car past Aaron's house, Sam scouted for a parking space on the cramped London road. The houses were all identical, all of them set back from the pavement, all of them narrow and tall as if they'd been stretched to accommodate more.

It was still raining.

It had been that morning when he had stolen his first car to leave Farnham, ducking down as he passed by three police cars, all screaming their arrival as they raced to stop him. He watched the law disappear in his rear-view mirror and found it symbolic for the life he had decided to live.

Everything he did was outside of the law.

But everything he did was for a reason.

While the police were busy trying to bring him to justice, he was rattling cages and fighting his way to a young girl whose life was about to thrown into a blender. A time would come, Sam thought, when he would face the music and pay for the crimes he had committed.

But not yet.

Not while people still needed him.

He had driven from Farnham to Tilbury in Essex, passing through Guildford and Ockham until he joined the M25. The ring of death that circled the capitol like a cramped, concrete moat was delightfully quiet at three in the morning and Sam had travelled the seventy plus miles in just over an hour. The Port of Tilbury was one of the few working ports in the UK, along with Felixstowe in Suffolk and Southampton in Hampshire. With the Thames running through it, it allowed for a number of 'authorised' shipments to venture down from the capital. Sam was certain that Jasmine would be here, locked away in a steel prison, trapped in the dark with nothing but fear to keep her company.

The rain was relentless as he'd stepped from the driver's seat, dumping the car outside of the gated entrance and doing his best to peer through the fence. A labyrinth of metal, corrugated containers were stacked high and irregularly. While to the dock workers themselves there was a knowledge and routine, to the outside eye there was no discernible system.

Blue containers stacked on red containers. Four to one pile. Six to another. This continued over the seven kilometres of the quay that comprised the port, all of it under the metallic arms of several cranes and winches.

Sam was looking for a needle in a haystack.

After a few moments of peering through the gate, Sam noticed a security guard rounding one of the containers and he stepped away from the gate, before looking around the surrounding areas. A large radio tower stood next to the port, long since abandoned and covered in graffiti tags and wooden boards. Sam eventually made his way inside and climbed to the top floor, his mind racing back to the evening this all began.

Him lying in a derelict building, aiming a rifle into a room full of criminals.

Now, as Sam pulled the car into a parking space at the far end of the road, he began to wonder exactly what would happen if he *couldn't* find Jasmine.

Aaron was relying on him to bring his daughter home. He had killed three men, wounded over a dozen more, and tortured a man to near death. He had gone to war with the police and left a number of them in the hospital.

The entire country was looking for him.

He was public enemy number one.

It would all have been for nothing.

He scolded himself for even thinking it. If there was even a half per cent chance he would be able to bring Jasmine home, then he would do it all again. If he ended up facing a lifetime behind bars or the barrel of a gun, then so be it. As long as there was a breath in his body big enough to push him forward into the fight, then he would gladly go.

He would fight. Until there was nothing left.

Sam pushed open the gate to Aaron's house and froze on the spot. Aaron was sitting on the steps, soaked through and with a bottle of whisky in his hand.

In the other was a gun.

Sam slowly stepped forward, one hand out protectively, trying to gauge the mindset of a desperate father who had clearly reached breaking point. As he stepped closer, Aaron lifted his head, his hair drenched and his eyes red through crying.

'Sam.' His voice was slow and slurred. 'It's about time.'

'Aaron.' Sam stepped forward carefully. 'Give me the gun.'

'I need to show you something,' Aaron spoke joyfully,

the alcohol clearly behind the wheel. He pushed himself to his feet. 'I need you to do something for me.'

'Let's just go inside.'

'No,' Aaron snapped, pointing the gun towards Sam. 'It's in the garage.'

'Garage?' Sam asked, alarmed. Aaron stumbled off the steps and towards the garage door. 'Aaron. What have you done?'

Without a response, Aaron lifted the metal door and woozily stepped into the darkness. Sam quickly followed, stepping in just as the lights pinged on and the door behind him began to close. As he adjusted his sight from the immediate blast of brightness, Sam saw the shape of a car. It was a newer model, with a logo of a rental company on a faded sticker stuck to the inside of the windscreen. Aaron shifted around the vehicle, pressing himself against the wall for support. As he reached the boot of the car, the garage door connected with the concrete, shutting them in.

'I've got him,' Aaron said, his words slurring like snakes coiling around each other.

'Who?'

'Him. The one who took my daughter.'

Sam took a few steps further, confused, his eyes locked on the weapon in the drunken man's hands. As he got to the rear of the car, Aaron stepped back, raising the gun once more.

'Open it.'

Sam kept his eyes on Aaron, watching as he took another excited swig from the bottle of whisky, a trickle dribbling down his chin. Sam searched beneath the logo for the latch, clicked it and lifted the boot. Sam soon realised that Aaron hadn't just reached the edge.

He had gone over it.

'What the hell have you done?' Sam asked once again, taking a step backwards. Lying in the boot of the car was a black, teenage boy. A horrible gash was pumping fresh blood over his blindfold and a gag was wrenched into his mouth. Both his hands were bound with thick layers of gaffer tape.

Tears stained his cheeks. Urine had stained his trousers.

The young boy quivered with terror, his muffled voice begging for help. The sound of the safety latch of the pistol clicking echoed around the garage like a gunshot and Aaron stepped forward, gun in hand. He aimed squarely at Sam's chest.

'I want you to kill him.'

CHAPTER TWENTY-THREE

Dana Kovalenko hung up the phone and a sickening grin spread across her full, red lips. Her extravagantly tipped fingers clutched the phone tightly as she turned, her heels clicking against the marble flooring as she strutted from the guest room of her brother's penthouse suite. A few of the armed guards who followed her family tried their best not to lay eyes on her tight, figure-hugging dress that high-lighted her phenomenal body.

Leering at Dana would have your eyes removed.

Andrei had blinded four of his own men for 'eye fuck-ing' his sister, and she took pride in both the danger she put the surrounding work force in and also the pedestal her brother placed her upon.

She approached her brother's bedroom door and rapped her knuckles against it. As she waited, she peered out of the large glass window at the city below. Lit up like a million fireflies, she adored the beauty of the city.

The life they lived was so far away from the one they grew up in that it lightened the load on her conscience. In a different life, she may well have been one of the young girls, tied up in containers and shipped off to warehouses in the derelict, run-down towns in the south of Ukraine. Her father was a monster of a man, and if selling her body would have brought in more cash, then he would have done it.

Thankfully, Andrei put a stop to that.

The door clicked open and her brother emerged, his shirt open and his hair messy. His body, once neatly sculpted, was now a little looser ,but the tattoos were still as prominent. Over his shoulder, Dana could see two women lying on his bed, their naked bodies entangled and a pile of cocaine on the bedside table. Andrei cleared his throat.

'What is it, sister?' he demanded impatiently. 'I'm busy.'

'Oleg called. He says that Sam Pope drove to the docks early this morning and scouted the place.' Dana's eyes lit up. 'Shall I give the order for Oleg to eliminate?'

'No, not yet.' Andrei lit a cigarette, taking a deep drag before tilting his head back pushing the smoke upwards. 'Where is he now?'

'Oleg says he is at a house in London. We believe it's the father that Wiseman spoke about.'

Andrei nodded and took another puff. Oleg had relayed the information he had beaten out of the young kid. The desperate father of one of the girls in his next shipment had caused a scene and managed to get Sam Pope hunting for her. Knowing that the city's most wanted man was hot on their tail should have been enough for him to change the schedule.

But Andrei didn't bow or bend for anyone.

Certainly not a man with a gun.

'We keep to schedule. Have the girls delivered to the port tonight. You stay here, in case anything does happen.'

'You're going?' Dana asked, her immaculate eyebrows raised.

'Yes. If this Pope wants to get involved in my business, then maybe I make him my business.'

Andrei's thick, Ukrainian accent had always added a hint of danger to his words and Dana hung on every one of them. Andrei finished his cigarette and turned back to his sister.

'Tell Oleg to keep following Pope. If he needs to intervene, tell him I want him brought to me. Alive.' Andrei's face twisted into a cruel grin. 'We can then post him to our partner, piece by piece.'

'That will certainly help his campaign.'

The two siblings laughed, their cruel humour only exacerbated by the complete ignorance of their partner. His ties to the city were huge and his involvement with the large businesses were what had funded his entire campaign. He had unknowingly opened doors that allowed Andrei to operate his business.

Soon, when the man was in power, Andrei would show him the evidence trail and secure him in his pocket forever. Andrei managed his crime empire like a game of chess, always thinking five moves ahead.

Two more moves and it would be check mate.

Behind him, a gasp of pleasure erupted from the bed and he turned, a sickening smile on his face.

'Duty calls.' He flashed a grin at his sister and turned back towards the bed, unbuckling his belt and dropping trousers as he did. As he positioned himself behind one of the woman, he shot a glance back to his sister, who watched on from the doorway. He knew she would be impressed at his display of power, and once he had sent off that evening's shipment, he would publicly kill Sam Pope and send a message loud and clear to his partner and to the Metropolitan Police.

London belonged to Andrei Kovalenko.

'No,' Sam said firmly, turning back to face Aaron whose eyes lit up with fury. He took another angry swig of the whisky and then slammed the bottle down on the tool bench at the back of the garage. The cupboards shook and the metal tools clanged together. He wiped his mouth with the back of his sleeve and stepped forward, gun raised.

'Kill him.'

'No.' Sam shook his head. 'He's just a kid.'

'The kid who took my little girl.'

'Aaron, this boy isn't the person responsible for what has happened to Jasmine. You need to calm down.'

'Fuck you,' Aaron spat angrily. 'This little prick lured my girl to a party and snatched her from me. So do what it is that you fucking do.'

Sam stepped away from the boot of the car, his arms up in surrender. Aaron's eyes were watering with anger, tears sliding over the lids and down his tired face.

'What do you mean?' Sam asked.

'This is what you do right? You find the bad people and you kill them. Or do you get to be the judge and jury as well as the executioner? Huh?'

'Aaron, you don't want to kill this boy…' Sam tried to mask the hurt in his voice, but Aaron's words were hitting him hard. Was that how he was perceived? Not as a force of good but just as a weapon of vengeance?

'Why do you get to choose who lives and dies? What gives you the right to decide whether one life is worth more than another?' Aaron's tears were full force now, his breathing intensifying as well as his grip around the gun. 'He took my daughter, Sam. The police did nothing. I appreciate that you tried but you haven't found her. She's gone.'

'She's still out there,' Sam pleaded. 'I've tracked the

people responsible and I'm waiting for a call to tell me where.'

'Waiting. Waiting. Waiting,' Aaron said drunkenly, swaying slightly as the whisky flowed through him. 'I'm tired of waiting. I might not have my little girl back, but I won't let them get away with it. So do what you do and kill him.'

'Aaron, you need to give me the gun.'

'Kill him.' Aaron repeated, his emphasis getting louder with fury.

'Killing a teenage kid isn't going to bring her back. Letting me go is.'

'KILL HIM!' Aaron screamed, lifting the gun once more. As soon as he did, Sam expertly swung a hand to the back of his jeans and pulled up his own pistol, both hands wrapped around the handle, his finger resting on the trigger. Aaron stumbled back, colliding with the bench and sending the bottle of whisky to an explosive journey to the concrete below. The sound of the smashing glass made the young captive jolt in the boot, his weeping increasing. Aaron, his hand shaking, lifted his gun back at Sam, who stood firmly.

'You do it,' Sam said coldly.

'W-w-what?' Aaron eventually stuttered, his words catching in throat.

'You want him dead. You kill him.' Sam kept the gun pointed squarely at the drunk's forehead. The eyes that were filled with furious tears were now wide with terror.

'B-but I…'

'You think it's so easy, then you do it. Like you said, your daughter is gone. This boy is responsible. So kill him,' Sam demanded, stepping forward towards Aaron who cowered slightly.

'B-b-but…'

'Come on, Aaron. Your daughter is probably being

217

raped or beaten as we speak and you did nothing to save her. Could do nothing,' Sam said through gritted teeth. 'This boy, this young kid who has been forced into the life by manipulative adults is the reason she was taken in the first place. So kill him.'

Aaron sobbed as he stepped forward, a wave of regret crashing into him as he looked at the outcome of his actions. The young kid wept uncontrollably, hearing every word of the two men arguing over who was going to end his life. After taking a few more short breaths, Aaron lowered his arm, the gun dropping to his side and he turned back to Sam, defeated.

'I can't.'

Sam clicked off the safety.

'Kill him, or I will kill you.'

Aaron stumbled back, his calves connecting with the bonnet.

'What?'

'You heard me. Like you said, this is easy for me. Killing people is what I do. You have made it clear to me that this boy deserves to die. So either you put a bullet in his head or I'll put a bullet in yours and leave your daughter to rot.'

Aaron shook. Sam's sudden, cold turn had blindsided him and he felt the wooziness of alcohol beginning to take control of his body. He thought of his daughter, alone and scared. He imagined her hands bound, her eyes covered, and the terrifying voices of two men who were deciding whether to kill her or not.

He realised then that he was no better than those who had taken his daughter. The young adult in the back of his car was as vulnerable as his daughter had been, only he had been taken in a different way. He had been coerced into gang culture by adults who preyed off the poverty of youth.

This young man had lured his daughter to a fate worse than death. But he didn't deserve to die.

'I can't,' Aaron finally uttered.

'Last chance,' Sam said, hating himself for every moment of this. 'Kill him or you will never see her again.'

At that moment, Aaron hunched over to the side and puked. Streams of vomit splashed against the concrete, ricocheting back against the car wheel. As he furiously threw up, he wept for the path he had fallen down. A week ago, he was just a single father, trying his best to establish a relationship with a hurt teenage girl who mourned for her mother.

Now he was holding teenagers at gun point and aiding wanted fugitives.

The last of the vomit hit the concrete and he stayed hunched on all fours, his back jack-knifing as he took in deep, full breaths.

Sam re-engaged the safety on his gun and tucked it back into the waistband of his jeans. He stepped forward and rested a comforting hand on Aaron's back. The last four years had ebbed away at his empathy, but it hadn't made him a monster. Sam knew he was no hero, but he also knew he wasn't the monster people like Singh made him out to be. As Aaron's breathing slowed to a more regular pace, Sam helped him to his feet. He smiled uncomfortably as Aaron dabbed at his eyes, regaining his composure.

'I couldn't do it,' Aaron eventually said, embarrassed.

'Believe me, you wouldn't have killed him even if you wanted to.'

'But I would have,' Aaron said, regrettably looking back at the young boy held captive. 'I really would have.'

'No, you wouldn't,' Sam reiterated, bending down to pick up the pistol Aaron had dropped on the floor. As he lifted it, he expertly slid the clip from the handle. It was empty. 'I took the liberty of emptying this last time I was here.'

Sam handed the empty clip to Aaron, who stared at it, then back at Sam in disbelief.

'What?'

'I figured you wouldn't be able to tell by the weight of it.'

Aaron chuckled, embarrassed.

'Then why the hell did you do all that when you knew I had no bullets?'

'Because you needed to see that this isn't your life. You were right. You're not like me. You can't kill people and that's a good thing. But I don't kill for the sake of it. I do my best not to. I promised my son a long time ago and despite the fact I've broken that promise a few times, I'm working hard to get it back. But trust me, Aaron, you're not the first Dad to feel completely helpless and then get desperate.'

'Yeah, but at least you got the guy who took your son from you.'

Sam turned away, his own pain drilling through his chest like a Black & Decker. Memories began to race forward, dominating his mind until he realised he needed to confront them.

Before he arrived back at that fateful night all those years ago, he responded.

'Not exactly.'

CHAPTER TWENTY-FOUR

The cool evening breeze danced around Sam seductively, doing its best to lead him away from the decision he had made. Edgware High Street was deathly quiet. The only sound was the intermittent noise of a train approaching Edgware Station, the final stop on the Northern Line. Sam strode up the street, zeroed in on the battered white door he had watched Miles Hillock enter.

As he approached, two youths stepped out from the chicken shop, a box of questionable meat in their hands. They made a point of stepping around Sam, one of them throwing an insult at him which failed to register. He wasn't surprised – his lack of hygiene and care for his appearance since losing his son was apparent even to him. His scratchy beard hung from his chin in fluffy patches, his dank, unwashed hair flopped over his ears.

Sam looked homeless, and the two youths made sure he knew it.

As they laughed at him, he hunched over, his hand tucked into the inside of his jacket. His fingers tightened around the serrated blade and he did his best to keep it covered. He approached the white door and took a deep breath.

He raised a fist up and hammered against the door.

Three hard, firm knocks.

Sam moved to the side of the door, stepping back slightly into the neighbouring doorway of the estate agents. He waited patiently for a few moments, watching as two cars shot down the road, not giving him a second look.

The sound of footsteps echoed from the wall behind him and Sam felt his entire body tense.

This was it.

Months of waiting and now the time had arrived.

Sam pulled the knife from his jacket and held it tightly, his knuckles whitening and his breath quickening.

The door opened.

Sam spun around the divider between the two doors and came face to face with Miles Hillock. The drunken murderer tried to focus on the homeless man who had just jumped out on him and he startled slightly. Sam glared at him, a rage coursing through his body like someone had opened the gates of hell. Hillock took a few moments until the colour drained in his face.

He recognised Sam.

Then he noticed the blade.

Hillock instantly reached for the door, pushing his weight behind it but Sam was too quick, slamming his shoulder into the door and letting the edge of it crack Hillock in the face, slashing open a gash above his eye and knocking him back into the dimly lit stairwell. Hillock fell against the stairs, his hands grabbing out at the tatty carpet to try to pull himself up.

Sam slammed the door shut behind him.

'Please. I'm sorry,' Hillock pleaded, but Sam swung a hard right hook straight into the man's kidneys. Hillock rolled over on the stairs, howling in pain and Sam reached out and yanked a handful of the man's greasy hair. He pulled Hillock's head back and then slammed it viciously against the edge of the stair, breaking the man's nose and watching with glee as blood gushed down his murderous face. Sam yanked the hair back again and then held the jagged blade to the man's throat.

'Slowly,' he whispered, his words striking fear in Hillock who wept feebly. Obligingly, Hillock rose to his feet and Sam forced him up the stairs, keeping the blade pressed against the man's unshaven neck. They stepped onto the landing, a cramped space with three doors leading off into separate parts of the rundown apartment. To the right, a mould covered bathroom shrouded in darkness. To the left, a sparse bedroom with cold, wooden floor boards and a crumpled mattress. Ahead, a cramped, grease stained kitchen with a broken, plastic table and an accompanying chair.

The place was littered with beer cans and fast food packaging. The smell was unbearable, a combination of sweat, bad drainage, and flat alcohol.

A depressing home for a pathetic existence.

Sam felt no sympathy, just a seething rage and he removed the blade from Hillock's neck before shoving him into the kitchen. Hillock stumbled into the room, sprawling across the rickety table. Panicked, he frantically reached for anything to use as a weapon, gripping the handle of a rusty pan smeared in week-old sauce.

He turned and swung.

Sam dodged, weaving underneath the blow before striking Hillock with an uppercut under the ribs, driving the air from his lungs. The pan clattered to the floor and as Hillock took a sharp intake of breath, Sam burst forward, hauling Hillock off the floor and driving him through the plastic table. It collapsed beneath their combined weight, Sam driving Hillock into the wreckage. Hillock yelped in pain, flailing his arms and trying to break free.

Sam rolled on top of him, straddling across Hillock's chest and pinning him under his weight.

'Please,' Hillock begged before his words were cut off by Sam's fingers reaching around his throat. Sam squeezed, staring rabidly into the terrified eyes of Hillock as he began to strangle him. All the pain of his loss came flooding back to him and Sam pressed harder, his hatred driving his weight down onto Hillock's larynx. Hillock weakly beat at Sam with pathetic slaps, clearly lacking in the notion of self-preservation. As Hillock's face turned a disturbing purple, Sam let out a pained yell and let go. Hillock gasped for air, greedily sucking in as much as he could. Sam, still atop him, stared at him with hatred and then the image of Jamie's broken, twisted body flashed in his mind.

He struck Hillock with a hard right. The already broken nose crumpled further, blood shooting out like a burst blood pack. Hillock rocked back, his eyes rolling, and Sam felt himself lose control.

He hit him again.

And again.

And again.

After the fifth blow, Hillock was barely conscious. His face had been brutalised, with his eye socket and cheek bone both fractured. Both eyes were quickly swelling like a champion boxer and his nose was shattered beyond repair. A faint wheezing noise emanated, the air waves damaged by the brutal beating. As he slipped nearer to unconsciousness, he feebly tried to speak.

'I'm sorry.'

'You killed him,' Sam said quietly, reaching for the serrated blade in his left hand and bringing it towards Hillock's throat. 'You killed my boy. You killed my boy.'

Sam repeated himself, tears flooding down his cheeks, and he grabbed Hillock by the hair, lifting his head and tilting it back, exposing his throat. The knife shook in his hand.

This man had taken away his son. Snatched him from the world due to his own selfishness.

Sam could end it right then and there.

Just as he gripped the knife, readying it to tear into Hillock's throat, the image of his son came back to him. Jamie was smiling, looking up at Sam with all the hero-worshipping adulation a son has for his father. They were playing in the local park and Sam was recovering from the bullet wounds that would end his career in the army.

Jamie asked him one thing.

'Daddy. Will you promise not to kill anymore?'

Sam burst into tears, falling back off of Hillock and leaning against the grimy cupboard. For what felt like an eternity, Sam sat in the dark, damp dwelling and wept, less than three feet away from the man who had caused him his pain.

The man who had killed his son.

Sam couldn't kill him. He had wanted to, more than anything, but it wouldn't have made him feel any better. His own pain wouldn't be numbed by ending this man's life. He'd spend the rest of his life in prison, another crime statistic, and no closer to anything resembling peace.

There was something else out there for him. Other people who, like him, had been let down not just by life, but by the people dedicated to protecting it. His son had died in a horrible accident, but the man responsible had broken the law. He had served a pathetic sentence and now Sam had delivered another kind of justice.

Hillock was a drunk driver. Sam wondered how many rapists or murderers still felt the sweet release of liberty while the lives they had shattered still remain unrepaired.

Sam knew what he had to do.

He had to fight back.

It wouldn't bring back Jamie. It wouldn't bring back Lucy or the life he had fought to protect. That was behind him and as he pulled himself to his feet, he realised just how close he had been to a different path. One that would have ended in a small, brick cell and a lifetime of incarceration.

A new path had become clear, and Sam shuffled towards the door, a new sense of purpose developing its own heart beat within in. A sudden wave of exhaustion hit him as if the closure he had experienced tonight had lifted the lid on every need in his body. His stomach growled. His throat was dry. He yawned.

The new purpose blossoming within in had triggered his body to survive, the basic needs he had neglected popped up like weeds and he was eager to return home for a good night's sleep before he contemplated his next move. The idea of shaving had never felt so good.

As he crushed another empty beer can on his way to the stairs, he heard the jostling of Hillock in the kitchen and turned back to the beaten man in the kitchen. The man's face was a living Picasso, the horrific injuries would require extensive surgery to repair.

Sam tried, but felt no guilt.

The man had killed his son.

Just as Sam went to descend the stair case, Hillock coughed, his throat gurgling blood.

'Kill me.' Hillock wept. 'Please.'

Sam stopped. The offer was tempting but it wasn't why he was there. The man was clearly suicidal, trying to drink himself to death. The demons of murdering a child, the horrific memories of a being raped in prison. The following morning, Hillock would be found, his wrists slashed vertically with a torn beer can. Sam said nothing, heading down the stairs and out into the night sky.

For the first time in a long time, the feeling of fresh air hitting his lungs was euphoric. He strode back to his car, massaging his broken knuckles. He got in, turned the ignition, and pulled out onto the High Street, heading to the next stage of his life.

———

Sat at Aaron's dining table, Sam shrugged and took the final sip of his cold coffee. Aaron sat next to him, a look of astonishment on his face.

'I've never told anyone that story,' Sam said, a look of shame on his face.

'Why?'

'Why?' Sam shrugged. 'I guess I never felt it was a memory anyone else needed but me.'

'No, I mean why didn't you kill him?' Aaron asked, the bags around his eyes getting heavier by the second.

'Because he was already dead. His life was going in one direction and whatever I did to him wasn't going to change it. It would have just sped it up.' Sam took a moment, swallowing the sadness that the memory was bringing up. 'There are good people in this world. I may not be one of them, Aaron, but you are.'

Aaron began to cry, turning away from Sam out of a senseless notion of macho pride.

'I'm not. I wanted to kill that kid.'

'But you didn't.' Sam pointed out as he stood. 'You didn't kill him, because that's not who you are. You're a good man and a good father. You've knocked on doors even I wouldn't knock on to find her.'

Aaron took a deep breath and wiped away the final tear. Sam reached out and patted him on his shoulder.

'I believe your daughter is being shipped out of Tilbury Port at some point this evening. I don't know when or where to. If you feel you need to call the police, let them handle it, then that's your prerogative as Jasmine's father. But I promised you I would get your daughter back, and that's what I'm going to do.'

Sam nodded, and then headed towards the hallway, making his way down towards the door. Aaron watched him march to the door, his eyes flicking to the business card of DI Singh who had visited him the day before. She had been so adamant that Sam needed to be stopped, but she would be able to bring the full fury of the Metropolitan Police to the location of his daughter.

Did he place his faith in one man? Or the entire justice system?

Sam opened the front door, taking one look at the downpour and then pulled the collar of his jacket up. Just as he stepped out into the elements, Aaron called after him.

'What are you going to do?'

Sam stopped and turned, the rain crashing into him, soaking him instantly and chilling him to the bone.

His words were even colder.

'What I do best.'

CHAPTER TWENTY-FIVE

Jasmine and the other girls were all huddled together in the dark. With their arms interlinked they did their best to keep calm. Inside the metal crate, the darkness had begun to feel like home. The foul smell of body odour and human waste all too familiar. Outside, they could hear the hustle and bustle of machinery, the warning beep of a truck, and a few voices shouting instructions. An hour before, they felt the crate begin to move as it was loaded onto a small boat, the restlessness of the Thames causing them to rock from side to side.

One of the other girls emptied her guts onto the floor.

It didn't matter. It was just enveloped by the rest of the foul stench.

Jasmine closed her eyes and tried to focus on her breathing. Two of the girls were weeping, the realisation that they were about to be shipped to an unknown destination had dawned on them. The words that no one was to touch them until they got to the other side raced around Jasmine's head.

Wherever they were going, it wasn't going to be nice.

Jasmine wasn't as young as the other girls and had

taken on the responsibility of keeping them calm. While few words were shared between the girls, their fear was.

They huddled together, knowing that wherever the crate was being transported to, their nightmare awaited on the other side of the door. A life of abuse and violation, so far away from home they would have no chance of returning.

As the two girls wept louder, Jasmine felt a lone tear slide over the edge of her eyelid, and she yearned for her dad. She had been so horrible to him, pushed him away when all he had wanted was for her to be safe.

When her mother had died, she'd blamed him.

She had never taken the time to realise that he had lost a wife.

Her lip quivered and soon, Jasmine was crying. The other girls snuggled closer to comfort her and the four of them agreed, that no matter what awaited them, they would always have each other.

But their time was running out.

———

The Port of Tilbury was spookily quiet as Sam Pope emerged from the building opposite. After he had left Aaron's house, he had gone home to grab a few hours of rest and then suited up. He had strapped a bulletproof vest to his torso, remembering the burning sensation of the bullets that had passed through his body before. He had liberated one of the Glock 20s from the wardrobe, and it now hung securely in the shoulder holster under his leather bomber jacket.

His trusted L85IW SA80 assault rifle lay across his back, the strap diagonally dissecting his vest.

His back-up plan was nine stories above him.

Sam had arrived in Tilbury just before five, intentionally missing the rush hour that turned the M25 into a carbon dioxide sponsored game of sardines. He had chuckled as he had broken into another car, wondering if maybe he should go into the lucrative business of boosting cars. It was a skill he had learnt years back while serving in the army when he and Etheridge had come under heavy fire.

It was Etheridge who had shown him how, which had saved his life.

Now, he was relying on Etheridge to save another.

Sam had his fingers clasped around his mobile phone, his hand stuffed in his pocket to shield the device from the relentless downpour. Sam had slowly walked around the outer fence of the port, trying his best to get an idea of the layout. It was the same as before, mountain after mountain of metal containers, all stacked up like an iron metropolis. Sam didn't like it. He always plotted and planned his attacks to the minutest detail. Nothing was trivial and every fine margin was well-scouted beforehand.

The last time he headed into a situation this severe with no preparation, he took down the entire High Rise, ending with him arresting a senior officer and unloading a clip into the chest of one of the most hardened criminals.

Now, he needed to avoid a shoot-out on unfamiliar territory while searching for a minor miracle.

The algorithm would display the container and its location at seven.

Etheridge would note it then wipe it instantly. Hopefully, that scramble would buy Pope enough of a head start to locate the container and get Jasmine and whoever else was locked inside ready to be shipped like a brand-new car.

Sam closed his eyes and let the rain crash against him.

He thought of Lucy. They were still married, and she laughed at one of his terrible jokes.

He thought of Theo Walker, his best friend, reaching across the table to cheers him.

He thought of Jamie, his son, riding his bike and begging Sam to watch.

Wonderful memories that Sam held onto like a lifeboat, worried that losing them would cast him adrift into a lonely ocean. His world now was nothing but pain, violence, and death. He relied on those memories, those warm moments of decency to pull him back.

To make things worth fighting for.

The scale of the mission wasn't lost on Sam.

He had travelled to many distant countries and fought violent terrorists on their turf. This was similar, he was entering unknown territory to face an unknown threat. The day-staff had long since clocked off, but just after six an evening crew had arrived. Sam was sure a few palms had been greased by those in charge to allow for some 'extracurricular' activities. Seven men had entered and after a few moments, Sam heard the forklift roar into life and the usual orchestra of beeps, clunks, and foul language he expected.

A car pulled up.

Sam pressed himself against the nearest wall, leaning back into the shadows. The rain was doing a fine job of obscuring everything, but he didn't want to be too careful. The front two doors opened in unison and two men stepped out. Their muscular physique and shorn hair screamed Special Forces and Sam could see they were both armed. They barked an order in another language and a few moments later, one of them opened the rear door.

Out stepped a well-dressed man with neatly combed blonde hair. The surrounding men stood to attention and the man barked at them, once again in a dialect that Sam was unfamiliar with. He could pinpoint it as Eastern European but wouldn't hazard a guess as to which country.

As the man pointed at two of the men to stay put, another black SUV pulled up, with four heavily armed men quickly filing out and following their leader through the gates and into the port.

Sam quickly realised he was looking at the man in charge. The one who had put all of this into motion.

He also drew the conclusion that they were expecting him tonight as there was no chance they would greet the police with such fire power.

Somehow, they knew that Sam was on his way, he was sure of it and that spelt danger for Jasmine. If they knew Sam was tracking them, then they would have soon realised why. With the bleak future laid out for the poor girls confined to one of those containers, Sam could only imagine the punishment Jasmine would suffer if Sam was unable to bring her out.

It didn't bear thinking about.

Inside Sam's pocket, the phone vibrated. Sam held his breath.

A message from an unknown number glowed brightly, luring Sam to his fate like a crooked finger. Sam swiped to the side to view it.

Lot 21235. Bay 64. Zone C.

Sam committed the location to memory and then slammed the burner phone to the ground below, watching the device shatter into a thousand shards. Beyond the fence, the rising sound of fury echoed off the thin, metal clad corridors of the port. Etheridge had wiped the location as soon as it had arrived, his hope of it giving Pope a head start had been fruitful. The algorithm would soon relay it back to the gang, but for now, they were searching for a needle in a haystack, while Sam was ready to zoom in like a homing missile. The odds were still shorter than he would have liked, but he thought back to his entire career, the number of shootouts he had been involved in overseas. Both High Rises.

Sooner or later, Sam knew that Lady Luck would pull the rug from underneath him. As with any form of gambling, the house always wins. But as he stood outside the port, the rain crashing against him, he knew he had to gamble one more time.

A young girl's life was at stake.

Sam reached to his side and grabbed hold of his rifle, pulling it around his body and allowing it to slip seamlessly into his grip. His fingers slid around the stock, one of them naturally falling onto the trigger. With a rifle in his hand, Sam was the deadliest weapon in the country.

The Takers were about to find that out first hand.

The commotion beyond the nearest stacks of containers grew loudly and Sam heard a series of crunching thuds, as if someone was being bludgeoned by something. Whoever it was, they'd messed up and Sam had a clear indication of the type of man he was dealing with.

There would be no negotiating. Not with these people.

Sam needed to make use of his head start, get in, get Jasmine, and get out.

Anything else, and he would have to break his promise once more, something that was happening with an alarming regularity. Sam took a deep breath and reached for the fence, pulling it away from the heavy, rust covered chain that attached it to the next panel. It budged a little, creating a small, uncomfortable gap for Sam to squeeze himself through. Just as he lowered himself to pass under the mighty links of the chain, a blue light lit up the horizon line. Flashing like a mobile disco, Sam felt his heart drop as a convoy of police cars and vans turned the far corner, racing towards the port like a heroic cavalry. Without their sirens, there was a morbid silence to their arrival that only added to the tension that was drifting through the downpour.

Sam's odds had just doubled.

The first two cars pulled to a stop to the side of the gate, a number of officers leaping from the car and taking positions against the barrier. Two vans pulled up, the back doors shoved open and two teams, armed with assault rifles and bulletproof suits leapt out, all of them following strict orders and forming a tight line, ready to go at the drop of a hand.

Sam wondered if somewhere among them Singh was barking out orders, her tiny frame juxtaposed by her ferocious leadership and will to succeed. On some level, he admired her, knowing what it was like to live an ideal. To run your life by a moral code that you fully believe was for the good of the people.

It was something they had in common. It was the line of the law that lay between them.

After a few moments, Sam heard the first gunshot, the Takers had realised they had unwanted guests and had opened fire on the boys in blue.

The police took up their positions and the incoming shoot-out was just moments away.

Another war zone that Sam was willingly walking into.

Sam's window of opportunity was dwindling, and before he could identify Singh in the crowd, he slipped through the gate and into the port, out of sight of the police, but under a watchful pair of eyes from the ninth floor of the clock tower.

CHAPTER TWENTY-SIX

Aaron Hill was shaking as Singh sat him down in the interview room earlier that evening. The man looked like a wreck, the last day or so weighing heavily on him. Singh had only been to see him the day before, yet he seemed to have aged drastically. Something must have happened, a horrible ordeal that had led him from being defiant about his business with Sam Pope, to knocking on her front door begging for help.

She had brought him a glass of water, and with watery eyes he told her everything. How Sam had been blazing a path through the London underworld to find his daughter and how now, with time running out, was running head on into a no-win situation to find her. While he would never condone the carnage Sam had created, he was thankful that Sam did what the police didn't.

He gave a damn.

When Singh tried to counter that statement, she was reminded of her own reaction when he first reported it. She had dismissed him as a drunk waste of time, caring more about her own career than the life of a teenager. It cut her deep, but she took it on the chin. She had made plenty of mistakes, but she was eager to put them right. While Sam did what the police didn't, she assured Hill that if he cooperated with her, she could deliver what Sam couldn't.

His daughter.

Battling with his own sense of betrayal, Hill had done what any good father would have done and put his daughter first. Despite his intentions, Sam Pope was still a dangerous criminal who had the means to cause serious damage to a lot of people. He would no doubt fight to the death for Jasmine, but Hill agreed that the full back up of the Metropolitan Police would lower the odds.

If it meant it would increase the chance of saving his daughter from a life of drugs, prostitution, and death then Sam was a sacrifice he would make.

Even Sam himself would understand, especially after what he had been through.

When Hill had made that remark, Singh had been confused and made a note to investigate later.

Was there something about Sam she didn't know? It was unlikely, considering her task of bringing him in was slowly becoming an obsession and being face to face with him but incapacitated had driven her to the edge.

She was determined to put it right and when Hill had told her where Sam was heading, she burst out of the room like she'd just found the last golden ticket.

She raced through the station, her little legs bounding the steps two at a time until she burst into Assistant Commissioner Ashton's office, earning a furious glare and a dressing down.

She didn't care.

It was her time.

When she explained everything, her superior had demanded to speak to Hill herself, stomping down the corridors with Singh in tow. A few minutes later, she gave the order for two tactical teams to head for the Port of Tilbury and that she would accompany them.

Singh was ordered to stay put.

As the sirens and lights burst into life and the Sam Pope Task Force raced towards his final showdown, Singh sat dejectedly in the interview room. Hill thanked her for her help and asked where he should wait. It was then that a new purpose bloomed in her.

This was her task force.

She looked up at Hill and smiled.

'You want your daughter back, right?' He nodded. 'Then get your coat.'

Forty minutes later, Singh and Hill were slowly crawling down a side road next to the Port of Tilbury, having broken several traffic laws in the process. She didn't care anymore, the chance to apprehend Sam and set everything right was driving her forward. An insatiable need to win.

Amara Singh didn't fail.

With her licensed firearm secured in her hand, she told Hill to wait in the car, slowly creeping out and along the side of the fence, casting an eye down the street to the tactical unit assembling in front of the gate. With her vision skewed, she decided to climb up a nearby industrial bin, trying to see over the nearest metal container.

She saw a luxury car and a group of men around it. One of them looked familiar, his expensive clothes doing little to cloak the sheer menace within. Just as she realised it was Andrei Kovalenko, one of the most dangerous men in London, two of his armed goons opened fire at the gateway, unloading half a clip from their automatic rifles at the police.

Her comrades.

As the adrenaline pumped through her like a house anthem, she paid little heed to the threat before her and clambered onto the top of the container and into the port. She slowly slid along the top, careful not to alert anyone to her presence.

As more gunfire rang out, she abandoned her quest for stealth and reached the edge of the container. The drop down was a sizeable nine feet, and she draped her legs over the side, turned and lowered herself down. As she did, her fingers slipped on the slick metal and she scrambled to keep hold. Her feet clanged hard against the metal and she dropped, taking the impact in her bent knees. Someone yelled out and through the torrential rain, she caught a glimpse of a burly man racing towards her, gun raised. A second gun man soon followed.

She turned and ran into the metal maze, cursing herself for running headfirst into a war zone.

There was no backing out now.

She needed to fight.

As she ventured further into the labyrinth, she knew they wouldn't stop until they had her.

That wasn't an option.

Rounding the next corner, she stopped and threw her back against the corrugated iron wall of the crate. She held her gun to her chest and took a few deep breaths.

Amara Singh didn't fail.

———

Sam had moved through the narrow walkways of the port, rifle held up at eye level, the stock comfortably pressed into the crevice of his shoulder muscle. Every corner was well scouted and he progressed further into the maze, the sound of the gunfight echoing in every direction like a stray bullet.

Sam approached an opening at the end of the passage-way, stepping out into the darkness, a lone floodlight illuminating the loading area. The rain was crashing down with a thunderous rage and Sam glanced at the sign.

Bay 26. Zone A.

Sam took another step forward, when from the dark corner of the opening, a bright light burst, followed by the echo of gunfire. The bullet hit Sam directly in the chest, a few inches below his scar. Spinning in the air, Sam crashed to the concrete, the impact into his Kevlar vest driving the air from him.

He lay still.

Footsteps splashed on the wet floor.

A hunter coming to claim his kill.

As the footsteps got closer, Sam's instincts told him that the man was raising the gun again, a second bullet of confirmation was soon heading his way. In one fluid motion, Sam swivelled on the wet concrete, his hand releasing the Glock from its shoulder holster and he lifted it through the illuminated rain drops.

He saw the man's eyes widen with a mixture of shock and fear.

That was replaced with pain as Sam unloaded two bullets from the handgun, both of them ripping through the man's chest like wet tissue paper.

The man collapsed, his final breaths struggling to leave his body as he wheezed, staring vacantly at the rain as the puddles around him soon turned red. Sam stood, wincing as he stretched his chest out, when another henchman raced into the clearing, drawn by the gunshots like a moth to a flame.

Sam spun quickly on his heels and slammed his back against the container next to his attacker's entranceway. As the splashes echoed louder off of the metal, the man darted through the opening towards his fallen friend. In a flash, Sam reached out and grabbed the man's collar, wrenching him backwards and off balance. Before the man could react, Sam struck a crunching blow with the grip of his pistol right between the man's eyes, shutting his lights out and leaving him in a collapsed heap on the floor.

Sam swung up his rifle once more, carefully stepped into the walkway, and ventured further into the unknown. Passing into *Zone B* Sam halted as two flashes flickered at the end of the corridor, before an armed officer dived recklessly into the walkway, a barrage of bullets whipping inches above him and into the giant storage container. The young officer tried to scramble back to his feet, but soon accepted his fate as two more armed henchmen stormed around the corner with an unquenchable blood lust.

Sam instinctively pulled the trigger.

The first bullet cut through the dark walkway, slicing through rain drops before ripping into the throat of the first henchman, severing the jugular vein in a stunning outburst of blood. The henchman collapsed to his knees, hands clasped to the wound as blood seeped through his fingers and he fell before the officer who tried to crawl away.

The second guard raised his handgun in Sam's general direction, shooting blindly into the dark. Sam had already dropped to one knee to change his position and a bullet soon imbedded itself into the man's stomach. As he stumbled back pressing his hands to the wound, a follow-up bullet to the chest sent him sprawling.

The officer pushed himself to his knees, splattered with the blood of the two men Sam had just eliminated. Reaching for his own gun as Sam approached, the officer was in self-preservation mode, having come so close to death. He raised it at Sam, who stepped forward, the young man realising that the very reason they were there was the same reason he was alive. The officer tipped back his helmet, revealing his youthful face and looked his saviour in the eye and nodded his appreciation.

Sam reciprocated.

The officer had no intention of stopping Sam, not when he owed him his life.

Sam plundered on, stepping over the now dead bodies in the walkway and approached the entrance.

Two officers lay motionless under the floodlights, their bodies riddled with bullets and Sam felt guilty for being a few minutes too late. He had avenged them, but seeing officers die in the line of duty was always hard to take, regardless of what line of the law you walked. As he squatted next to them and shared a silent moment of respect, two more officers burst into the clearing, one of them trying to reload his rifle while the other was marching backwards, gun aimed into the darkness of the walkway.

The rain was playing havoc with any visibility, and the officer on guard didn't see the two men on the metal walkway above the containers, their rifles aimed down at them.

Like shooting fish in a barrel.

A gunshot exploded behind the officers, followed swiftly by another.

Both men flopped over the edge of the walkway and to the hard concrete fifteen feet below. They were dead before they hit the floor.

Sam Pope had aimed for the head.

He didn't miss.

As the officer spun on his heel, his gun still up, Sam drove his own rifle into the officer's gut, disarming him before flipping him over onto the concrete. The second officer reloaded his rifle, but Sam aimed his own at the officer's head.

'Drop it.'

The officer obliged and Sam motioned for him to move next to his fallen comrade, who was gingerly pushing himself to his knees. As they regrouped having come seconds from death, the two officers looked across at their fallen comrades and realised how lucky they'd been.

Sam ventured into the darkness of the walkway from whence they'd run, only stopping as he caught a glimpse of the sign ahead.

Zone C.

———

As the footsteps approached with impending doom, Singh realised she was holding her breath. As the first gangster stepped out from the walkway and straight past her, she kept her composure, ensuring she kept deathly quiet. A moment later, his comrade followed, a heavy assault rifle in his arms.

'Police. Drop your weapons,' Singh commanded, stepping up behind him and pointing her own gun in his direction. The man held his hands up, turning slowly with a sadistic smile on his face. He was a broad man, with a thick physique and a unibrow that slithered across his beady, grey eyes. Singh kept the gun pointed on him, but with the rain obscuring her vision, struggled to see the first gunman.

She took her eye off him for one second.

The man dropped his rifle and lunged forward reaching for her gun, his powerful fingers snatching at her wrist. Singh rocked backwards, her boots slipping in the rain and her finger squeezed the trigger.

The echo of the gunshot in the metal confines was almost deafening.

The roar of pain from her attacker equally so.

The bullet tore through the man's shoulder, a clean shot that had passed right through. With blood pumping from the wound, the man yelled aggressively in Ukrainian before lunging at Singh, his heavy fists fallen down like the hammer of god.

Singh dodged the first blow, the man's flat knuckles cracking the concrete with a bone breaking thud.

The second blow caught her hard on the side of the head, a high pitch ringing drilled into her brain. Her vision went bright and she quickly regained composure, ducking the follow-up strike and reached up and thumped the man in his fresh bullet wound.

He fell back in pain and Singh arched her back and planted both boots as hard as she could into his granite-like chest.

The man doubled over onto his back, but as Singh tried to get to her feet, the second man slipped his hands under her arms and wrenched her up off the ground, using considerable strength to hurl her recklessly to the side. She collided with the metal container, her lip splitting on impact and it took everything in her not to fall to the floor. The man approached and as he reached out for her, she spun to her left, drilling a vicious kick to the side of the man's knee, knocking him off balance. Quickly, she grabbed his hair and with her full force, drove him face first into the metal.

The explosion of blood from his broken nose was like a grenade and he limply dropped to the ground, dabbing at his shattered face with fear in his eyes. Singh readjusted and turned back to her first attacker who had risen to his feet, his bullet-ridden arm swung loosely from his body.

His eyes were wide with murderous rage.

She raised her fists and as he approached, she blocked his wild swing, before catching him with two swift hooks to the kidneys, ducking another erratic fist and lunged forward, driving her knee into his stomach. As he hunched over, gasping for air, she searched the glistening concrete for her weapon.

Any weapon.

A sickening thud was closely followed by a searing pain

in the back of her skull and Singh slumped forward. The henchman with the broken nose adjusted his grip on the rifle, the collision of its stock with her head had nearly driven it from her hands. Singh woozily pushed herself up onto her hands and knees, her brain felt like it had been shunted loose. Her vision was blurry, and the freezing rain splashed over her entire body.

As she reached feebly for her handgun, a large boot pressed down on her forearm, the weight of it testing her bone strength. One of the men then reached down and lifted her gun from the floor.

Singh knew she was defeated.

Her head throbbed and Singh forced herself to look upwards, determined to look her killer in the eyes. She may have failed, but she would never cower. She had fought through too much in her life, beaten every obstacle that had been thrown in front of her. She had never backed down and now, as she lay on the soaking wet concrete of the port, she wanted to look death in the eye before it took her.

With blood dribbling down her lip and her eyes squinting from the throbbing pain in her skull, she locked eyes with the burly man who stared down at her. His face was a crimson mask, the damage she'd caused made her heart swell with pride. Beside him, his comrade grunted his fury, his hand pressed to the bullet wound in his shoulder.

She had gone down fighting.

That was enough.

The man removed his foot from Singh's arm and then raised his rifle, the barrel a mere inch or two from Singh's forehead.

Singh closed her eyes. A myriad of images flashed before her eyes, memories of her childhood leaping through each other like she was whizzing past on a roller coaster. She found herself passing through fond moments of her life, from winning a netball championship in high school to passing out as a policewoman.

A life well-lived.

The man rested his finger on the trigger.

The rain crashed down around her, and Singh felt a sense of calm.

A gunshot rang out.

Singh opened her eyes as the man spun to the side, half of his skull splattering the concrete surrounding her. His wounded companion spun in a blind panic, his one good arm nervously holding her pistol out at the darkness. The body that had crashed next to her was still, blood spilling from the gaping hole in the man's head.

A second shot rang out.

The bullet caught the man between the eyes, whipping through and out the back of his skull in an explosion of blood, brain, and bone. It splattered the concrete like an upturned can of paint, and he was dead before he hit the floor.

Singh tried to regain her thoughts, the blow to her head had scrambled her brain. As she slowly pushed herself to her feet, she heard the purposeful footsteps of her saviour. As the blurring began to subside, she looked out into the clearing at the figure marching through the dimly lit rain, reloading his rifle.

Sam Pope.

Still woozy, she stumbled forward, trying to recover the gun from the dead grip of the recently deceased.

Sam approached quickly.

'Don't even think about it.'

'Sam Pope, you're under arrest. You do not have to say anything…' Singh said, pressing one hand to the back of her head. She pulled it back and thankfully, there was no bleeding.

'Stop it,' Sam ordered. 'Right now, there are bigger things going on here than you and me, have you got that?'

'I'm taking you in,' she said, aware of her own desperation. Her obsession to catch Sam Pope had put her life in danger. She had been seconds from death and at that moment, the shock of what had just happened hit her.

Sam had seen it before many times when he'd served overseas. The first time someone is forced to face their own mortality and still walk away is a harrowing experience.

'Look, you and I can settle up later. But right now, these people have Hill's daughter and goodness knows how many other girls locked in a container. I know where it is but it's not going to be long until they do too.'

Singh took a deep breath and turned to Sam.

'What do you need me to do?'

'I need you to take this and get to that container first.'

Sam smiled warmly and held his hand out, offering his own handgun. A conflict collided in Singh's brain, as the dangerous vigilante she'd become obsessed with catching had not only just saved her life but was placing his trust in her enough to arm her. It annoyed her but he was right, there were bigger things at hand. She gingerly reached out her hand and took the gun, her knuckles aching from the furious punches she'd landed on her now-deceased attackers.

Sam told her the location of the crate before expertly snapping the new clip into his assault rifle. He pulled it up to his chest and began to head towards the pathway Singh had just emerged from, heading directly towards the battle zone.

'Where the hell are you going?' Singh asked, perplexed at her concern for Sam's wellbeing. Without looking back, Sam slowly walked towards the walkway as he responded.

'To buy you some time.'

CHAPTER TWENTY-SEVEN

Mark Harris sat at his desk, his eyes scanning the speech he had commissioned the second he had got off the phone with Assistant Commissioner Ashton. She had informed him that they knew Pope's location, as well as a possible shipment of abducted women. They were heading to put the entire situation to bed and Harris was preparing to milk the situation dry. He had nailed his colours to their mast, promoting the 'Sam Pope Task Force' publicly. After each failure, he himself had shielded the police, taking all the criticism on his perfectly structured chin.

Now it was time to reap the rewards.

The speech spoke of the bravery and dedication of the city's finest officers. He even demanded a credit to DI Singh, despite her failure to get the job done. Harris still maintained a romantic interest in the fiery policewoman and pulling her up from the wreckage would surely work in his favour.

A polished grin flashed across his face as he imagined taking her out for dinner, knowing she would be indebted to him.

Harris always got what he wanted. It was what made

him such a great politician and a shoe-in for the mayor's job. Everything was falling into place and as he finished reading the final line, he decided he had earned a treat.

He pushed himself out of his leather chair and strode across his plush office to his drinks cabinet, rows of expensive liquors all promising sweet inebriation. Harris removed the glass lid of the decanter and the scent of a twenty-year-old single malt Scotch wafted seductively towards him.

A liquid pat on the back.

As Harris tilted the decanter and let the rusty liquid splash into the expensive, crystal tumbler, he wondered whether he should call for Burrows. The man had worked diligently behind the scenes, managing the partnerships with his biggest benefactors. All Harris had to do was smile for pictures. What those companies did or how they impacted the city were of little consequence to him.

The only consequence that mattered was him being sworn in as Mayor of London, and then he would open as many doors for those who had opened them for him. Harris chuckled as he sipped his drink, the warmness tickling his throat as it smoothly slid towards his stomach. The amusing thought was how little he knew of his stuffy assistant. The man was meticulous in how he went about his duties, which Harris found commendable. Any document he needed was always delivered before time, all meetings set, and photo opportunities sussed out. Benefactors donated large sums to the cause, all of which Burrows initiated and had done for the past three mayors to come from Harris's political party.

Burrows had been the one who had strapped the rocket to Harris's back and let him fly up the political ladder. Perhaps, Harris chuckled once more, he would let Burrows have the weekend off.

'Drinking alone?'

A surprising voice snapped Harris back to reality and he turned, startled. Adrian Pearce stepped into the office, his coat soaked through and his hands stuffed deep into the pockets. Harris raised his eyebrows.

'I was. Fancy one?'

'Very kind.' Pearce flashed his warm smile, sliding his arms out from his long jacket and letting the warmth of the room envelope him. The weather had taken a horrible turn, the lashing rain hitting like freezing daggers. He recalled being in the office a few days before, the politician demanding that Pearce help him bring in Sam Pope.

If Harris had been trying to get Pearce onside, he had pushed all the wrong buttons. He wasn't anti-authority by default, but Pearce knew he had a problem with being told what to do. Especially when it didn't follow the chain of command. Harris's infiltration into an almost advisory role with the police was a testament to his gift of the gab and Pearce found it a little disconcerting that the higher ups were pandering to him so much.

It was clear why. The man was the Mayor elect.

It was a formality.

At least it had been.

Harris handed Pearce an identical tumbler and lifted his slightly. Pearce followed suit, gently clinking the glasses together before he took a large swig.

'Whoa,' Harris said smarmily. 'Don't rush it.'

'Long day,' Pearce offered, placing the empty glass back on the drinks shelf before striding back into the centre of the room. Harris frowned, following.

'Is there a reason you're here, detective?' Harris asked rather curtly. 'I'm assuming you didn't pop in just to have a drink with me?'

'I'm afraid not,' Pearce said, looking around the room. 'Question, how long did you think it would take when you were in office, for the press to find out that you're supporting the abduction of young girls?'

Harris spat his Scotch across his desk, the brown liquid splattering the laptop and loose papers.

'Excuse me?'

Pearce turned on his heel, his dark eyes locking onto Harris like a heat-seeking missile and he saw fear in the politician's eye. Pearce had interrogated more men than he cared to remember, and he knew that when he flicked the switch, his charm was swiftly replaced with a quiet fury.

'Let me rephrase that. How long have you been paying money into this bank account?'

Pearce placed a piece of paper on the desk, spun it to face Harris, and pushed it across. Harris looked at it, his eyes wide with horror.

'Burn Group Inc.?' Harris stammered. 'What the fuck is that?'

'Come on, Mark. You're a bright chap. That's the bank account belonging to The Acid Gang. The ones who throw the acid at people. I think you gave a speech about it when you realised it could help your campaign.'

'Fuck you,' Harris spat, his hand shaking as he polished off his Scotch.

'It's also the bank account that receives five grand for every snatched girl, paid by Transcendence Holdings, which, if I'm not mistaken...' Pearce pulled out another sheet of paper and confidently tossed it onto the laptop. 'Is the campaign management company that has your name as the CEO.'

'I don't know anything about this...' Harris began and slumped into his chair, running a nervous hand through his hair. Pearce stepped around the desk and stood before him, feeling the confidence draining from him with every tick of the grand clock on the wall.

'I've connected these dots so you're going to have to

connect a few more, Mark. As this will either be handled behind closed doors or your name will be dragged through the mud, with your entire political career not far behind.'

Harris glared at Pearce with venom in his eyes.

'I have nothing to do with this. Just because you've been shelved and your career is wasting away, you think it gives you the right to threaten me? After everything I've done for this city? Everything I've done to get the people to believe in your beloved Metropolitan Police?'

Harris stood, trying to assert his authority. With one, swift, open-palmed shove, Pearce knocked him back into his seat. Harris looked shocked, the fear at being physically restrained evident. Pearce leaned in close.

'I don't give a flying fuck about your career. Teenage girls are being taken off the streets. Do you understand me? They are being snatched from their lives and sold to some godforsaken hell hole and into a life that would make Satan himself shit his pants. So if I have to rip you and your fucking career into a million pieces to find them and the people responsible, then you can bet every penny in your campaign fund I will. Do you understand me?'

Pearce stepped back, taking a deep breath. He knew his words had shaken the man who was so used to having his ego stroked. Pearce watched as Harris's eyes darted back and forth, the man running every possible outcome to what he had just been told. Pearce watched as Harris broke.

Harris began to cry.

'I don't know anything about this,' he said through sobs. 'I swear. Ask Burrows, he knows how little I get involved with the business side of things. I don't even fucking sign anything.'

Pearce frowned with confusion.

'But this is your signature.'

'It's electronic. They paste it into documents to save

time.' Harris dabbed at his eyes with his sleeve. Pearce rubbed his temple with frustration.

He hated being wrong.

'Who authorises these payments then?'

'The only person who has access and authority to use my signature is Burrows.' Harris had regained a little composure. 'I'm sure he can clear this up.'

Pearce stomped across to the chair and lifted his coat, sliding his arms back into the drenched sleeves as Harris leant forward and pushed the top button on his phone.

The speaker phone beeped to life.

'Carl, can you come in here please?' Harris waited. Pearce was already heading to the door. 'Carl?'

'Don't bother.' Pearce stopped at the doorway, shaking his head with anger. 'He's already gone.'

'Gone? But why?' Almost immediately the realisation hit Harris like a lightning bolt. 'No? Not Carl?'

'I need to find him. Now!' Pearce shouted, turning to leave.

'But what about me? My campaign?' Harris whinged. The self-centred nature made Pearce clench his fists with anger.

'Like I said, I couldn't give a flying fuck.'

With that, Pearce marched back out into the hall, fishing for his police radio to put out the search on Carl Burrows. In his office, Harris slumped into his chair once more, tears flooding his eyes. In a moment of rage, he lifted the crystal tumbler and hurled it across the room, the glass shattering into hundreds of pieces and crashing to the ground.

A horrible similarity to his political career.

He wept.

———

Sam burst out from his dark shadow and into the opening of the port, three of Kovalenko's armed guards instantly raining heavy gunfire in his direction. The barrage of bullets rattled the metal just behind him and he leapt through the rain and crashed down behind a forklift truck. More bullets rattled off the frame work of the vehicle and he readjusted his grip on his rifle, the relentless rain causing it to slip in his hand.

The gunfire would undoubtedly alert more henchmen and armed police.

He was a sitting duck.

As he'd raced through the port, he'd done his best to draw the attention of Kovalenko's men, luring them away from their intended cargo. If all the gunfire was aimed in his direction, then there was none aimed at Singh as she made her way to Jasmine. Beyond the three men was the outer fence, and Sam could see the radio tower.

His back-up plan.

Three more bullets ricocheted off the metal and he knew it wouldn't be long until his time ran out. Sam slipped the magazine from the gun and checked.

Five bullets left.

He snapped it back in and scrambled to his feet, his back pressed against the side of the truck. Somewhere behind, he could hear footsteps slowly splashing in puddles. As he had darted into the clearing, he had clocked the location of the three men, committing to memory their standing points.

He made a logical conclusion as to how far they'd moved by the slowness of their steps slapping the wet concrete.

It was something he had done a number of times when buried deep under cover on a cliff face, his rifle aimed at a moving enemy target. Anticipating the movement was what had made him so deadly.

Anticipation and his clarity of thought. Sam never second-guessed himself and as he spun out from the life-saving cover of the vehicle, he saw that he had been correct. The floodlight above hindered his view, but the three figures were approaching in his anticipated formation, their rifles ready.

One bullet slammed into the metal a few inches from Sam's body.

Sam sent his bullet directly into the shooter's forehead. Spinning on his heel, Sam dropped to one knee as three bullets skimmed past him, the last one grazing the sleeve of his jacket.

Sam unloaded two more. They embedded in the second shooter's chest, lifting him off the ground and two red sprays bursting out of his back and into the rain. The man was dead before he crashed into the ground.

A gunshot rang out.

Sam felt the burning sensation ripple through his left thigh as the metal ripped through his flesh and muscle. The bullet burrowed through and out the other side of his leg, a spray of blood chasing after it. The memories of Project Hailstorm came flooding back, the searing pain of being shot and the feeling of your life escaping your body with every pump of blood.

Sam collapsed to the side, swung his rifle up, and sent his penultimate bullet into his attacker's knee cap. The man screamed in agony as he collapsed forward, and Sam pulled the trigger for the final time.

He watched as the bullet pierced the man's eyeball before blowing out the back of his skull. He collapsed forward, his back arched and blood overflowed from the gaping hole in the back of his head.

Sam groaned with pain as he pushed himself up, pressing his hand firmly against his thigh. He felt the thick, warm blood filter through his fingers, and he tried to run, his leg buckling and he limped unsteadily towards the fence. Behind him, he could hear furious voices screaming commands and the incoming patter of footsteps.

Quicker, Sam.

Every step caused him to wince, but he hobbled through the bloody battlefield and made his way to the fence, falling against the chain-link panel and trying desperately to catch his breath. He could see the flashing sirens further to his right, the final few officers retreating to think up a new strategy. Beyond them, four more SUVs were gunning down the road towards the war zone.

Kovalenko had called for the cavalry.

A bullet clattered the fence post next to Sam and a few more whizzed by. Another band of armed men had flooded the area, all of them training their guns at Sam. Ignoring the pain Sam pushed himself upwards, scaling the fence and dropping to the other side and into the shadows below.

He felt woozy, the blood loss nipping at his consciousness like an over eager puppy.

With painful steps, he hurried across the dark street to the abandoned radio tower, dislodging the wooden panel he had loosened earlier and he slipped in, just as a fresh bout of gunfire polluted the airwaves.

Sam pulled off his jacket as he fell against the wall, ripping the sleeve from the seams and wrapping it around his thigh. He gritted his teeth and pulled it tight, grunting with agony as he stemmed the flow of blood. The makeshift tourniquet quickly stopped the blood oozing out and he took a few moments to catch his breath. His body was screaming for sleep, the blood loss had weakened him nearly to the point of collapse.

But he couldn't.

Jasmine was still in the port and he needed to make sure Singh got to her and got her out.

Sam limped to the stairs, grimacing as he forced himself up, stopping on each floor for a slight bit of respite from the pain. Eventually, he stumbled through the door to the ninth floor, the abandoned control room was a mausoleum of dusty desks and glass screen panels. Part of the roof had been removed, a tribute to the work that had never been completed. The rain crashed through, splattering the desks with freezing water. From the metal beams that had been exposed, a number of chains swung down, some of them with rusty hooks which rattled in the wind.

Sam assumed they were set up as a makeshift winch at some point, but with the renovation clearly abandoned some time ago, they now acted as nothing more than heavy wind chimes.

Sam weaved through the desks to the far window, the glass panel giving a wide view of the port below. Flashes of light drew his attention, machine guns spitting bullets with murderous intent.

The war was still continuing.

In some ways, Sam felt like it had never stopped.

He reached beneath the windowsill for the black sports bag he had stowed there earlier that evening. Inside it, his Accuracy International Arctic Warfare bolt action sniper rifle waited patiently.

Behind him, the chains rattled, and wind whistled through the empty building. The sounds camouflaged the surprisingly soft footsteps of the behemoth, Oleg Kovalenko, as he slowly approached Sam Pope from the shadows.

CHAPTER TWENTY-EIGHT

Oleg Kovalenko had followed Sam the moment he'd left Aaron Hill's house. The opportunity to enter the property and beat the truth out of the civilian had been mooted by his sister, who always seemed to want to hurt people. Dana was so very pretty, but Oleg knew that an evil rested within her.

Not like his brother, Andrei.

Oleg idolised him and obeyed every word. Ever since they were younger, nasty boys had called Oleg names. Despite his size, none of them were scared of Oleg because his brain didn't work as quickly as theirs did. They would hurl abuse at him whenever he was alone, calling him a freak and saying all sorts of horrible things about Dana. Oleg would cry, not knowing why they would hate him so much.

When Andrei found out, he would scream at Oleg to shut them up, to show them how strong he was. Oleg was too afraid, but everything changed after that blood-filled night. Andrei had taken beating after beating from their father, not allowing him near his younger siblings. Oleg knew, that even as a teenager, he was bigger than most fully grown men, but their father terrified him. The man was an animal and Oleg had witnessed him brutally kicking Andrei in the ribs, his older brother coughing up blood but refusing to cry.

He was so brave.

When the time came, and Andrei told both he and Dana that Papa was dead, they knew he had done it for all of them. After that, Oleg promised to always listen to his brother, who had encouraged him to join the army. There, despite his mental limitations, Oleg proved to be a physical specimen beyond most and his lack of compassion made him a cold and calculating killer. Even under extreme torture when the Russian Special Forces melted the left side of his face with a blow torch, Oleg had stayed quiet.

Because his brother had told him to be the best soldier he could be.

It was why, when he joined his brother in London, he followed every order. He had thrown every punch he had been commanded to and he had killed ruthlessly whenever asked. Oleg had tortured, beaten, maimed, and murdered at the behest of his brother. It was a loyalty, bound by blood and the reason why, as he watched Sam Pope stumbled towards the windowsill, he knew he would kill him.

Andrei wanted Pope dead.

So Oleg would kill him without thinking twice.

As he crept forward from the shadows, Oleg felt proud of his ability to hide, the skills he had learnt during his seven years in the army had kept him off of Pope's radar and had taught him what Sam was doing. Sam had placed a weapon here, in case things got out of hand. By the sound of gunfire outside, Oleg realised it had descended into a war zone. He was worried for Andrei, but he knew his brother could take care of himself.

As Pope pulled open the bag, Oleg could see the fabric tightly wrapped around his leg, the left side of his jeans dark with blood. Pope had clearly been shot, and he grunted with pain as he unzipped the bag, the barrel of a sniper rifle visible under the floodlights from outside.

Pope was going to shoot Andrei.

Oleg lunged.

Abandoning his subtlety, the monstrous Ukrainian emerged from the darkness like a demon from the gates of hell. Sam turned just in time, his eyes wide with shock as the mutilated face snarled at him, two massive hands reaching out and grabbing him by the lapels of his jacket.

Sam felt his left leg buckle, and the man crashed his solid, charred skull into his face, the blow snapping Sam's head back and sending his entire brain into a whirlwind. Oleg swung Sam by his jacket, crashing the side of his head against the metal window frame before hurling him back into the room, Sam stumbling back until his injured leg crashed into the side of a dusty desk. He cried in pain as he flipped over the wood and crashed to the hard floor below, willing himself back to his feet.

The man mountain stormed around the desk, reached down and grabbed Sam by his shoulder, but as Sam found his balance, he dropped his shoulder and tipped the large man over his head. He crashed through the desk, but instantly got to his feet.

All it did was piss him off more.

The man threw a few punches that Sam blocked with his arms, each impact crashing into his muscles like a sledgehammer. The man was a trained fighter, but his size and strength advantage was something unlike Sam had ever experienced. As the man landed a sickening thump into Sam's ribs, he thought back to the brawl he had experienced with Mark Connor in the High Rise. The vicious East End gangster, affectionately known as one of the Mitchell Brothers had fought him to the death, the two men beating each other to a pulp until Sam had lodged a knife into the man's eye and then through to his brain.

This would be different.

As Sam stumbled backwards from the blow, he collided with the wall behind. His huge attacker launched forward at full force, driving his fist straight for Sam's face. At the last second, Sam ducked, his leg slightly buckling and the man's knuckles cracked into the plaster, puncturing the wall and colliding with brick work.

The bones cracked.

The man didn't react.

Oleg retracted his hand and used his left to grab Sam by the throat, pulling him back up to his feet. As Sam rained hard punches down on his monstrous face, Oleg felt the trickle of blood from a gash above his burnt eye.

He reacted by grabbing Sam's left leg with his right hand, digging his fingers into the fresh bullet wound. Sam roared with pain, but the man tightened his grip around his throat, choking the pain right out of his voice.

Then, in a display of terrifying strength, he spun, lifting Sam off of the ground and hurling him through one of the glass screens that was embedded in the wall. Sam smashed through the divide, collapsing into a pit of sharp, broken shards that punctured into him like a pin cushion.

The tourniquet had come loose on his leg and he could feel the blood begin to ooze to freedom, taking his energy and chances of survival with them. Sam began to crawl through the broken glass, the shards slicing his skin. He thought of Jasmine somewhere below, locked in a crate and what her life would be with monsters like this man.

The drugs. The abuse. The rape.

He couldn't let another child's life be ended by his inability to act.

He couldn't save his Jamie.

He had to save Jasmine.

Sam heard the crunch of glass behind him, the heavy footsteps stamping the glass to dust. Above him, Sam heard the jangle of the chains, the rain slipping in through the gap in the roof and splashing against his face.

A hand reached down and grabbed the back of his collar and Sam was hoisted from the ground. He scrambled in the glass and as Oleg turned him around to deliver another bone-crunching strike, Sam slammed his fist into the chest. The man's eyes widened with agony as Sam stumbled back, the shard of glass embedded deep into the side of the man's pectoral. Blood began to spill out from around the sides of the wound.

It only provoked him.

The man stormed forward, cracking Sam with two, hard, right hooks before wrapping both hands around his throat and hoisting him clean off the ground. Sam began to choke, his eyes watering and straining from his head, his feeble kicks having no impact. He could feel his life ebbing away, the immortal fingers of death beckoning him towards the afterlife.

It would be easy just to let it all go.

The war would finally be over.

As Sam began to fade, he saw flashes of his life dart before his eyes, ending on his wife walking away from him, disappearing into a field of whiteness. A voice caused his head to look downwards.

His son. Jamie.

'Not yet, Daddy.'

Sam's eyes opened, and with a renewed vigour, he hammered at the thick, tree-like arms of Oleg, who snarled crookedly. The man was a cold-blooded killer, and Sam was moments away from being another successful encounter.

Sam scrambled and his hand reached out and grabbed a metal chain. Instinctively, he wrapped some of it around

the thick, triangular neck of his attacker and Oleg, realising Sam was fighting back, pressed his fingers deeper into
Sam's larynx.

Sam was seconds from passing out.

With the chain wrapped around Oleg's throat, Sam
used the last of his energy to wrap his fingers around the
rusty hook that hung from the end of it.

Darkness began to blur the edges of his vision.

He swung his arm with all the strength he could
muster.

The hook rammed into the soft flesh beneath Oleg's
chin, the hook bursting up into his mouth and embedding
in its roof.

Oleg's grip instantly loosened, and Sam reached out
and snatched a handful of chains as he dropped, clattering
to the floor in agony. As he fell, he pulled the chain taut,
lifting Oleg off the ground, the metal links around his
throat tightening. As his feet kicked in panic, the blood
burst from his mouth and cascaded down his throat like a
crimson waterfall.

As his airwaves were choked, his lungs filled up with
blood and Sam held on tightly, watching as the gargantuan
attacker drowned on his own blood.

Oleg stopped kicking.

Sam fell back, releasing the metal. Oleg crashed to the
floor, dead and Sam used the nearby desk to pull himself
to his feet. He could barely stand; the bullet wound was
still pumping blood, and he reattached his makeshift
tourniquet to see him through. The man's grip had
certainly done some damage to his throat, and his body
ached from the cuts and bruises.

He looked like hell and felt like he had been dragged
arse backwards through it.

As he stumbled to the window, he collapsed to the floor,
his body buckling under its injuries. He hauled himself

across the floor, leaving behind a smear of blood like a dying slug.

He needed to stay alive.

At least until they'd freed Jasmine.

With the evidence of their fight to the death behind him, Sam reached for his bag, his fingers finding his rifle.

———

Andrei had been furious as the location of his container had been scrambled. Dmitri, the superintendent at the port who had implemented the system, had promised him it would help to evade the watchful eyes of the authorities. If they couldn't pinpoint their own shipments until the moment of delivery, how could the authorities?

Dmitri had met them as they arrived, assuring Andrei his shipment was well protected and that he had hired ten heavies to patrol the port.

Sam Pope had been followed to the port by Oleg. It meant he was going to try to stop the shipment, which was something Andrei couldn't allow. Ever since he had suggested the move to the UK to their uncle Sergei, Andrei had never missed a shipment. He had ruled with an iron fist, he had ordered a lot of pain and torture and been responsible for a lot of death.

All in the name of business.

As soon as Dmitri reported that the location had been hacked and scrambled, Andrei had put a bullet in the man's head. He reviled incompetence and the man's solution to their problem had backfired.

Andrei demanded his own men filter out into the port, team up with the hired guns already patrolling, and call for further backup. The shipment would be going out as scheduled and he would make his way to Zone C, the usual location. From there, he would need to wait for the system to resend the location of his shipment. It would be the final time he would use it, the idea of spending a small fortune on a cleaner system had become unbearably preferable. As Andrei had headed towards Zone C, a series of gun blasts echoed out behind him and he watched in horror as armed police began to enter the port through the gate.

His men had engaged and now, despite his insistence on professionalism and subtlety, they were locked in a gun fight with the police themselves.

Andrei decided then that he would escape with the shipment, demanding the captain of the boat take him to his uncle and they could rethink. Prison wasn't scary to a man as powerful and as cutthroat as Andrei, but it was time consuming. The moment he stepped away from the table, there would be a power-hungry upstart ready to take his seat.

Andrei ruled over the human trafficking in London and he wasn't ready to relinquish his throne.

Entering Zone C, he walked slowly through the dark corridors, the containers stacked high and casting ominous shadows across his path. A few floodlights loomed over the port, their beams of light fogged by the relentless downpour. The echo of rain danced around him like chattering teeth, intermittently broken by the explosion of gunshots from somewhere behind him.

He didn't care.

His phone buzzed and he smiled evilly.

Lot 21235. Bay 64. Zone C.

Looking up at the nearest sign, Andrei could see he was only ten bays from where he needed to be. He broke into a quick jog, his drenched suit chafing against his thighs. It didn't matter, the adrenaline of getting away with the shipment and his freedom consumed him and he raced through the final few walkways until he emerged into a large opening. The floodlights burst down like a raging sun, illuminating the crates before him.

Bay 64.

With measured steps, he approached the blue crate emblazoned with the Transcendence logo. The senior official working with the Mayor-elect had worked diligently to ensure the waterways were clear. Andrei's donation to Harris's campaign had been sizeable and kept secret from the man himself. The man would be mayor within the next month and Andrei knew having evidence that he had been in cahoots with his executive would make him a very powerful man.

It would open other avenues and would be extremely helpful when he needed to return to the country. With his men opening fire on the police, Andrei knew he would join Sam Pope on their list of most wanted men.

All he hoped for was that one of the men on the receiving end of those gunshots was Pope himself.

Andrei approached the front of the container, the small keypad slick with rain water.

A timer was counting down on the small screen, the red numbers informing him he had just over two minutes before the lock would disengage and he would be able to view his merchandise. Once he had inspected the girls hadn't been abused, he would usually give the team the go-ahead to transport them to the ship and begin the short voyage back to their homeland.

This time, he wouldn't be giving orders. He would be the merchandise itself.

If he got bored on the trip, maybe he could even experience the girls for himself. He chuckled at his own twisted version of quality control.

Behind him, the safety latch of a gun clicked.

'Don't move.'

Singh's word were laced with menace and she stepped

a few feet closer, narrowing the twenty feet gap between them. Andrei turned slowly, his piercing blue eyes were wild with excitement. He raised his hands in the air, refusing the temptation to reach for the gun inside his jacket. The woman before him wore a furious scowl, but she was fiercely attractive. Her slim, defined frame was evident through her drenched clothes and her brown skin added an exotic beauty.

Andrei smiled.

'How do you think this ends for you?' he asked, his thick accent carrying every word.

'Open the crate,' Singh demanded, taking a few steps to the side, her arms straight ahead, her eye trained on the sight of the pistol.

'I do not want you to be killed,' Andrei said, a sudden confidence taking over him. 'But my men do.'

Singh glanced over her shoulder and felt her heart drop. Behind her, four men approached, their rifles trained on her chest. They walked with the practised symmetry of an elite military squad and Singh realised she was out of options. As they approached, Andrei pulled out a gold-plated Bowie knife, tossing it up and down in his hand, feeling its weight. It had been cleaned since he'd murdered Peterson with it, and now the shiny blade shimmered under the floodlights.

'You kill me, and you'll have the entire Met after you,' Singh said defiantly. 'You don't just kill a detective and get away with it.'

'I don't want to kill you,' Andrei said, a cruel grin across his face. 'But after you join me on my trip home and I'm finished with you, you will wish that I had.'

Singh felt her heart race, the claustrophobic feel of her captors closing in caused her hand to shake. She was outnumbered, outgunned, and had no way out. The man would take her, do god knows what to her and then probably sell her into the same deplorable life as the teenage girls behind the metal door.

Singh knew she was screwed, but she refused to lower her weapon, even as Andrei approached.

Behind her, the men stopped, the four of them fanning out to cover her from all angles, all of them ready to unload an automatic burst that would wipe her out.

Andrei's eyes twinkled with a demonic delight as he stepped nearer, his hand gripping the knife tightly.

Singh felt her finger twitch on the trigger.

Amara Singh didn't fail.

A booming gunshot shook across the port like a roar of thunder and then one of the armed men behind her flew across the ground, his skull exploding by the velocity of the bullet that had been sent crashing through him. Andrei startled, hopping back a couple of steps before he angrily screamed something in his native tongue.

All three men turned their guns to the shadows of the port, the rain and darkness shielding their attacker.

They scanned helplessly.

Another explosion echoed through the air and another one of the armed guards fell backwards, the top of his skull instantly turned to paint.

As Andrei panicked, the timer behind him beeped and the lock of the metal crate swung open with a mighty clunk.

At the top of the abandoned tower that overlooked the port, Sam expelled a considerable amount of effort to pull the chamber back, exposing the empty shell casing of the bullet he had just fired.

With one eye planted against the scope, he watched as Singh chased Andrei towards the opening crate, as the two other men nervously aimed their guns in different directions.

He reloaded.

CHAPTER TWENTY-NINE

Every gunshot sent a shiver racing down Aaron Hill's spine, as he sat in the passenger seat of DI Singh's car. Every time one of the blasts echoed through the air, it hit him like a gut punch. Every shot sent a fresh memory to the forefront of his mind as he recounted how far his life had unravelled.

Bang.

The intense panic when he realised his daughter had been taken.

Bang.

Stupidly buying a gun and staggering drunk into a criminal hot spot.

Bang.

A gun being pointed at his head by Elmore Riggs, followed swiftly by the man's head exploding.

Bang.

Sam Pope saving his life.

Bang.

Stupidly pointing a gun at Sam and trying to force him to kill a teenage kid.

Every gunshot was like a reminder and Aaron felt sick.

Somewhere in the vast, metal maze before them, his daughter was waiting. He couldn't bring himself to imagine the state she was in. Had they beaten her? Or worse? All he wanted, was to wrap his arms around his daughter once again. Nothing else mattered anymore and although he felt guilty for giving Sam up to the police, he knew he had stacked the deck in Jasmine's favour. He watched as the armed police regrouped and entered, their rifles flashing like cameras as they unloaded rounds of bullets into the unseen enemy.

Aaron felt himself shaking, knowing that he was sitting on his arse doing nothing.

Sam Pope had fought and killed to find his daughter.

DI Singh had potentially thrown her career away to make sure she was brought back safely.

Sitting still wasn't enough.

Aaron threw open the car door and stepped out into the torrential rain. Glancing up and down the road, he didn't care who had seen him. He ran to the fence and began to climb, reciting his daughter's name as he battled the slippery metal structure and his chronic fear of heights. As he made his way across the metal container, he took deep breaths as he lowered himself down and dropped to the wet concrete below.

The gunshots would guide him and as he wandered further into the dark, deadly war zone in search of his daughter, he realised just how far he would go for her. With careful steps, he continued onwards into the dark.

———

The final henchman spun in the air, the left side of his chest ripped open by the velocity of Sam Pope's final shot. The man fell face down, dead as a door nail and the pool of blood quickly seeping outwards like an unstoppable wave. It quickly joined the puddle forming around the head of the third guard, which Sam had eviscerated with pinpoint accuracy.

Singh had heard the final two shots but not seen the impact, knowing full well that survival was unlikely.

Sam Pope didn't miss.

That much was clear.

Her heart pounded against her chest and her lungs burned as she sprinted to the large, dark opening of the container, her gun raised in front of her. Andrei had reached the threshold a few moments before, allowing the darkness to envelope him. From the horrifying blackness, Singh heard the terrified screams of the teenage girls and stopped in her tracks.

The vulgar smell of a weeks' worth of waste filtered out of the crate and a few seconds later, Andrei emerged. His right arm was wrapped around the thin waist of a teenage girl, her ribs prominently showing after a week of near starvation. Her dark hair was greasy and matted and her eyes were red from crying. A few bruises were visible on her arms and legs, the brown edges indicating they were on the mend.

Singh knew it was Jasmine Hill. Her doting, desperate father had shown her the photos before he had disobeyed her direct orders.

She screamed for help, her eyes squinting at the first sign of light for days, and Andrei wrenched her towards him.

In his other hand, he held the knife.

'Let her go,' Singh yelled, her arms aching but holding firm. The sight of her gun was aimed directly at his chest.

'Put down the weapon or I will slice her fucking throat,' Andrei screamed, his words alive with fury. There was nowhere to go.

A man with nothing to lose.

The most dangerous kind.

Singh kept her weapon trained on him. She carefully took a step closer, and he lifted the blade, placing the sharp edge against the pale, gaunt throat of Jasmine who froze with fear.

'I mean it,' Andrei yelled, his words crazed. 'I'll carve her open right now.'

Singh relented, opening up her hands and letting the pistol swing around her finger. She stared at Andrei with hatred before looking at the terrified Jasmine.

'Jasmine. I'm DI Singh,' she said calmly. 'I'm here with your father.'

'Dad?' Her voice croaked.

'Yes. I'm going to take you to him.'

'She stays with me,' Andrei barked, pressing the knife firmly into her neck. The tip broke the skin and Jasmine cried out as a line of blood dribbled down her chest.

'Let her go,' Singh ordered. 'Let her go and we can work this out.'

Andrei's eyes widened with fear as, through the darkness, the armed police officers emerged, having successfully taken down or arrested the rest of his men. They stepped out from the shadows, their helmets and vests soaked through and they all trained their rifles in the direction of the standoff.

A woman strode forward, her seniority as clear as his own and Andrei glared at Assistant Commissioner Ashton. With her rain coat wrapped around her shoulders and a plastic cap over her own hat, she raised her megaphone.

'DI Singh. Stand down,' she commanded. 'Stand down or you will be arrested.'

'I can't do that, Ma'am,' Singh yelled over her shoulder. 'Not until he lets her go.'

'DI Singh, this is a direct order.'

Singh ignored her superior, knowing full well she was

271

flushing her promising career down the drain. As much as she'd obsessed with catching Sam Pope, she'd realised that it was driven by their similarity. He did what was needed to help people. While she would never condone taking the law into her own hands, she realised now that Jasmine's life was worth more to her than her sparkling reputation.

Andrei's eyes were manic, darting from rifle to rifle that was trained on him. Singh knew it was only a matter of seconds before something tipped him over the edge.

Something would cause him to snap. The man was a powerful criminal who would not bow nor bend over for anyone.

He would kill Jasmine and follow her swiftly to the afterlife.

She needed to act.

Just as she went to flick her hand back around the pistol that swung from her raised hand, that very reason Singh was dreading appeared. Through the rain-soaked metal corridors emerged Aaron Hill, stepping out behind the armed officers and he followed their aim towards the situation ahead.

He saw four dead bodies, all of them ripped open by an unstoppable force.

He saw Singh, standing with her hands up.

Then he saw her.

Jasmine.

The barbaric man who clutched at her with tattooed fingers held a knife to her throat, his other hand wrapped around her waist as she feebly struggled for freedom. Aaron felt the magnetic pull of parenthood, his need to be with his daughter causing his feet to pick up speed.

He raced past the armed officers and their superior officer, who barked something at him.

Probably an order to stop.

He ignored it. As he got within twenty feet, he screamed her name.

'Jasmine!'

Singh turned and looked over her shoulder, her wide eyes warning Aaron to stay back. As he raced forward, Andrei realised that the moment had arrived and that his final stand had begun.

In Singh's mind, everything slowed down.

As Aaron raced towards his daughter and her captor in slow motion, she spun and launched forward, hoping to get to Jasmine first. Andrei readjusted, his fingers tightening their grip, and he lifted the knife for leverage, before bringing it down towards Jasmine's throat.

Singh watched as the blade sliced through the rain drops, the blade millimetres from ending the young girl's life.

A gunshot echoed.

The rush of wind that followed the bullet whipped past everyone and in a horrifying instant, the impact hit Andrei directly in the right shoulder. The explosion of blood and ligament erupted forward and his right arm fell to the floor, the shot severing his arm completely. The knife clattered out of his hand as it hit the floor and Jasmine screamed before racing past Singh.

Andrei paled, the shock of the severance dominating the pain and Singh raced the final few steps, knowing full well Ashton and her officers were quickly approaching.

With all her might, she swung and rocked Andrei with the hardest punch she'd ever thrown. His nose broke instantly and he fell backwards to the wet concrete, his body shaking with pain. As she shook the impact from her hand, Singh turned towards the open container.

———

Through his scope, Sam watched Singh shut Andrei Kovalenko's lights out and couldn't help but smile. The woman was a relentless pain in his arse, but he admired her tenacity.

With extreme discomfort, he swept to the right and he felt the hairs on his arm lift as Jasmine's bare feet slapped against the concrete, carrying her far away from her captor. A few feet away, a weeping Aaron raced towards her and Sam felt his heart stop as she leapt forward.

Aaron caught her, wrapping his arms around his daughter and falling to his knees. Sam watched as the man stroked her hair, holding her as tight as possible. Although Sam would never hold his own son again, he felt no envy for Aaron's reunion.

He felt proud.

Proud that he had ripped the city apart to find the littlest details to get her back, to save her from a terrifying future. As he watched Aaron and Jasmine hold each other, he smiled, wishing them the very best and hopeful that she would be able to recover from her ordeal.

Jasmine had been through hell and come out the other side. She had a father who was willing to run head first into the abyss for her.

Sam smiled once more before sweeping his scope once more to the container. Four of the armed officers stood guard, as the others rushed in with foil blankets, wrapping them around the shoulders of the malnourished girls they were escorting out. While they were not greeted by their fathers, Sam knew the police would return them to their families and do whatever they could to ensure it never happened again.

As the pain from his injuries flared, and he gritted his teeth, he swore he would do the same.

Watching Andrei writhing in agony on the floor as two

paramedics tended to his missing arm, Sam knew he was just the delivery man.

Sam needed the head of the snake.

Knowing his work was far from finished, Sam pushed himself to his feet and lifted his sports bag. Before he put his trusty rifle back in its case and disappeared, he allowed his curiosity to get the better of him.

He lifted the rifle once more, placed his eye to the scope, and focused in on DI Amara Singh.

As the circle frame of the scope settled on her, he could see her standing, back straight, chin up as her superior officer clearly read her the riot act. As the rain tirelessly splashed against her pretty face, Sam smiled.

In another life, perhaps?

Singh reached into her back pocket and handed her badge to her boss, a clear punishment for her actions. But Sam couldn't help but feel proud of her, she'd done exactly what he had done. She had raced into a war zone to find Jasmine.

Whether or not she had an ulterior motive to bring him in, it didn't matter.

She had done the right thing.

He observed Singh looking at Aaron and his daughter, the two of them wrapped in a foil blanket and he watched a beautiful smile crack across her face.

He hoped he would see her again.

At that very moment, Singh looked up at the tower, as if she was looking directly at him. Slowly, she raised a middle finger, causing Sam to chuckle.

It was his permission to leave. To disappear.

Because the hunt for him would only intensify and Sam knew then that his life would never allow him to go back.

Within a few moments, the radio tower was empty.

Sam Pope was gone.

CHAPTER THIRTY

Amara Singh awoke the following morning, her head still ringing from the harsh blows she'd taken in the heat of battle. She groaned as she lifted herself from her bed, the Egyptian cotton sheets sliding from her, mocking her decision to leave with their extreme comfort. She made her way to the bathroom and inspected herself in the mirror.

A dark, purple bruise lined her toned stomach and her back ached. A bandage was wrapped across her breasts, the pain of a cracked rib causing each step to be questioned. As she brushed her teeth, she felt something dislodge, and spat a large mouthful of blood into the white, porcelain bowl.

A tooth rattled around and she plucked it from the water, inspecting it with a shake of the head.

She felt like shit, but it had been worth it. All the girls were returned to their families, the immediate reports confirming that while they were suffering from malnutrition and some signs of physical abuse, none of them had been violated or sexually assaulted.

Singh had saved them.

Begrudgingly, she had to credit Sam Pope as well.

Thinking of Sam sent a strange feeling through her body and she gently made her way to the kitchen, clicking the button on her Tassimo coffee machine and watching as the glass filled up with the warm, welcoming brown liquid and the accompanying smell of luxury. As adamant as she was about catching Sam, he had saved her life.

He had risked everything to save an innocent girl from a life not worth living.

She could never find it in herself to call him a hero, but there was much about his stance against the evil in the world to be admired. What bothered her most, despite the myriad of 'decent men' who desired her courtship and the countless number of crimes he had committed, Singh found herself attracted to him.

In another life, perhaps?

With a disappointed sigh, she took a sip of her coffee and wondered how she would spend the first day of her two-week suspension. It had been such a long time since she'd taken time off that she didn't know how to relax. Maybe she would go to the cinema and see which comic book hero was being force fed to the nation? Maybe she would book into a spa and put her broken body through some well-deserved pampering?

Singh would have loved to have been excited by any of them.

But she knew what she had to do.

While her punishment was well deserved, she knew that the review committee would look favourably on her thanks to her past record and the fact that she did save four teenage girls from a lifetime of sex slavery. To restore her reputation, she needed to get back on the horse.

She needed to catch Sam Pope.

As she booted up her MacBook, she lowered herself onto one of the breakfast stools that lined her kitchen. She clicked onto BBC news, intrigued to see how the

Metropolitan Police had spun what had happened. With her appetite non-existent, Singh popped a couple of pain killers into her mouth and washed them down with the remains of her coffee.

A headline flashed up that caught her eye.

'Mark Harris, leading candidate in the Mayoral Election, has withdrawn his candidacy amid wide-spread rumours of illegal operations.'

Singh began to scan the article, smirking as a picture of the smarmy politician looking bedraggled filled the page. Apparently, his robotic assistant, Burrows had been dealing with nefarious businessmen to secure funding.

Singh clicked the button again and the Tassimo machine rumbled to life, eager to provide her with another helpful shot of caffeine.

If she was going to catch Sam Pope, she was going to need all the help she could get.

———

A week had passed since he had brought Jasmine back to the house and Aaron was still unsure what he should say. At first, she'd clung to him, not leaving his side all day and spending the nights curled up next to him. But as he tried to reintegrate her back into normal life, he could see the pain in her eyes.

Whenever the doorbell went, she jumped. If a cupboard door slammed shut, she screamed.

Aaron had been forced to put his phone on silent, just to keep her heart rate down.

He didn't blame her. He couldn't.

His precious daughter had been snatched, beaten, and stuffed in a metal prison, forced to sleep and shit in the same room and given barely enough to survive. All they were promised was a life of drug abuse and sexual degradation. It was horrifying, and he had sat next to her every night, watching her toss and turn with tears falling from his eyes.

Yes, he had gone to extreme lengths to get her back, but he hadn't saved her. She still saw demons when she closed her eyes and she still feared every person who came anywhere near them.

He sighed deeply as he took his seat at the dining table, envisaging the cup of tea he had had with Sam Pope, begging the stranger to help save his daughter. Aaron would forever be indebted to Sam for the lengths he went to save his Jasmine, the unspeakable acts he committed all in the name of her survival. Even when Aaron himself had stepped dangerously close to the edge, Sam had reached out and pulled him to safety.

For a man who was trained to ruthlessly kill, Sam Pope was the most caring person he had ever come across.

It saddened Aaron that he had never got to thank him. To shake his hand and tell him, despite the horrors of his own past, that Sam Pope was a good father.

As he tried his best to sip his cup of tea, Aaron wondered if he was. Jasmine had asked to return from their walk early, unsure of the two youths who had gathered on the pavilion across the field. They had posed no threat, were over two hundred yards away and hadn't even clocked their presence.

But Jasmine was terrified.

Now, she was locked in her room, crying until she fell into a light, horror-filled sleep.

Aaron began to cry, tipping his tea down the sink. It was a long road back for the both of them.

He had got Jasmine back.

But he hadn't saved her.

————

Pearce thanked Etheridge for the drink and rose from his seat, offering a warm smile and a firm handshake which was returned with gusto. Pearce liked Etheridge, the multi-millionaire was still a soldier at heart, and they'd casually spoken for over an hour about their careers before Pearce had complimented him on his home. Pearce had joked about the demolition job Pope had done on the place when he had disabled a tactical unit. Etheridge had played along, agreeing that he had been held at gun point.

So said the medical report, which had found the bruising of a gun barrel being pressed against his skull.

Both men knew that they would never turn on Sam, but Pearce had to follow up his own investigation, especially when his own digging had uncovered a mayoral campaign with cancerous veins inside it. As they approached the front door, Pearce nodded towards the *for sale* sign in the front garden, the large, blue card looming over the pristine Porsche below.

'Not sticking around, Paul?' Pearce asked, popping his arms into his jacket. The rain had finally given up but had been replaced by a bitter cold that chilled to the bone.

'I think it's time for a change,' Etheridge commented, his limp noticeable to a trained eye. 'This life isn't for me anymore.'

'Oh?'

'Well, what with Kayleigh leaving, I've decided to sell the business and maybe do a bit of good.'

'A bit of good, eh?' Pearce raised his eyebrows. 'I have a question?'

'Shoot.'

'How would someone get forged documents nowadays? I mean, with all passports going digital and the whole word deciding to live in the cloud, how would someone bypass all of those things? You know, so they were still official documents.'

'Good question.' Etheridge rubbed his chin. 'You'd probably have to be able to configure a profile within the government database and manipulate the information to render historically as well as digitally. It would be very tricky.'

'I bet,' Pearce said, zipping up his coat. 'Thing is, I doubt Sam Pope has that kind of knowledge on a computer but would definitely need someone to do it for him.'

Etheridge nervously chuckled.

'Probably.' Etheridge swallowed. 'Is there anything else I need to think about?'

Pearce smiled and offered his hand once more. Etheridge took it.

'Don't worry about it, Paul. I'm not much of a computer person.'

Etheridge smiled and Pearce patted him on the shoulder before exiting out into the freezing cold, but was warmed by the idea that Sam Pope had an ally in his ever-growing war against organised crime. The things Etheridge could do with a computer and the doors he could open would be vital and as Pearce drove from Farnham back to Bethnal Green, he decided to close any case against Etheridge, to give him the best possible chance he could to begin his new life.

To do 'something good.'

As the sun set on the first Sunday of December, Pearce arrived outside the Bethnal Green Youth Centre slightly late, the sky already dark and the temperature dropping rapidly. Although he still had forty-five minutes until the doors opened, he usually liked to have a cup of tea and a read of the Sunday news. The local youths who attended were always so talkative and alarmingly knowledgeable about current affairs.

While many would dismiss them as estate kids or

'hoodies', he was often surprised with how intelligent they were and the conversations he had had around politics and the law were fascinating. It was a testament to Theo Walker, the former soldier who had partnered Sam in his past and who had set up the project to help the kids who had to survive on the streets.

Pearce had done his best to honour him, but age and time restraints were making it harder to do it beyond once a week.

As he got out of his car, he took a moment to stretch his back, Father Time reminding him of his age as more aches and pains infiltrated his reasonably athletic body. He stepped through the gate and towards the door of the community hall when a young man climbed off from the steps and approached him. Pearce assessed him and quickly offered him his warmest greeting.

'Hello, young man. Can I help you?'

The young man had been severely beaten, his face was slashed and bruised. His right hand was wrapped in bandages and he twitched nervously. Pearce thought he recognised him but couldn't place him.

Wiseman approached Pearce, nervously chuckling.

'Err, I don't want to get into any trouble,' he finally said.

'There is no trouble here, son. I don't allow it.'

Pearce's joke caused Wiseman to smile, his youthful exuberance peeking through the brutal scars.

'Well, I was sent here by Sam Pope.' Wiseman waited a moment then continued, 'He said this was a place to come to if I needed help.'

Pearce stood still for a moment, shaking his head slightly as his respect for Sam grew even more. The most wanted man in the country was probably its most caring.

Pearce offered his handshake.

'He wasn't wrong.'

Wiseman took Pearce's hand, solidifying their friend-ship with a shake before following the wise detective into the community centre, the warmth of the building welcoming him in from the cold and ushering him into a new life.

EPILOGUE

Burrows spat the final remnants of vomit into the toilet bowl and then reached for the chain. He sighed with relief that the ordeal was over and pulled himself up, his beady eyes flashing around the cubicle. A few numbers were scrawled across the wall, all of them offering a lewd outcome and he stepped out into the airport bathroom.

It had been two weeks since he had gone dark, using the money he had been stockpiling for the last fifteen years to hide away in the darkest hole in the country.

Having worked for the Kovalenkos for a decade and a half, Burrows had over two million in a personal fortune that he kept hidden, choosing to live off of the generous salary provided by the UK taxpayer.

He had seen the end coming as soon as Sam Pope began taking down some of the major crime brackets in London. Once Frank Jackson's High Rise fell, he knew that unless something was done, Pope would connect enough dots to lead him to their doorstep.

Then the game would be up.

He was right.

But Burrows had managed to slip through the net,

reading with little remorse that Harris's bright star had been extinguished and he had retired in shame. As the weeks went by, more stories of their misdeeds had flooded the broadsheets, with Burrows' links to Kovalenko exposed. Harris, despite his campaign benefitting from the money, had been put forward as a victim of their betrayal, but his life was still spiralling out of control.

With their chance of fifteen minutes of fame and a potential pay out, a number of women came forward, selling their stories of their affairs with Harris to anyone willing to buy them. It wasn't Burrows' problem anymore, and he blamed Harris for not pushing the task force earlier.

Burrows had been in his ear every day, telling him to base the campaign around bringing Sam Pope to justice and tackling the rise of crime in London the right way. He had sold it like it was Harris's idea, that he was the one in charge. But Burrows had pulled the strings and the odd lavish gift or dinner date with Assistant Commissioner Ashton had been most beneficial.

There had been nothing in the papers regarding their links and despite her rejection of his advances over the years, Burrows wasn't willing to sell her down the river just yet.

An announcement echoed over the speakers, asking all final passengers for the non-stop flight from Birmingham to Kiev to make their way to gate sixteen. Burrows splashed water on his face, not recognising the plump man before him. The tufts of hair that framed his head had overgrown and his grey beard was overdue a trim. The green contacts had changed his eye colour, but he cursed having to put them in everyday.

Sergei Kovalenko had been in touch when news of Andrei's passing became public. Despite their best efforts en route to the hospital, the paramedics had declared Andrei dead before they'd arrived.

Sergei hadn't been best pleased, but he didn't blame Burrows. He wasn't anything more than a facilitator, but the man had been incredibly loyal to him and his family.

Therefore, he had offered Burrows a safe haven in Kiev, where he would protect him from the authorities who wanted him crucified.

A few days later, state-of-the-art documentation had arrived, giving Burrows a new identity as Gregory Baker. He didn't hate it, but he felt like a snake, ready to shed its skin. Along with the new passport and birth certificate, they'd falsified his dental records, his finger prints, and removed any record of his DNA from the government system.

Kovalenko's reach was huge and it terrified Burrows just how powerful a man he was.

Powerful and cruel.

Burrows had arranged for the safe transportation of his fortune, purchased a one-way ticket and now, having thrown up the last of his nerves, he felt like he had finally stepped from one life to another.

It was time to live as Gregory Baker.

A retired ex-pat who settled down in Kiev with the massive fortune he'd made as a stock broker.

It was better than living the rest of his life in a prison where he would be singled out as part of the system that had let most of the inhabitants down.

He made his way through the gate and boarded the plane, finding his seat and locking himself in place. He wasn't the best flyer, but he was ready to leave it all behind.

His crimes.

His life.

His country.

All of it.

As the plane shot down the runway and lifted into the sky, Burrows felt liberated, that all of his indiscretions had been left on the ground and he was a man reborn.

He had got away with it.

He was free.

Four rows back, sitting in the window seat, Sam Pope lifted the bill of his cap and shot a look in Burrows' direction. Etheridge had sent him all the information he needed to track Burrows down and also furnished him with a state-of-the-art passport.

As Sam watched Burrows order a gin and tonic, he took a sip of the mineral water he had ordered. The seat was uncomfortable, the beating he had taken from Oleg Kovalenko was still echoing throughout his body. The bullet wound in his leg still sent painful reminders whenever he tried to move in his cramped confines.

But it would be worth it.

In just over four hours, they would land, and Sam would introduce himself.

Sam wanted the head of the snake.

And Burrows would lead him straight to him.

As Burrows sipped his drink, Sam glanced out of the window, and England faded from his view.

It was time to take the fight to them.

GET EXCLUSIVE ROBERT ENRIGHT MATERIAL

Hey there,

I really hope you enjoyed the book and hopefully, you will want to continue following Sam Pope's war on crime. If so, then why not sign up to my reader group? I send out regular updates, polls and special offers as well as some cool free stuff. Sound good?

Well, if you do sign up to the reader group I'll send you FREE copies of THE RIGHT REASON and RAIN-FALL, two thrilling Sam Pope prequel novellas. (RRP: 1.99)

You can get your FREE books by signing up at www.robertenright.co.uk

SAM POPE NOVELS

For more information about the Sam Pope series and other books by Robert Enright, please visit:

www.robertenright.co.uk

ABOUT THE AUTHOR

Robert lives in Buckinghamshire with his family, writing books and dreaming of getting a dog.

For more information:
www.robertenright.co.uk
robert@robertenright.co.uk

You can also connect with Robert on Social Media:

facebook.com/robenrightauthor
x.com/REnright_Author
instagram.com/robenrightauthor

Cover by Phillip Griffiths

Edited by Emma Mitchell

Proof Read by Lou Dixon

Printed in Great Britain
by Amazon

45723246R00172